MONSTER

S. E. GREEN

PART ONE

Annabelle grabs my hand, and giggling, she tugs me across the field of wildflowers. "Come on, Caroline, hurry!"

Behind us, Mom yells, "Dinner in thirty!"

"Okay!" I yell back, waving.

In the distance, the train's horn sounds, signaling its approach, and Annabelle lets go of my hand as she picks up the pace. I'm right behind her when we break from the field, race through the bordering trees, and come to a stop a few feet from the train tracks.

She stands in front of me, as she always does, and together we stretch our arms out wide. The horn sounds again, letting us know it's almost here, and up ahead it rounds the hill to begin its gentle slope toward us. My gaze rolls over the number of cars. It's a short one but we'll make the best of it.

My twin and I have done this a zillion times over the years but my heart never ceases to bang my ribs as the ground vibrates with the incoming train.

Annabelle casts me a quick smile over her shoulder and I grin back. We brace our feet wide, the ground rumbles, the horn blows telling us it's passing, and the air around us becomes alive as the train whizzes past.

I close my eyes, arch my back, and lift on my toes. I swear I'm flying. My sundress suctions to my body and my cheeks wobble as I laugh. I stretch my arms longer, cupping my hands, and almost stumble back with the weighted wind.

Another horn, the train now saying goodbye, and then it's gone. Hopefully, the one tomorrow will be longer.

Laughing, Annabelle turns to me, flicking her long dark hair over her shoulder. "I hope we—" Her voice fades away as her gaze moves beyond me and her smile gradually dies. "Caroline," she whispers.

But I don't know what she sees, because everything goes black.

ONE

Present Day

Tires crunch across my driveway and Dr. Vincent DeMurr pulls his dark SUV in and cuts the engine. It's been three months since I've seen or talked to him. Three months since I stopped helping him with cases. I told him I needed a break but something tells me he's about to talk me into another.

His car door opens and brown oxfords appear first, followed by a three-piece navy suit and burgundy tie. Always the snazzy dresser, my foster father. Wearing his usual gray flat cap, he takes his silver shades off and places them on the dash, before closing the door and crossing over to me.

"Caroline," he greets me with a nod and polite smile like it was just yesterday we saw each other and not three months.

I return the greeting, "Vincent."

Taking his cap off, he slides long fingers over his clean-shaven head and, not for the first time, I wonder what he would look like with hair. But not Vincent, not once has he ever sported bristle on his cheeks or head.

He glances at the little farmhouse my boyfriend, Fallon, and I are renting. All around us span acres and acres of isolated Tennessee land. In the distance on a hill sits the home of the woman who owns this place—Suzi Derringer. Good people, as my grandpa used to say.

"I hope you're getting out," Vincent says. "I know it's not easy for you to be social."

I nod, even though I'm not getting out. I prefer my own company. Or Suzi's. Or Fallon's. Or the multitude of dead people sitting in files on my desk. Cold cases I haven't looked at in months.

"Classes going well?" He asks.

"Yes." Truth is I'm looking forward to graduating and taking a break. But he wants me to roll right into a master's program. *A master's in criminal psychology will take you much further than a bachelor's.* Words he has said to me entirely too many times.

"I saw one of your professors at a conference last week. He couldn't stop talking about your talent. About your ability to understand and empathize with sociopaths. 'Like nothing I've ever seen,' he said."

"I'd call it more an unwanted and active imagination." Brought on by things better left in the past. But I don't say this and instead smile. "Now why are you really here? It's not to talk about my classes, I'm sure."

Propping his loafer on my porch, he leans in. "I've missed you."

"I've missed you, too."

"I know we agreed you needed a break but you're going to want in on this one."

With a sigh, I shake my head. "I can't. Not yet."

"Caroline, we think it might be cannibalism."

A stillness settles through my body and for several long moments I don't move. I don't respond. He knows cannibalism is the absolute only thing that would draw me back in.

Reaching into his inside suit pocket, he pulls out a series of documents folded lengthwise and hands them to me. Turning away, he takes a seat on the porch steps and I open the papers.

Three girls from three different private schools abducted in the past three months. Abducted as in no bodies, except for the third one found returned to her dorm room, dead, portions of her organs removed and then put back in.

"Why is Detective Uzzo linking them?"

"They may not be but the private school connection had her drawing some preliminary connections."

"And why do you suspect cannibalism?" I ask.

"Because unused portions of the organs were returned with traces of seasoning."

Might be something ritualistic versus cannibal. Either way, I'm intrigued. I flip a page, looking at each of their pretty smiles. One with blond hair, another brown, another dark. The dark one with her pale skin and light eyes looks close enough to me that we could be sisters.

I flick the page containing the photos, getting some initial thoughts. "If they are connected, then these are replacements for something that didn't go right or a reliving of something that did."

Vincent shifts to look at me. "And the returned body?"

"Other than the seasoning on the organs, what does Detective Uzzo have?"

"It's a fresh body so not a whole lot. Yet."

I shuffle the papers, pulling out the picture of the returned girl. "Why did he return you?" I mumble to the dead girl.

"He?"

"Just a pronoun to use until I know more. What about the parents?"

"We haven't been able to reach them."

I hand Vincent back the papers. He came here to lure me in and he succeeded. I'm officially on board with finding this killer. "Let's go look at the scene."

TWO

It takes us an hour to drive from our town in southeast Tennessee north to the private school where the third girl was found returned to her bed. While Vincent drives, I study the files on the three girls. This one we're about to see was strangled but, according to the report, it wasn't the cause of death.

Three girls. Three different schools. All within an hour's drive of our town of Mockingbird, Tennessee. The killer either lives in our town or he's trying to make it look like he lives in our town.

"The killer has skills," I say, zeroing in on the familiar cut marks.

"Though they are done with a—" I pause, needing a second, "a hunting knife, the cuts have been made with expertise."

"Yes, I noted that as well," he says. "A doctor, a nurse, a mortician—"

"A hunter, a butcher, a chef."

With a nod, Vincent pulls onto campus and winds his way through the brick buildings, eventually pulling into a parking lot. Among the sea of student vehicles and news crews, I pick out Detective Uzzo's old green and white Chevy truck and a couple of cop cars but I don't see the white CSI van and assume they've come and gone.

Zipping up my white windbreaker, I keep my head ducked, hoping the news crews don't catch sight of me. Luckily, they don't as I exit the vehicle and follow Vincent into the dorm. Girls crowd the lobby, some crying, some standing blank in shock, and yet others are on their phones chatting like a girl wasn't found dead right here earlier this morning.

We head through the lobby, ducking under crime scene tape and stepping into the now empty dormitory hall. Two cops stand guard and Vincent shows them his official ID, saying, "She's with me."

They step aside and we walk toward a door where Detective Uzzo stands.

Tall with thick gray hair and matching thick gray-framed glasses, Uzzo lifts her tired gaze to watch us walk toward her. We come to a stop at the eighth door on the left, a single unit like most seniors have.

"Dr. DeMurr, Caroline," Detective Uzzo greets us. "Thanks for coming." She steps aside. "The team has combed it and already removed the body, so you're free to walk in."

Already removed the body. That's not normally the case but Uzzo knew I was coming. Uzzo knows I can't handle the actual bodies. It's too much for me. It's what sent me toward the nervous breakdown I had three months ago. For now, I'll do just fine with crime scene photos.

Still, I eye the open door warily before sliding past Uzzo and stepping inside. Afternoon light from the window streaks across the floor over to the empty bed to light up the spot where the girl's body was found. I stand just inside the door, immediately noting the first-floor window is open.

"Take as long as you want," Vincent quietly says allowing me some space.

Knowing I'll have a headache afterward, I pull prescription capsules from my front jeans pocket and swallow two dry. I need to remember to bring water with me to these things.

Crossing the room to the window, I inhale the fresh winter air cleansing the smell of death from my senses. Then taking another breath, I exhale through my mouth and close my eyes.

In my mind I bring up the picture of the body that Vincent showed me, dressed in a long sleeping tee and lying face-up on top of the comforter as if she were about to crawl under and go to bed. All sounds dull, replaced by the steady thump-thump-thump of my heart.

I become the abductor, standing outside the window peering in. The campus is dark and quiet, most gone home for the weekend. Opening the unlocked window, I crawl through and I stand by her bed, staring down at her sleeping body.

Then I move, lightning-quick, and my hands go around her throat. I squeeze, sudden and violent, knowing the adrenaline will shoot epinephrine through her body, richening the taste. The girl startles out of sleep, struggling, her face swelling with bursting capillaries that spread into the whites of her eyes. She tries to scream but it comes out as a croak instead and I continue my grip until she passes out. I don't want her dead though, the organs are better when you take them out of a live body. So I release her throat and take a step back.

My throat involuntarily opens and I gasp for breath as I

come back to the here and now, staring down at the spot where the body was found. My gasp brings in a new scent—honey, sweet and rich—and my stomach muscles clench. "Did the killer treat the wounds?"

Vincent and Detective Uzzo step into the room, ready. "Yes, with honey and charcoal."

Exactly what I was treated with.

Vincent hands me a homemade cookie that he pulls from his suit pocket. "Please eat this. I saw you take pills and you're not the best about putting food in your stomach."

He's once again got his foster-father cap on so I appease him as I peel back the plastic wrap and take a bite.

He gives me a few seconds to eat and swallow before asking, "Why return her? Why not just dispose of the body?"

Detective Uzzo moves closer to the bed studying the stained sheets. "Because the killer wants to be caught."

I nod but I think it's more the person who returned the body wants the killer to be caught. I don't say that though, because I'm not entirely sure and I don't want to muddle things.

With a sigh, Uzzo looks between us. "You should know the press is already dubbing this killer with a name. The Organ Ripper." Turning, she strolls from the room. "I need to go make a statement."

Turning away from the bloody bed, I look up at Vincent and he reads my mind when he says, "Honey and charcoal."

With a nod, I press my fingers to that spot above my left brow that aches as a memory floats in...

Our captor grips Annabelle's head, a hunting knife poised at her neck, staring at me over her head. My sister struggles against his hold and my heart lurches as a prick of blood trickles from her skin.

"*Run*," she whispers.

"*Do that*," he speaks, "*and I will remove her organs one by one, all while I keep her alive.*"

Her scent wafts across on a breeze, honey coating her raw skin, heavier than usual with her fear and sweat.

I could run. I could get away. But I don't. I won't leave my sister.

THREE

When we were babies, Annabelle walked before me. But I was the first to speak. I was also the first to read. While Annabelle was out running the farm, fishing and chasing goats, I would be on the porch reading.

When I was two, I asked my dad to read me the dictionary and every night we would cuddle in his big brown chair, him reading while my head lolled on his chest as my eyes followed the words. It didn't take long before I started saying the words ahead of him and my parents knew there was something different about me.

When I was four, my mom found me in the yard with my grandfather's sextant measuring the angle between the moon and the horizon. When she asked me where I learned to do that, I told her I read about it in one of my grandfather's encyclopedias.

When I was six, I stopped going to school with Annabelle and started attending an academy for the gifted. The first few days were scary but, after that, I couldn't wait to come home and tell Annabelle about all the stuff I was learning.

Grinning, she'd always say the same thing. "Caroline, I wish I was as smart as you."

"You are smart!"

"Yes, but one day you're going to be famous smart. You wait and see."

Those words go through my mind as I stand in my shower, letting the hot water stream down my neck and back. At the time I thought I would be "famous smart" like my grandfather in a mathematical or scientific field. The only thing I'm "famous" for is my ability to crawl into the mind of a killer. It's not a famous I want but one destiny has slapped me with.

I left the vent off and the steam rises and collects around me. As it does, the air around me shifts and I'm no longer here in the shower. I'm there in the woods where he kept us.

I see him, our captor, walking toward me through the fog, his face obscured by the hood he always wore. A new girl lays lifeless across his arms and I look away. I can't watch what's about to happen. He whistles, just those three slow eerie notes he always did, and they carry through the mist.

Shaking my head, I force myself back to the here and now as I shut the water off and grab a towel. After drying off, I pull on long plaid pajamas and then I go through my nightly ritual of checking every door and window before setting the alarm. Fallon will be back tomorrow from a research trip he took with his forensic science professor and a few other students. I sleep better when he's here.

Zane, Fallon's elderly mixed-breed Great Dane, lumbers in from the living room, heading straight over to his giant memory foam bed that lays in the corner. He turns exactly one circle and then eases down into the lamb's wool with a groan. At nine years old, he's defying a big dog's life span and I'm sure it has everything to do with the mixture of breeds running in his blood.

Petal, my gray cat, is already curled on our bed waiting for me in her usual spot right smack dab in the center of the left side of the bed, the side I always sleep on. I found her last year alongside the road, matted, starving, and huddled up hiding in a clump of flowers. We adopted each other and here we are.

I pull the white comforter back and slide in between the purple striped sheets, my legs circling Petal's plump body. For a few seconds, I watch the tree shadows cast by the moon stretching along the walls of my bedroom, swaying slightly with the chilly night breeze. I glance at the digital readout on my clock. 11:23 p.m.

With a heavy sigh, I close my eyes, already feeling the weighted pull of sleep.

Another person's breathing fills the room and my eyes flick back open. I take and hold a breath, listening, wondering if I'm hearing things—but there it is again—another person's breath.

Turning my head, I see the girl from earlier lying beside me, still alive and breathing. I'm used to this. I'm used to seeing the victims of the killers that I hunt.

I reach out to touch her and her body shifts and stretches, lifting off the mattress. Blood seeps from everywhere, darkening her white oversized tee, and as her body gets sucked into the darkness, her face slowly becomes my sister's.

She's huddled in the darkness where our captor kept us and I'm right there beside her. Something to the right scurries and I lunge. There's a squeak, a snap, and then a rip. I swallow and what little saliva I have coats the inside of my cheeks.

Sliding back over, I give my sister her portion of whatever it is I just killed. Together we rip into it, slurping and eating the blood and raw meat and sucking the bones dry. From the weight, size, and fine hair, I can tell it's a small mouse.

The first time we did this, we both threw up afterward. Now, neither of us even gags, and the hungry acid in our stomachs settle.

For now.

With a jolt, I shoot straight up in bed, zooming back to the here and now. *Annabelle*. It was a nightmare. Just a nightmare. I'm used to getting them. I expect them, especially when I'm helping with a case. Except...

They've never once involved my sister. She visits me in my dreams and she's always in my thoughts but she's never once mingled with a dead person from a case.

Not once.

This is the first cannibalism case I've worked on though, my mind must be making connections. That has to be it.

FOUR

The next morning I'm on my front porch sipping coffee, idly watching the birds zip and zing around the feeder that Suzi Derringer hung. She sits beside me knitting tiny booties for her granddaughter. Beyond her in the distance on the hill sits her multi-leveled brick and wood farmhouse. Between our two homes runs a narrow trail that she walks every morning to join me.

Fallon has lived here going on a year now and me three months. I moved in right after my nervous breakdown, soon after that Suzi began wandering over. I had, of course, met her several times when I visited Fallon but it wasn't until I moved in that we began our morning ritual.

Yes, I've gotten used to my morning front porch time with Suzi as I sit quietly taking in the scenery and she sits quietly knitting. It reminds me of all the times Rachel, my foster mom, and I used to sit on her and Vincent's porch. This is exactly why I let Suzi lead the conversations and am careful with what I say. I don't want to unsettle Suzi. I don't want to run her off.

Like I did Rachel.

Fallon and I spent our childhood years together in Vincent and Rachel's home. Fallon started talking about moving away together years ago but I didn't feel right leaving Vincent all alone in his huge home up on the mountain, especially with Rachel gone.

It was Suzi actually, who encouraged me to do it. "Vincent will be fine," Suzi had said. "Be brave. Be strong. Be independent. Don't be afraid to make decisions for yourself. You owe Vincent nothing and I'm sure he would agree with that. He took you and Fallon in because he wanted to. Not because he felt you owed him something. Just like my children owe me nothing but love. If you want to move in here with Fallon, then do. Tragedy brought you two together. Now let love move you forward. Enjoy being together. You deserve happiness."

It was those words that prompted me to have a difficult conversation with Vincent. A conversation that went surprisingly well. Or perhaps Vincent made me think it went well.

"I hear you're helping Vincent with a case," Suzi says, bringing me from my thoughts.

Taking a sip of coffee, I glance over at her kind and gentle round face. I don't question how she knows that. Detective Uzzo and Suzi are longtime friends. I'm sure Uzzo told her. "Yes," I say.

"Make sure you take care of yourself," Suzi tells me as she continues to knit. A retired teacher and a widow, she happily spends her days' knitting and gardening—and subtly reminding me to take care of myself.

"I will. I know my limits."

Suzi doesn't respond to that, just nods, and for a few seconds, I stare at her long wavy hair with its swirls of auburn and white. Creamsicle. That's what it always reminds me of.

"Did you know children are born with mirror neurons?" she asks. "It helps them socialize and usually the neurons fall away. But some people, like you, keep them or they come back after a traumatic event, like what happened with you and your sister. Sometimes this makes it difficult to know the real you because you're constantly reflecting those around you. It's also what makes you good at connecting with killers."

Vincent has said as much so I keep looking at the side of her face, waiting for her point.

Suzi glances up then, smiling. "I always want to know the real you, Caroline. Always."

I nod, needing to hear that more than I realize. "Thank you."

"I meant it."

She goes back to knitting and idly I watch her as my mind tracks back to three months ago and my nervous breakdown. Vincent was helping the state with a case in West Tennessee surrounding a couple who held their six children captive in a basement. They tortured and eventually killed all six kids ranging in age from two to fourteen. I couldn't take it. The bodies of the children. The torture they had endured. I snapped. I completely crumbled. Seeing adult dead bodies is one thing but seeing those small bodies tapped a part of my psyche that I never want to be touched again.

The purr of a motor fills the quiet morning and it doesn't surprise me in the least when Vincent pulls in, effectively disrupting our time.

Suzi doesn't glance over at his SUV when she asks, "Shall I go?"

With a sigh, I nod. "Probably for the best." Though neither Vincent nor Suzi have said it, I get the feeling they don't care for each other. I think Vincent feels Suzi is replacing him, both as a parent and a confidante. And Suzi feels Vincent has too tight of a hold on me.

With that Fallon would agree.

The thing is though, Vincent knows my darkest secrets. Things I would never tell Suzi. And Suzi knows my current thoughts. Things I don't want to share with Vincent. Like the fact I'm questioning my major in Criminal Psychology. I don't want to get my masters. And I'm not sure profiling is the career I want.

Vincent. Suzi. It's a balancing act, for sure.

The one thing I do know is that I love the normal conversations that I have with Suzi, like about her grand-daughter or her pet pig or plants that grow in different environments. I can't recall the last time I had a normal conversation like that with Vincent.

Standing, she wraps a long green scarf around her creamsicle hair, tucks her knitting down inside a wicker basket, gives my shoulder a gentle squeeze, then walks down the front porch steps. With only a nod of acknowledgment to Vincent, still sitting in his SUV, she cuts across the dried winter grass heading for the trail.

Vincent hangs up with whoever he's talking to and, before he's even closed the door of his sleek SUV, he's saying, "You're not returning my texts. Is that your way of telling me you don't want to be involved in this case?"

"No, that's my way of telling you my phone is inside and I haven't heard your texts." Really, it's my way of stalling. I don't like what happened last night and I'm still not sure if it was a nightmare or a hallucination.

Propping his loafer on the porch, Vincent leans in. "I was hoping we could talk through a few things."

"Okay."

"What's your take on the honey and charcoal?"

I give myself a second, not allowing my brain to go back in time, to focus on the here and now. "Someone who believes in natural remedies. Our killer is justified in his way."

"I thought you said he wanted to be caught."

"You know as well as I do that we're in the beginning stages of this. I'm bound to change my mind as I work through things."

"A killer who is a naturalist." Vincent takes his gray flat cap off, trailing his fingers over his cleanly shaved head, thinking through things. "Okay, going with that, a naturalist would—"

"Use everything." I sit up in the rocking chair, feeling that surge that comes with knowing I'm heading down the right path. "Three dead girls with only the third returned. We're not sure the first two girls are connected to this case."

"Yes, but it's a working theory."

"Then going with that and the naturalist idea, I'm not sure we'll find the first two bodies because there's nothing to find."

Vincent wedges his hat back on. "Go on."

"Three similar girls over the past three months, meaning Caucasian and roughly the same age, sixteen or so. Before that, nothing. Or at least nothing we know of yet. So the killer, The Organ Ripper, is either new to the area or his prior victims aren't on our radar yet. We've already established the cuts were made by someone with skill and, now going down the line of a naturalist, I don't see it being a medical doctor or a nurse. Alternative medicine perhaps..."

I take a sip of my coffee, rolling it around in my mouth, thinking for a second.

Vincent takes a step back, folding his arms and looking down at his loafer, also thinking. "As you said, the three girls are similar and that would hold significance to The Organ Ripper. But the returned girl wasn't raped so defiling isn't what this is about."

"He's trying to replace something lost or something he is about to lose. We're likely looking for someone with a daughter around the same age. With the cannibalism aspect, he's either eating the girls himself or he's feeding the girls to his daughter."

"This case may be over with before it even starts."

"Let's hope." I grab my coffee mug and go to get up when the sound of a familiar engine rumbles in the distance.

I glance toward the horizon to see Fallon peak the crest. The morning sun backlights the black Camaro's silhouette as he cruises down the hill, making his way toward us. He's only been gone a few days but still my heart flutters. I smile and wave as if he's been gone weeks or even months.

A few minutes later, he pulls in beside Vincent's SUV and cuts his engine. Opening the door, he runs his fingers through his shoulder-length blond hair and swings his long leg out to stand. Tossing his aviators onto the dash, he unzips his brown leather jacket and his eyes stay level on mine as he carefully approaches.

Vincent extends a hand to shake. "Fallon, it's been a while. How are you holding up? School going good?"

Fallon nods, his eyes flicking between us, curious.

"I'm doing another case," I answer Fallon's unspoken question.

"You aren't ready for this," he tells me, kicking into

protective mode. "Need I remind you what happened three little months ago?"

Vincent holds up his hand. "It's just this one."

Fallon scoffs. "And then it'll be another and another and another."

"The price of my imagination," I say, making a lame joke.

Fallon just looks at me. "That's not funny."

I sober. "I know it's not. I have to. It's likely cannibalism."

Fallon sighs. He looks at Vincent. "Promise me you'll watch her."

"I promise," Vincent says.

FIVE

The next morning I open the front door, eager for my time with Suzi, and Vincent stands there. With his fist up to knock, he's holding an insulated tote. My gaze goes beyond him to see Suzi walking away toward her home on the hill. She must have seen Vincent and turned around.

Disappointment moves through me but I mask it as I look back at Vincent.

"Been a while since we ate together," he says. "I made yours vegan and extra special."

I motion him in and, while he sets up at our rustic dining table, I pour him a cup of coffee. I add a little stevia to his and, with mine black, I take the seat across from him. He's already peeled the lids off two warm Tupperware bowls and the spicy scent of a cooked breakfast makes me salivate.

I note the third Tupperware bowl. "Fallon's already gone to class."

"I figured. I brought one just in case."

Picking up my fork, I survey the bowl. I push around the quinoa, fresh herbs, black beans, and stir-fried veggies, before scooping up a heap and taking a big bite. Vincent watches me, smiling, and I close my eyes with a slight moan.

He chuckles. "I take it you like it?"

"I forgot how good your food is. Thank you. If you think of it, I'd love some of those seed bars that you make."

"Of course, I'm happy too." Picking up his fork, he takes a few bites and together we eat in silence.

A few minutes later and done first, I lay my napkin over my empty bowl and grab my mug. "Two mornings in a row you've come here. There's another body, isn't there?"

"Yes." With a nod, he takes his flat cap off and sets it aside. "Naked and laying out in the middle of a park and decorated with flowers and herbs. Female, sixteen, Caucasian, organs removed but this time not put back. Strangled like the other one. Cut marks the same."

"Honey and charcoal?"

"Yes."

"What kind of flowers?"

"Wildflowers."

My favorite.

Laughing, Mom puts a crown of wildflowers on first my head, then Annabelle's. "There, now you're princesses."

I slide up in my chair, uncomfortable with the parallel my mind just drew. I focus on what Vincent just said. "The first two girls unaccounted for, the third returned to her bed, and now a fourth on artistic display."

"What's your gut telling you about this fourth one?"

"Seasoning on the organs of the returned girl so we would draw the lines to cannibalism. Wildflowers on this one with the organs missing which means he'll do something with those organs. The flowers show appreciation, a thank you, which cycles me back around. I think our killer wants to be caught. Or I think someone wants us to find the killer."

"Great, so we're dealing with two people, one is The Organ Ripper and one is a person who knows who it is?"

"Perhaps. What I'm sensing is that the killer isn't about show-and-tell, at least not to the public. To himself, yes. With the skill of cutting in and removing the organs, this is something practiced and fine-tuned over the years. The two returned bodies are unusual. He's either trying something new or as I said, someone else has stepped in. Our killer has a motive for wanting those organs. But something has recently changed in his universe."

Finished, Vincent wipes his mouth and puts the lid back on his now-empty bowl. He studies me for a few quiet seconds. "Fallon's very protective of you."

I find the abrupt change in topic a bit odd. "As I am him."

"He sees you as something fragile. You're not fragile, Caroline."

I never thought I was. "And how do you see me?"

"Like I always have, as a great white shark circling, studying, waiting for the moment to strike."

Vincent packs things back up and I think about that analogy, smiling a bit at the accuracy.

I glance outside at the barren winter trees. "A body decorated with flowers and herbs...it's wintertime. There are no flowers and herbs except in greenhouses." Looking up at Vincent, I smile. "We're looking for greenhouses."

"Your neighbor, Suzi Derringer, has a greenhouse."

"As do you," I say.

His lips quirk. "Touché."

SIX

Light flashes across my face in sweeping blue arcs as I stare down at the blood drying on my fingers. All sound dulls to just the thump-thump-thump of my heart. With shaky legs, I lean against the SUV, numbly watching the circus of cop cars, paramedics, and officers streaming in and out of the cozy-looking cabin and the detached garage and greenhouse.

A few simple hours ago I was in my kitchen eating with Vincent and now I have blood on my hands of a man who may have been The Organ Ripper.

With a deep breath, I close my eyes and I dive into the darkness of my mind, trying to make sense of what just happened.

Vincent puts the SUV in park. "Organic farmer, nutritionist, chef for hire, lives within driving distance of all the recent abductions and has a teenage daughter who is dying from cancer. His name is Harley Laine and his daughter is named Becka."

Unbuckling my seatbelt, I survey the A-frame cabin nestled into the woods some fifty yards away. Beside it sits a

*garage and in back a greenhouse. "Is there another body?" I
ask, dreading the answer. But there has to be, otherwise, why
would I be here? "And where's Detective Uzzo and her
team?"*

*"No body and Uzzo will be here soon. I thought you
might want to see this side of things. You're always looking at
photos, reading files, visiting the crime scene afterward, but
you've never been present when a search warrant is issued."
Vincent taps his finger to the clock on the dash. "The team
will be here any minute."*

*I glance over my shoulder and through the back window,
gazing down the winding gravel road looking for Uzzo. That
spot above my left brow thumps and I'm not sure why.
Usually, my headaches come on when I'm actively involved
in a scene, not just sitting and waiting.*

*Still, I reach in my jacket pocket for my prescription
headache pills. I take one, not two, washing it down with the
coffee I brought along.*

*Vincent eyes my movements. "How often are you getting
them now?"*

*"Not often," I fib. "I've learned to take the pills before it
gets debilitating."*

*"You should carry crackers. Those pills on an empty
stomach are never good."*

*I take another swallow of the cooling coffee. "You forget
the excellent breakfast in my system."*

*Vincent smiles. His phone rings then and he checks the
display before opening the SUV's door. "Need to take this.
You stay here."*

*He wanders back down the gravel road, eventually disap-
pearing around a curve in the road. I glance again at the
cabin nestled into the trees some fifty yards away. When will
the team be getting here?*

Grabbing the binoculars he keeps under his seat, I survey the area noting the dark wood garage tucked back to the right. The door to the garage opens and I jump. Out steps a man, tall and thin, with a burgundy beanie crammed down over straight dark hair. He locks the door behind him and with purposeful strides, he walks through the woods back to the A-frame cabin, not even glancing my way.

It's faint, the cry I hear, and if it wasn't for the quiet of the woods I probably wouldn't hear it at all. But it's enough to make me open the door, step out and stand for a second to listen.

There it is again, the cry, this one a little louder with a muddled and wheezing, "Please," to it.

I take off running toward the garage, my arms coming up to knock branches out of the way. I get closer and closer and the woods around me tilt and warp. They look different now. Familiar. Thicker than a second ago. Fear and panic clench through my stomach with awareness. But this can't be real. How did I get back here? No, I have to get to my sister before he returns.

I hear it again, the muted whimper, and I smash my shoulder against the locked door. It's hard to tell if the resounding crack is the wood or my bones. Either way, I don't care. I kick it, and I kick it, and little by little the door splinters around the lock.

One last time, I throw my whole body against it and I rush inside. Adrenaline pumps through me and I don't see the blood defacing the table or the floor. I stop cold at the sight of my sister chained in the back corner, her wrists shackled to the wall. "Help me," she pleads.

"Annabelle," I whisper.

She rattles the thick chain. "Hurry before he comes back."

I come down in front of her, grabbing the shackle and yanking. "Where's the key?"

"I don't know," she sobs, her hand coming out to grip my wrist. I try not to see the flickers of fear on her face. It will only distract me. Gently, I pry her fingers from my skin and she nods up to a shelf. "There's a knife up there."

I jump to my feet, grab the hunting knife, and a shadow falls over me. Turning, I see our captor, his face a blur, light pulsing behind him. I lunge, not giving him a chance to speak or move, and I sink the knife into his lower abdomen. I yank it out and thrust it in again. Out, and in again.

Time slows to a crawl and each of my movements become sluggish. He doesn't go down and I slide the knife out and then back in again, sobbing now. Finally, he grasps at me with jerky halting movements, then his body spasms as he falls forward, heavy and hot, to land with a dense thud on the garage's floor.

He struggles to breathe, his air wheezing in and out, hissing at me through jagged dying breaths. He becomes blurry as his life ebbs away and I sing "This Little Light of Mine" as I remove his organs.

Then all around me, the movement begins. Someone touches me, pulling me away. I look down at the body, only it isn't my captor. It's a man, violently stabbed to death, his organs removed and left in a pile beside his body.

"Caroline." Vincent touches me and I blink from my haze. "Are you hurt?"

Looking around, I note that I'm standing next to the SUV. I'm not in that garage anymore. I look down at the blood drying on my hands and then up into Vincent's face. I see pity but also regret. He's regretting bringing me.

In the distance sits the garage, the cabin, and the team

moving in and out of the crime scene. The ambulance pulls away.

"That wasn't Annabelle in there, was it?" I ask.

"No. Your sister is dead, Caroline."

"I know," I breathe, but the truth is, I don't know. Her body was never found. But I don't argue this point because I don't want the back-and-forth with Vincent about it.

From the garage steps a handful of cops carrying a body bag. It's the man. I turn my head so I don't have to look at it. My mind fuzzes between reality and the hallucination I just experienced, and I'm too afraid to ask the question, *did I kill him?* What exactly happened?

Vincent has worked with me long enough that he recognizes the confused look on my face and fills in the gaps. "You found Harley Laine in the garage, dead with his organs removed. There was a nearly unconscious girl chained to the wall, presumably the next victim."

I look down at my bloody fingers. "But why..."

"The girl was whimpering and you heard it. You ran to help. You tried to resuscitate Harley. That's how I found you." Vincent grabs a water bottle and a towel from the SUV and uses both to clean my hands.

I try to force my mind to make connections between Harley Laine, The Organ Ripper, the chained girl, and the other dead girls but my brain is too fatigued. "But I saw him alive, the man. He was walking from the garage." Though even I say this, I know I didn't see him. I was hallucinating.

Fallon appears at my side, grabbing my shoulders and turning me to face him. With his light brown eyes, he searches my features, and his jaw clenches at whatever he sees. I don't know why he's here. I guess I called him—or maybe Vincent did.

"You said you'd watch out for her," he speaks to Vincent. "This is *not* watching out for her."

"I-I'm fine," I tell him but Fallon ignores me.

"Detective Uzzo's already questioned her," Vincent tells him. "You can take her."

Uzzo questioned me? I don't remember any of that.

"Let's get you home," Fallon says, wrapping his arm around me and leading me away.

But as I walk with him, "This Little Light of Mine" echoes through my head...

"It's okay, Annabelle," I whisper, stroking her greasy hair. "I'm right here."

"I was just thinking about Grandpa and how I didn't say goodbye to him."

When Grandpa was dying of cancer, Annabelle was too scared to say goodbye. "It's okay, I said bye for the both of us." And when I did, Grandpa made me promise to always take care of Annabelle. That promise was the last thing I said to him.

Annabelle shifts and, in the blackness of the basement, my fingers flex into my sister's emaciated body. Somewhere above us I hear growling and sniffing. Am I imagining it?

"This little light of mine," Annabelle sings softly, "I'm gonna let it shine. This little light of mine, I'm gonna let it shine. This little light of mine..."

"I'm gonna let it shine," I murmur, "let it shine, let it shine—"

"Let it shine," our captor rasps from outside the door.

SEVEN

The following day, Fallon drives me back out to the cabin. And while he quietly navigates the back-country roads, I sit with my eyes closed, my body swaying with the gentle curves.

Reaching up I grasp my sister's peridotite necklace with her initials, *AC,* engraved on the back of the stone. Our captor had taken both of them for a ransom that Dad said never happened. The word "ransom" was meant to give us hope. Our captor never intended on giving us back to our parents.

Yet somehow when I was found I was wearing Annabelle's necklace, not mine. To this day I don't know why or how. But I'd like to think wherever her body is, she's got mine.

The August-born without this stone, tis said, must live unloved and alone. That was the poem Mom included with our 8th birthday gift. I sometimes wonder if she brought on our fate by giving us the gift.

Fallon touches my arm. "We're here."

Opening my eyes I stare out at Harley Laine's cabin,

the detached garage, and the greenhouse that lies beyond. This time yesterday this place was crawling with cops, paramedics, investigators, and Uzzo's team. Now only scene investigators move through the A-frame home and the detached greenhouse, carefully collecting and inspecting.

Vincent is already here, standing at the entrance to the garage. A crisp wind kicks in, blowing dry leaves up and around.

Fallon turns off the engine to my Mini Cooper. "You sure about this?"

"No." Unbuckling my seatbelt, I open the door. "But the bodies of the first two girls are still unaccounted for and I'll do whatever I can to help find them." To give their families closure. A closure my family never had. "Plus, I need a clearer picture of yesterday."

Closing the door, I look at him over the roof. "Thanks for coming, you didn't need to."

The side of his mouth kicks up in a half-smile as he shuts the driver's door and together we walk through the woods toward Vincent.

"Good morning," he greets us both, handing me a tin container. "The seed bars you asked for."

"Thanks." With a deep breath, I glance into the garage taking note of all the white and yellow investigator markers. "They're done in here?"

"Yes, we're cleared to go in the garage only."

"I'll want to see the house when we can," I say. "And the greenhouse."

Vincent nods. "All the herbs found on the bodies can be traced to Harley's greenhouse."

"And the flowers?"

"Nothing yet on that."

Fallon clasps my fingers. "I'll be right here if you need me."

With a nod, Vincent steps aside and I move forward and into the garage. My gaze falls first to the blood-stained floor where, just yesterday, Harley Laine's body laid.

Next, my eyes track across the walls filled with pictures of his slaughters. There's one of Harley and Becka next to a deer, one of Harley beside a bear, one of Becka holding up a dead rabbit, and on and on. Becka, the daughter with cancer.

From the pictures, some depict a healthy Becka and others a sick one, it appears as if she has been in and out of remission since she was a tiny girl. When healthy, her light brown hair shines glossy and her naturally tan skin shows off her pretty dark green eyes.

"Any trophies?" I ask. "Antlers, stuffed dear heads, bear claws, skins..."

"A few in the cabin," Vincent answers.

"Yes, I'll want to see the cabin when Uzzo clears us."

A large stainless steel sink occupies the back corner with various knives hanging above it on a rack. A wooden table stained with blood sits beside it with a commercial-sized freezer. Next to that is the horrifying shackle and chain where I hallucinated Annabelle was being held captive when in reality it was the girl Harley was planning on killing. A girl that is safe and alive thanks to whoever killed Harley.

"The girl in the chains was found nearly unconscious?" I ask.

"Yes," Vincent says. "With a hood over her head. Uzzo has questioned her but isn't getting much."

"Fits the profile age-wise. Is this animal or human blood?" I ask, stepping closer to the stained table.

"Animal."

"Which means Harley has somewhere else. Perhaps he was simply keeping the girl here with intentions of moving her. Harley was a personal chef. Detective Uzzo should look at clients. She should also look to see if Harley owns any other properties. Where is Becka now?"

"In the oncology ward at Tennessee Holistic Hospital. She was questioned yesterday and doesn't know anything."

Opening the freezer, I peer inside to find it empty. "How long has she been sick?"

"This time, three months."

"Which is when the first local girl was abducted." Turning, I look at Vincent standing in the doorway with Fallon hovering uneasily just outside. "I doubt we're going to find the two bodies, or rather we'll find parts of them if that."

"Harley knows what he's doing with animals, with humans. He's a naturalist. He knows how to use all the parts and pieces of them. Medicinal cannibalism versus dominant cannibalism." I know all about the aggressive and terrorizing latter but this isn't that. "Harley practices the former."

Vincent tucks his gloved hands into his coat pockets. "This seems too easy. Harley abducts two girls, kills, and uses the parts of them. He returns a third because he wants us to know cannibalism is at play. The fourth one we find on artistic display in a park. The fifth almost-victim chained up and ready to be slaughtered. What am I missing?"

Slipping a ponytail holder off my wrist, I pull my long hair up into a quick messy bun as I think through things. My brain latches onto my previous thought that two people are involved. "One who does the kills and one who covers it up."

"Which one is Harley?"

"I can see it going either way but I'm leaning toward the killer. The one who covers things up is tired of being manipulated. That person planted girl three in the dorm and girl four in the park, showing us how to find Harley."

"Are you thinking the killing will now stop?" Vincent asks.

"It's either going to stop or it's going to be different now that Harley is dead. The one who covers things up may be eager for his chance. Eager to do things his way now that he's not being manipulated anymore." Turning, I look up at Vincent. "The question is, how does the sick daughter, Becka, factor into this?"

"Detective Uzzo questioned her yesterday and got nowhere," Vincent tells me again.

"Then it's our turn." I walk from the garage and Vincent stops me with a gentle hand on my arm.

His voice is low when he says, "You can be done with this. Because of you, we found Harley. You can let Detective Uzzo take over and know with confidence that you've done your job."

Shaking my head, I say, "You know I have to see this through."

An understanding smile tickles the corners of his mouth. "Okay, but take caution with the emotional burden. I showed you the way out of the dark corners of your mind before and I can do it again. I prefer though, that you not get to that point."

You know exactly what's going on inside your head which is why you don't want anyone in it. He told me that years ago and he was spot on. "I'm okay," I assure him.

He holds both hands up. "Fair enough."

I turn away from him, looking again at the blood-stained floor. I stop cold when I see Harley Laine lying there, his organs piled beside him. All sound falls away and I stare, caught in a vacuum, unable to breathe. I squeeze my eyes shut inhaling a jagged breath and telling myself it's not real. It's not real.

Opening my eyes, I find the floor empty, save for the stain, and I let out a relieved breath.

Vincent moves in. "What did you just see?"

I shake my head not wanting to say anything, especially after the words we just exchanged.

"It's just stress," he assures me. "Harley is dead. Very simply dead."

"There's nothing simple about death," I whisper.

EIGHT

That night I sit silently in the oncology ward at Tennessee Holistic Hospital, nibbling on one of Vincent's seed bars and staring into the room where Becka lays asleep. Other than photos, this is the first time I've seen her, and I don't know why I'm still here. I came to talk to her but I can't do much of anything when she's asleep. Perhaps simply being near her will give me a sense of who she is.

If Harley was indeed practicing medicinal cannibalism, then he would have been bringing food in for Becka. I'm sure he came every day to visit his daughter. And he probably brought food each one of those days. This is something I need to ask a nurse.

My phone beeps with a text from Fallon: HAVE YOU SEEN THIS? Attached to the text is a link that I bring up. It's a picture of me from earlier as I stood on Harley Laine's property, taking everything in. From the angle of the photo, whoever took this was hiding behind either my Mini Cooper or Vincent's SUV.

TAKES ONE TO KNOW ONE is the title of the photo. I go on to read, *It takes a demented mind to know a*

demented mind. Tennessee state police used Caroline Chris-
tianson to help solve the recent private school abductions.
Many of you may remember Miss Christianson who, along
with her twin sister, Annabelle, were abducted from their
home some thirteen years ago. Missing for a year...

I stop reading and lay my phone face down on my knee.
Closing my eyes, I take a few breaths. I knew this was
coming. Every time I help Detective Uzzo and Vincent the
press latches on to me. It's been thirteen years. When will
they stop trying to make connections?

The haunting sound of the wind blowing through
winter trees echoes down the hall. Opening my eyes, I look
up to see Annabelle gliding toward me from the far end. All
the breath in my lungs suspends and I don't move as she
comes closer. Closer. And closer still.

I'm hallucinating but I don't blink. I don't make it go
away. I want to see her. She's eight years old, the same age
when we were abducted. Her long black hair blows out
behind her and her sundress presses to her body with the
wind. She draws closer still and reaching out, I try to touch
her but her image flickers, and then she's far away again.

I see her hunched in the darkness, her back to me and
her side leaning into the corner of the dirty brick wall. The
sound of sucking and guttural slurping echoes through my
brain. I don't ask her what she's doing, I already know. She's
eating her clothes, her hair, the skin around her nails.

She's so hungry.

I'm so hungry.

Above us and beyond the wood walls of the dilapidated
house he's keeping us in, the wind whistles. The last time he
took us outside it was colder than before. Winter. He took
us in the summer. Are Mom and Dad still looking for us?
Have they given up? Why haven't they paid the ransom?

It's been so long since our captor fed us. It's been so long since we've seen him. Has he been caught? Is he dead? Hope surges in me that he is, to immediately be replaced with the desire *to* see him. Because if we see him, then at least we get a little bit of food.

The grunting sounds of my sister stops, to be replaced by soft sobs that come shaky and remorseful. "It's okay," I tell her, as I always do, and she leaves the corner to crawl back over to me.

Her skeletal body touches mine and I grimace as the jutting and sharp bones pinch my skin. She presses against me, her bones cutting and jabbing, and I wonder when she's going to die. The thought used to frighten me, now it feels only numb. I can't save her and she can't save me. If she's not dead, I pray she goes soon. I can't take much more of her pain.

She puts her finger on my lips and I taste blood. "It's okay," Annabelle says, this time to me, and my tongue comes out to taste.

My lungs compress on a gasp as I zoom back to the here and now. I look up and down the hall that was empty before but now an elderly man stands several feet away propped up on a walker and dressed in a blue robe.

He coughs and it fills the area with the sound of mucus and the scent of rot. I breathe through my mouth and I do something I haven't done in three months—I ground myself in the present, just like Vincent taught me to do.

I whisper, "My name is Caroline Christianson. I am in a hospital. It is 7:21 at night. I am alive. I am okay."

A faint eerie whisper flitters through my thoughts and draws my gaze back toward the end of the hall where I saw Annabelle a few seconds ago. But she's gone and darkness moves in, carefully enveloping the gleaming tile, crawling up the walls, and washing everything in a midnight wave of dread. It moves closer, closer still, and my whole body shakes as it pulls away from the wall to touch me.

I say it louder this time. "My name is Caroline Christianson. I am in a hospital. It is 7:21 at night. I am alive. I am okay."

"Caroline?" Vincent speaks and my eyes fly open.

I look past him to a nurse writing in a chart and beyond her to the elderly man slowly walking away in his robe. I see a janitor mopping and an orderly wheeling a gurney into a room.

Clearing my throat, I scoot up in the chair. It was a dream. I wasn't hallucinating. I was dreaming. What is going on with me?

"You were grounding yourself," Vincent says. "What's going on?"

"You heard me?" I must have been talking in my sleep.

"Yes." Concern etches the corners of his dark eyes. "Anything you want to tell me about?"

I scoot further up in the chair. "It's Annabelle. I'm dreaming of her. I'm hallucinating her. I'm dreaming that I'm hallucinating. It's this case. I know it is."

Vincent slides into the seat beside me. "Yes, of course. It's natural for your mind to draw the parallels with your sister given the content we're dealing with. You did the right thing, grounding yourself. Just make sure you keep talking to me. Don't close me off to what's going on, okay? And don't push yourself beyond your limits. I'm not inside your head so I'm trusting you to know those limits."

Blowing out a breath, I pat my cheeks. "I got this," I say, more to assure myself than him.

Vincent studies me closely for a few seconds, then

apparently appeased with what he sees, he says, "Have you had a chance to talk with Becka yet?"

"No, she's been asleep. But I want to talk to the nurses to see if Harley brought her food each day."

Vincent smiles. "Great minds and all that. I did talk to the in-charge nurse a few minutes ago, and yes, Harley visited Becka every afternoon and brought her a container of food."

"You and I both know what was most likely in that container."

"Yes, but Harley took those containers with him and so we have nothing to give Detective Uzzo to test."

My phone still lays face down on my knee and I pick it up to show him the text from Fallon.

Vincent glances at it. "I'd wondered if you'd seen this. You're not surprised are you?"

"No. I hate the image these articles create of me though."

Crossing his left leg over his right, Vincent glances into the room where Becka lays asleep. "It does but what you need to remember is that catching Harley was a success, no matter what people say about it—or you."

"Yeah, well, Becka's life sure isn't a success. Look at her in there."

"Are you feeling sorry for her?"

"Of course."

"Does it feel good that Harley's dead, or does it feel good that the girl found in chains is still alive?"

"Both," I answer without hesitation.

"Good. Never feel sorry for your honest thoughts." Uncrossing his legs, he shifts to get a better look at me. "Tell me, when you found Harley in that garage, who were you seeing?"

Vincent is trying to get inside my head and so I shake it, silently telling him I don't want to answer. Emotionally, I can't handle this right now. I don't want him to know that I saw my captor.

"Did you see the ghost of someone?"

"Harley being dead feels just," I say instead of answering his probing question.

"Which is why you're sitting here. To prove that justness."

I stand up and move a few steps away. Even though I don't want Vincent in my head, he's still somehow getting there.

"You've told me before that you can get inside of a killer's head and live the scene of the crime because you feel as if you understand that killer. Did you do that with Harley? Did you see what he's capable of?"

"It takes a demented mind to know a demented mind," I repeat back the words from the article. "Why are you doing this right now? Pushing me. We're not in one of our sessions."

"It's a beautiful thing, the mind." He smiles. "Forgive me. You know that I'm constantly in awe of you."

I hate it when he says that. There's nothing to be in awe about. "I shouldn't have agreed to help out. I needed more of a break before diving back in."

"Is that what Suzi Derringer said?"

To that, I don't respond. I merely look at him. I don't want him talking about Suzi.

A few quiet seconds roll by as he keeps his gaze on mine like he's weighing his next words. Finally, he says, "This is what you're good at and you know it. What happened to you in the past has formed you into the person you are now. You can use that for good or for bad and here you've used it for good. You saw yourself killing Harley and that's what has you in this mood. It felt good. It's okay to admit that to me. You know that you can say anything to me and I never judge."

I look into his familiar long face with its equally long creases as I weigh his words, then I say, "Okay, yes. I felt like I was stabbing Harley and it felt good. It felt just. Because I was stabbing Harley, yes, but also my captor. And both deserve what they got."

"It made you feel powerful."

"Yes," I say, wishing it wasn't true. "So powerful." I look into his face, his expression more interested than concerned. Even when I don't want him to, he still manages to get inside of my head.

"Word of advice?" He asks.

"What?" I stand up, ready to leave because Becka's still asleep and I'm not going to get a chance to talk to her tonight.

"I'd be careful what you tell Fallon. You know how he gets."

NINE

My eyelids flutter open and I stare, disoriented, at the ceiling of our living room. It takes me a few seconds to remember that I came home from the hospital, laid down here, and then I must have gone to sleep.

A sleep, thankfully, with no dreams.

Early morning winter sun drifts in from the window above the red striped couch and, rubbing my eyes, I swing my legs over the side and sit up.

Through the great room, I look over into the dining room to see Fallon sitting at our rustic wood table with Petal curled in a gray lump on his lap. His long jean-clad legs stretch out under, crossed at the ankles, his top barefoot keeping the beat to whatever music he has in his ears. With a quiet sigh, he flips a page of his textbook and keeps reading and I use the few seconds to silently study him.

Brother and sister. That's what Vincent and his wife, Rachel, insisted we were during the years we lived with them. It was just the four of us in that big mountain mansion and neither Fallon nor I have a family. Everyone is gone.

Vincent and Rachel were trying to make a family, and I get it, but I have never once thought of Fallon as a brother or Vincent as a father. I did, however, think of Rachel as a mother.

Fallon glances up and, with a little smile, takes the earbuds from his ears. "You're up."

"Yep." I glance outside at the just-dawning morning. "How long you been awake?"

"About an hour. What time did you get home?"

"Late. I was at the hospital, looking in on Becka, and then I drove around for a bit." Trying to clear my head of the conversation I had with Vincent. "I just crashed here when I got home. I didn't want to wake you."

"I never mind if you wake me." He nods through the dining room and into the kitchen. "Coffee's on."

I make my way into the kitchen, stopping by Zane's bed to give his warm ears a little rub and go about pouring a cup of dark brew. "I was just thinking about how Vincent and Rachel always called us brother and sister."

Fallon chuckles. "Until Rachel caught us in bed. You would've thought we were re-enacting *Flowers in the Attic* with the way she sat us down and discussed it all in length."

I chuckle, too, as I grab tofu from the refrigerator and a skillet from under the oven. "We'd been living with them for three years by then. I was fifteen and you were sixteen."

"I remember. All we did was sleep though. We didn't get busy for another year." He smiles as he marks the page in his textbook and closes the spine. "So was Vincent there when you saw Becka?"

Sliding a knife from the counter rack, I cube the tofu. "He showed up, yes."

Gently, Fallon places Petal on the carpet, then pushes back from the table and crosses the dining room into the kitchen. He comes up behind me putting his hands on my hips and propping his chin on my shoulder. "He presses you too hard."

Fallon's protectiveness makes me smile and I tilt my head to kiss his clean-shaven cheek. "I'll be okay," I assure him, though Vincent's parting words drift through my mind.

"Did you get a chance to talk to Becka?"

"No, she was asleep the whole time."

Moving away, Fallon turns the heat on under the skillet and coats it with oil. "She sort of reminds me of us."

"How so?"

"Tragic loss has led her to be alone. I mean, does she have any relatives that are going to take her in?"

"I have no clue." I grab a handful of cubed tofu and lay it in the warming skillet.

He folds his arms, leaning up against the counter beside me. "Then she'll fit right in, won't she?"

TEN

With a soft knock, I follow Vincent and Detective Uzzo into Becka's hospital room. Unlike last night, she's sitting up in bed playing with a doll. Or not playing, she's hand sewing one. Interesting hobby. She must be responding to whatever they're doing to her in here because her skin tone appears healthy and her weight, too.

She glances up at us and her dark green eyes go straight to me. They widen a bit in recognition and I can only assume that she knows me from the news, the blogs, the articles that perpetually surround me whenever I get involved in a case.

Vincent extends his hand. "I'm Dr. DeMurr and this is Caroline Christianson." He nods to Uzzo. "You've already met Detective Uzzo."

"What kind of doctor?" Becka asks, not shaking Vincent's hand, and ignoring it with an air of superiority fit for someone royal.

He takes it in stride, tucking his hand into his gray trouser pocket and assuming a casual pose. "I'm a psychiatrist. I often work with the authorities in profiling cases. Caroline does as well."

I'm so glad he didn't introduce me as a former patient.

Becka gives me a good solid up and down. "You look awful young to be a profiler."

"I'm twenty-one. I've been helping Dr. DeMurr for years now."

"Yes, I know. I've been reading about you. You have some magical connection with killers."

"I wouldn't call it magical."

She sets the doll aside. "Detective Uzzo says that you're the one who found my father?"

Her words hang in the air, weighted, and tears gather in her eyes threatening to spill over. I find the abrupt appearance of them odd. I search her expression, trying to get a read on her. She's both relieved and sad her father is gone. Interesting.

"Yes," Uzzo quietly says and Becka's wet eyes dry just as quickly as they became wet.

"He was crazy," Becka tells us.

Vincent slides into a chair beside her bed. "Is that something you want to tell me about?"

Shaking her head, she turns to look at me and silently I return her stare. I wait for her to ask a question but she doesn't. She seems very practical about everything.

"Becka, you need a place to stay. Would you like to come to my house?" Vincent glances over at me and I don't hide my surprise at that question. I wasn't aware he was going to extend her that invitation. "Caroline grew up there."

Becka looks at Uzzo. "Does he have your approval for that?"

Detective Uzzo nods. "Dr. DeMurr and I have already

talked. The only other option is to put you in a foster home and we both think you will be better off with DeMurr."

Becka shrugs. "Okay, I guess, but you know I'm dying, right?"

Vincent says, "Your doctor says you have one more round of treatment but, no, they have not told me you are dying."

Becka scoots up in bed, her senses more alert now. "If I go with you, what are you going to expect from me?"

Vincent doesn't immediately answer her as he weighs her words. "Nothing, Becka. I want you to be your true self. That is all."

Her eyes move over to me. "Is that what you were when you lived with him, your true self?"

"Yes," I say with complete honesty.

Her green gaze goes back to Vincent. "Will you lie to me?"

"I will never lie to you."

Becka huffs a laugh. "Only liars say that."

"You don't know me," Vincent says. "But in time you'll see you can trust me. I want you to be whoever you want to be and if you're not sure who that is, I can help you fill in the blanks."

She fiddles with the white blanket laid across her legs in her first display of uncertainty and nerves. She folds and refolds the seam, apparently thinking through whatever it is she wants to say. I eye her carefully, still trying to get a read.

Finally, she lifts a hesitant gaze. "Do you think everyone will think I'm like my father?"

Vincent doesn't hesitate. "I think it doesn't matter what others think but perception will drive that. Which is why I can help you with the things you say."

"Help me lie?" she asks.

"No, help you survive and not be held responsible."

Becka seems to absorb that. "I hear you have to think like a deranged person to hunt a deranged person." Her eyes track back to me and though she hides it well, I see a slyness in them.

I have a quick image of Harley Laine lying gutted on the garage floor and I move my gaze off Becka needing a few seconds.

With a weak sigh, she scoots down a bit in her bed. "Sometimes I can't articulate what I feel."

She doesn't seem to be having a problem to me.

"That's okay," Vincent assures her. "It's okay to show it if you can't speak it."

"I don't know. Nothing seems real right now."

"Did your father tell you about the girls he killed?" Uzzo asks and this surprises me. She's normally direct, yes, but tends to be a bit sneakier in her queries. She's taking a different tactic with this girl. Likely because Vincent told her to.

Becka falls silent. "I hate when people ask me questions I don't want to answer. I already told you I don't know anything. Who do you think killed my father? A vigilante?"

I wait to see if Vincent and Uzzo will tell her that I believe Harley had a partner in the killings. The Organ Ripper is plural and the second half of the team turned on Harley.

"We're not sure yet," Uzzo chooses to say. "We're working on that."

Interesting.

Becka looks between all of us. "It's a good thing I'm dying of cancer because this type of thing, finding out your father is a killer, is the type that would mess me up for life."

Vincent shifts, uncrossing his legs and leaning forward a

bit in his chair. "I'm curious, Becka. Do you feel betrayed by your father or do you feel mad at him?"

Becka gives that some thought. "I suppose it's like my cancer. I mean, what's the point? Cancer is what it is. It's just trying to survive and do its job. It's trying to kill me."

Curious analogy. I take a tiny step closer to her bed. "You never get used to trauma. It *should* bother you, that's why it's called trauma. You will replay the things you've seen over and over in your head. You'll question them. You'll wonder about them."

Becka studies me with scrutiny. "It's been two days since you found my father gutted. Have you replayed finding him in your head?"

"Of course I have."

"And did you feel bad about his death, even though he deserved it?"

"Yes," I lie, feeling Vincent's gaze on me. I find it odd that Becka is asking me the same questions as Vincent. Is it possible she heard us talking last night outside of her room?

Becka's eyes leave me, shifting back over to Uzzo. "Will you take me back to our home? I want to see everything with my new knowledge."

Uzzo nods. "We can do that for you once the place has been cleared for entry."

"I'd like to be there as well," I say. I've yet to see the cabin and I'd planned on doing that but now I want to do it with Becka. I want to see her reaction.

Done with us, she picks up a remote and turns on the TV hanging in the top corner. "I don't want to be rude but I want to watch my soaps."

With a nod, Vincent stands, and together we three exit her room.

"She's odd," I say when we're out in the hall.

A smile curls through Vincent's lips. "So were you."

I say to Uzzo, "I didn't think you were going to ask her about the missing girls."

She walks down the hall. "I didn't either but I was gauging her mood. Vincent's right. She doesn't trust us enough to speak the truth."

I glance over my shoulder and back down the hall toward her room. "She's a bit too practical about everything."

We come to a stop at the elevator and Vincent presses the down button.

"Are you sure about her staying with you?" I ask Vincent.

"She'll be safe there," Uzzo answers instead. "Whoever killed Harley could very well be targeting Becka next, especially if she knows more than she's letting on."

"You're putting a guard on the house?" I ask.

"No," Vincent answers. "No need. I have my home security unit and no one but us three know that she's there. She's safe."

"Agreed," Uzzo says.

It's true, Vincent's house is like a fortress up on the mountain. "Any luck with Harley's client list?"

"We haven't found anything yet. However, some clients have already come forward. With words like 'cannibalism' hanging in the air, they are understandably concerned Harley's fed them humans. We've taken some samples from those who had leftovers and are analyzing."

"There's no telling how many cold cases this might connect to," I say.

Uzzo sighs. "I know. If teenage girls are his thing, there are sadly way too many reported missing each day, week, month, and year."

The elevator door finally opens and we step inside the empty elevator. Vincent turns to me. "I want you to be careful. Whoever killed Harley may come after you if you get too close."

Uzzo nods. "As is with any case you help on. Do you want protection?"

I shake my head. "It's a risk we all take. Not just me." I press the button for the garage. "I know all about monsters and I'd like to see the bastard try."

ELEVEN

The next afternoon, we three check Becka out from the hospital and take her back to the A-frame home where she and her father lived.

As we climb from Vincent's SUV, I ask her, "From the photos hanging in the garage, you and your father hunted together. Did you have a certain place you liked to hunt more than another?"

Becka shrugs. "Not really. We tried all kinds of areas."

I follow that with, "Did you always bring the kills back here to gut and process, or did you have another place you did that?"

She walks toward the garage. "Here, if I hunted with him. But sometimes he went off by himself and would bring the meat back."

Uzzo and I exchange a knowing glance. There is some other place Harley is connected to.

I motion to the greenhouse that sits behind the cabin. "Your dad grew a variety of things. How long has he been a home chef?"

"As long as I can remember." Becka points to a white

van parked beside the garage. "He always takes that when he travels."

Perfect to abduct someone with.

"We're trying to find his client list." I step around a recently cut tree trunk. "Any idea where that might be?"

"No clue. But I know he had clients from all over." Becka comes to a stop just outside the garage. "What's with all the questions?" She looks at Uzzo. "Aren't you the one who is supposed to ask questions?"

"Caroline and Dr. DeMurr are consulting. It's what they do. They're trying to get a picture of the whole story. Please cooperate and answer."

"I'm just trying to get to know you," I tell her.

Vincent opens the door to the wood garage and stands aside. "Whenever you're ready," he says to Becka.

I expect her to hesitate but she doesn't. She simply steps right into the place where her father's body was found. Standing for a moment, she stares down at the rust-colored stain where Harley Laine was gutted.

A few tears brim in Becka's eyes, hovering but not spilling over, just like yesterday in the hospital. I take my attention off her and look down at the stain, too. My heartbeat elevates, thumping my ears, and I see Harley there again, blood gushing, his removed organs glistening.

"This is where Dad died?" Becka asks, even though she already knows the answer.

"Yes," Vincent tells her.

She seems to take a second to wrap her brain around it, then whispers, "Goodbye, Dad," before turning away.

She leads the way across the yard that separates the garage from the A-frame cabin. Tucked back to the right sits the small greenhouse, the door open with forensic tags visible inside. I make a mental note to ask Uzzo what they found but, other than verification of the herbs, my gut says nothing. He wouldn't have stashed bodies in there. But if Harley has been doing this as long as I suspect he has, then he's good. The fact is, if it weren't for the returned girl in the dorm and the one found on artistic display in the park, Harley would still be killing and getting away with it.

Becka used the word vigilante and perhaps she's right. Perhaps The Organ Ripper isn't a killing pair. Perhaps Harley was the one and only killer and his murder was an act of vigilance. I can only hope that's the case because that would mean there will be no more girls turning up dead. However, way down in my soul, I know it's not the case.

Yet that would explain why the girl in chains was found alive. A vigilante would leave her alive and well. I'll be curious to get Vincent's thoughts on this.

Crime Scene tape obstructs the side door to the cabin and Vincent removes it, balling it up and tossing it to the side. Becka's hand goes to the knob but she doesn't turn it.

"If you're not ready for this," Vincent assures her. "We can go and try again another day."

Becka can do what she wants but I am for sure going in there.

"No." Becka shakes her head, turning the knob and stepping inside. For a few seconds, she lingers in the doorway and I glance past her into a living room that has been thoroughly combed over by the investigative team.

"It doesn't look the same," she says, stepping inside. "It's a mess." She looks up at the ceiling and the second story above our head. "Did they go through my room?"

Uzzo nods. "Yes."

Becka's still looking at the ceiling when she asks, "Do you and Caroline do this a lot? Go places and look at crime scenes?"

"We do," Vincent tells her.

Becka looks at me. "How do you figure things out?"

"I can look at things and recreate it in my mind. I get to know the killer on a more personal level. I try to look at the killer from the inside."

An odd smile curls her lips. "So you're like a serial killer whisperer?"

I don't like that analogy but it seems to amuse her so I try not to take it personally.

"What does it feel like to be inside their head?" She asks, truly fascinated.

I give that some thought before answering. "Like I'm a shadow with weighted feet, trying to make my way into the light."

"With what happened to you as a child, there's no wonder you're so in tune with killers."

I'm used to hearing people say as much so it doesn't faze me when Becka does.

She turns a slow circle, looking around the country decorated living room with its blue plaids and shades of brown. "None of this seems like my dad. He was good-natured, funny, liked by everyone. He wasn't strange."

"Most serial killers are well thought of until they're not." I step around Becka and further into the living room. "Where would they be, Becka?"

"You mean the first two girls? I don't know." She tilts her head back, looking again at the ceiling. "My room looks out over that garage."

Vincent and I exchange a glance.

"Yet I never once saw a thing. Then again, I've been pretty sick these past months. If something was going on in that garage, I was probably in bed or the hospital and didn't realize it."

She wanders around the living room, picking things up and setting them back down. In the corner sits an oversized doll propped up in a small rocking chair.

"Did you make that?" I ask.

She glances at it. "Yep. It's one of my best." She keeps walking, continuing with the inspecting. "About a year ago we killed a deer and Dad made a big deal about using every single part of that deer. We ate it, of course, but he also used it for sewing, jewelry, and small tools. He even used the bladder to carry water..." Becka's voice trails off as she realizes something. "Dad fed me those dead girls, didn't he?"

I don't respond because the question seems staged. Like she's already worked the answer through in her head.

"It's probable," Uzzo answers.

A soft knock on the open door has us all turning to see a slender, red-haired girl around Becka's age. Her eyes go straight to Uzzo. "Are you the cops?"

"Yes. Can I help you?"

"You were in chains," I say, recognizing her from the follow-up photos.

Her gaze tracks over to me and she sucks in a breath. "Thank you." She takes a hesitant step toward me. "Thank you for finding me. Thank you for—" her lips tremble and she presses them together to contain her tears.

Gently, I assure her. "It's okay. It's all over. You're safe." I glance out the cabin's front window and down to her car, looking for a parent. Did this girl come here alone?

"What are you doing here?" Becka asks. "This is private property."

"Becka," Vincent quietly admonishes her with a shake of his head.

The girl glances over her shoulder and out the open side door in the direction of the garage. "I can barely remember anything. They tell me I had a hood over my head but I thought he was the one with a hood over his head. Maybe we both did."

She did have a hood over her head. Harley did not, though. "Do you mean the person who killed Harley? That person had a hood?"

The girl shrugs. "I guess I thought if I saw the place, it might jog something loose."

That I understand, though sometimes the things jogged loose are not what you want. The word "hood" catches and clings in my brain. My captor always wore a hood.

"It's very brave of you to come back here," Vincent assures the girl. "Do your parents know where you're at?"

She shakes her head. "No, and they would not want me here."

Vincent takes a step toward her. "Why don't I escort you out? You shouldn't be here without parental permission."

Ignoring Vincent, the girl turns, her gaze going to Becka again. "Wait, do I know you?"

Becka's attention doesn't waver. "I don't believe so."

"Your hair was different. Short and black. You were standing by my car."

"You've got the wrong girl." Becka shakes her head.

The girl takes a step back, stumbling. "I don't think so."

Becka keeps shaking her head. "You're mistaken."

The girl turns then and she runs.

"Wait!" Uzzo yells, running after her, but a few seconds later a car engine roars to life and tires peel out.

Shifting I look out the front window to see Uzzo unclipping her cell from her belt and making a call.

Becka defends herself. "She's crazy. Black hair and standing by a car? I've barely been anywhere but here and the hospital these past months." She sits down on the brown leather couch, dragging a fabric pillow over to hug it to her chest. "I don't know what she's talking about." She lifts pleading eyes. "I promise I don't."

Clutching the pillow, she silently rocks, staring at the colorful woven rug beneath her feet. Her breath catches and Vincent turns away, giving her a moment. I don't though. I keep watching her, trying to gauge if the emotion is fake or real.

Then she stops rocking, and something must dawn on her because she throws the pillow aside and drops to her knees. She claws at the woven rug and my heartbeat elevates to thump in my ears as her thin fingers dig up and under the various colors, ripping them from the pattern. With shaking hands, she holds up a clump of multi-colored thread.

I come down beside her, leaning in to look.

Only it's not threading. It's human hair.

TWELVE

That night I sit on my porch, staring out at the rolling hills that lead up to Suzi's house. To the side sits her greenhouse glowing a soft green. Inside a shadow shifts as she moves from one plant to the next, tending. Maybe I'll wander over and say hi after I get off this phone call with Detective Uzzo.

Uzzo's saying, "The problem is that, yes, Harley had clients all over and he's been a home chef for years. What clients we know of so far cross state lines. He also operated quite extensively in cash only. Cross-checking all of that with timelines and missing girls—"

"Makes tracking cold cases nearly impossible."

Uzzo sighs. "It's going to take time for sure. There is one heck of a lot of missing girls. I've placed a call to the FBI."

I take a sip of my herbal tea. "Good, you need the manpower."

"For now, all we can do is focus on the ones here. That rug was a huge find," she says. "Thanks to Becka. We're currently dismantling it but there's a lot of human hair in that rug. It's going to take a while to trace it all."

"And the girl from earlier?"

"Her parents are bringing her in for another round of questioning. Also, I wanted to get your take on something. Why high-profile private school girls? Why not just home-less girls who would be less likely to receive the media's attention?"

"The quality of the meat," I say without hesitation.

Uzzo pauses. "I think I just threw up in my mouth."

"You asked."

"That I did."

"I know there are a lot of moving pieces right now but anything on other properties Harley may have owned?"

"Nothing yet. Listen, we'll touch base later. I've got another call coming in. I need to go." She clicks off.

I take another sip of my herbal tea. In the distance, Suzi leaves the greenhouse crossing over into her home. She'll be going to bed soon. I'll catch up with her tomorrow.

From my lap, I pick up the woven threads of my latest bracelet and braid in a black bead. Rachel taught me how to make jewelry. When I first moved to their home I didn't talk and Rachel used jewelry-making as a way to spend time with me. Even though we worked in silence, somehow our art helped us to communicate.

Eventually, I began talking but I never gave up with the jewelry, and every time I start a new piece I think of Rachel. Where is she and what is she doing? Does she still make jewelry? Does she think of me as I do her?

As I finish weaving in the black bead and start on the next section, an eerie silence falls in the darkness around me. The blood in my veins moves, humming through my head, and I hear a rustle over to the right.

Glancing over I see my sister, her feet bare, walking quietly across the dried grass toward me. She's not eight years old this time, she's twenty-one, just like me. I hold my breath, hoping it's real but knowing it's not.

She stops and she watches me for a few seconds before her lips move. "Hold still. Still. It'll all be over in a second. Second."

Those words and hearing them again freezes me in place. She backs away and I shift forward in my chair, not wanting her to leave. The image of her shifts and changes, and now she's Harley Laine dressed in a flannel and jeans. Blood darkens his shirt right where his abdomen is and with shaky fingers, Harley presses against the wound.

The image shifts again and now I'm looking at our captor, dressed just like Harley but with a hood over his head. He reaches up under his hood and his fingernails scrape across the bristle covering his neck. Those eerie three notes he always whistled float through the air...

The exterior light on our farmhouse clicks on and I'm once again alone on our porch. There is no Annabelle. No Harley. No captor.

Hold still. Still. It'll all be over in a second. Second.

Those words and their cadence. I would never forget them. Nor that whistle or the sound of him scratching the whiskers on his neck. Annabelle. Harley. Our captor. My mind wouldn't be putting them together if they weren't all somehow connected.

In my peripheral I see a squirrel leap from a nearby tree onto our porch rail and, despite where my mind just was, I still smile a little. "Hi there, little guy."

He comes to his haunches to study me.

"You hungry?" I ask, already standing to gather some seeds from the bird feeder. Carefully, I toss them his way and I continue to smile as he eagerly gathers them up. He turns a little and I catch sight of several white dots speckling his tail. Rover had white dots...

I stand alone on the playground, my back to all the 5th graders, tossing sunflower seeds at the family of squirrels that have come to be my only friends. Before the woods, I had friends. I had a best friend, a sister. Now I have the squirrels.

Behind me, all the kids in my class compete in a T-ball game that the P.E. teacher banned me from.

I don't "play well with others".

Through the air floats the scent of tater tots on today's lunch menu. It's not my favorite but I'll smother it in salt and ketchup to make it palatable.

One of the squirrels, whom I've come to call Rover, ventures closer to me than the others. I hold my breath, afraid to move, afraid to frighten it away. I drop a sunflower seed just inches from my shoes and Rover glances up at me as if weighing his options.

Behind me I hear shoes shuffling through the grass and leaves, followed by snickers, and I brace myself for what is coming.

"Look at the retard and her squirrels," someone says.

Ignoring the kids in my class, I toss more sunflower seeds, this time farther away, encouraging the squirrels to scat. Something hits the back of my tee-shirt and I glance down to see a rock land between my shoes.

"She's not a retard, she's mute," another kid says.

"Same thing," the first one replies.

In the distance, the P.E. teacher blows her whistle. "Let's go!"

Behind me, I hear the kids scurrying away. "Come on," one says. "Let the retard, mute, whatever be late."

"I'll catch up," the first one says.

A few seconds go by and I stare at Rover and his family as they pick up the remaining seeds. In my peripheral vision, something small flies past and I glance over right as a rock cuts through the air to ping Rover directly in his back. He jumps and races away and slowly, I turn to face whoever stands behind me.

It's a boy in my class. I don't know his name. I don't care to know any of their names. I prefer making up names. This one I call Bleach because his hair and skin are always pale.

Bleach catches my gaze and he snickers. "What are you going to do about it, retard?"

I don't respond with words. He's taller, he's bigger, and I don't care. I lunge forward, shoving him hard, and Bleach goes down fast in the dirt and grass. Stunned, he doesn't even fight back and I scramble on top of him. Holding his shoulders down with my knees, my fists fly, driving my knuckles into his face again and again.

The edges of my vision narrow to just Bleach and his cruel face and I zero in on his pale eyes and the true fear I see in them. Blood spurts from his nose and it gives me a tiny bit of satisfaction.

He wrangles an arm free and lands a scratch to my neck. Bleach tries for another and I block him, digging my fingers into his forearm and driving it back under my knee.

In the distance, I hear yelling, then there are hands on me pulling me back. I don't take my eyes off Bleach as he scrambles in horror away from me. My hands flex and I feel the strain in the bones and muscles. I think I broke a finger.

Someone shakes me. "What is wrong with you?"

I don't respond. I just keep staring at Bleach and the bruise quickly forming around his now bloodshot eye. I hope it swells shut.

The P.E. teacher drags me to my feet. "You're an animal."

She's right. I am. My captor made me one.

THIRTEEN

Later that night I lay beside Fallon in bed and while he sleeps soundly, I stare at a framed photo of my family. Of Grandpa seated with me and my sister, each propped on one of his knees and my parents standing behind us. I study each smiling face, trying to remember that day. Trying to remember the sound of our laughter, or our words, or the smell of Grandpa, or even who took the photo.

But nothing comes.

Instead, I hear only my dad's voice. "I wish I could put Annabelle's body to rest. I wish your mother was still here. I wish I didn't have to be the strong one. Why did your mother have to kill herself? Why aren't you talking yet? If you could just be nice to people like you are to animals, Caroline." A sigh. "I can't do it anymore. I don't know how to help you. It's time to take you someplace else."

I wish—

Why—

I can't—

Nearly all of Dad's sentences started that way.

I can hear Suzi's gentle voice next. "Caroline, if your father was here right now, what would you ask him?"

That's easy. I'd ask him "why." Why did he leave me? Why did he give up?

Why?

PART TWO

Nine Years Ago

With my forehead pressed to the chilled glass, I stare out at the trees and thick greenery as we wind our way up the mountain to my new home. The home where I grew up sits about sixty miles to the west.

It's time to take you someplace else. I never imagined Dad meant the institution where I've been living for the past six months.

When he came to visit me there, he told me that he sold our home and that a new family was living there now. Though he didn't tell me why he can't stand to be there. Neither can I. Too many memories.

My sister's death. My mom's suicide. Me coming back broken. If I would've just died in those woods with Annabelle, Dad wouldn't have to deal with me. He must be happy that Dr. DeMurr has agreed to take me in. I'm no longer Dad's problem.

Dr. DeMurr points to the right. "Just up there. Do you see it? I think you're going to love it here. It's very peaceful."

For the six months that I was institutionalized, Dr. DeMurr met with me every single day. I like him okay. He doesn't treat me like a child. But mostly he lets me be whoever I want to be.

He's been talking nonstop since he picked me up but I don't mind. I like the sound of his voice, deep and mellow with a lilt to it. It matches the way he looks with his vest, flat cap, and the deep dimple in his chin.

We round the last curve and his SUV pulls through an open wrought-iron gate with a simple wood sign that reads THE DEMURR RESIDENCE attached to it. A long, gravel driveway winds through a manicured lawn, around a fountain big enough to wade in, and comes to a stop in front of a white stone mansion.

He puts the SUV in park and turns to look at me over the front seat. "If at any time you don't like it here, you only need to tell me. We're all about honesty and communication." Turning the engine off, he opens the door. "Now, let's have a look around."

My door opens and I glance up to see a beautiful black woman smiling down at me. For a second or two, I think I might be imagining her, and with the sun illuminating her from behind, I think she might be an angel.

Then she speaks. "Hi, sweet girl. My name is Rachel and I am Dr. DeMurr's wife. We are so very delighted to have you here in our home."

She shifts back to give me room and her long dress drifts with her movement. Unclipping my seatbelt, I slide free from the leather seat and my feet touch the gravel driveway as I stand.

I'm not sure what makes me look but I glance to the right past the manicured lawn to where a row of trees borders the property. A boy stands there, a little older than me, with shoulder-length blond hair. He's dressed in light jeans and a white tee. Beside him sits a mixed breed puppy that looks like a combination of Great Dane and Rottweiler.

"That's Fallon," Dr. DeMurr tells me, opening the trunk and grabbing my suitcase. "He's been here a few months and is one year older than you. He's thirteen. And that beautiful puppy beside him is Zane."

Zane. I like that name. Holding my hand out, I silently beckon Zane to come but he doesn't move from Fallon's side.

Rachel nods to the steps that lead up to the front door. "Come on, let me show you to your room."

I follow behind Rachel but I never take my eyes off Zane and his control. Stepping through the wide-open door and into the air-conditioned and pristine interior, my gaze trails over the details—the polished tile floors, the flowered wallpaper, the gleaming and curving stairwell. The scent of lemon lingers in the air and I surmise it has more to do with the cleanliness than well-placed air fresheners.

Dr. DeMurr steps in behind us and closes the door. "It's a large place but we're a small family." He climbs the stairwell. "Let me show you to your room."

Rachel heads off to the left and through an archway that leads into a formal dining room.

"We're removed from the world up here," Dr. DeMurr keeps talking. "No television or computers or iPhones. Just us, open doors, and nature."

Open doors. I like those words.

I take the steps one at a time, thirty in all until we come to a landing. To the left stretches a carpeted hall with open doors on both sides, everything done in burgundy and white. Same to the right.

Dr. DeMurr nods his head toward the end where white double doors sit open on both sides. "That's the master suite." He comes to a stop at a room on the left. "And this is yours."

Walking in, he places my suitcase beside the bed and I step through the doorway into a room done in light greens and blues. A full-size bed sits centered against the wall with nightstands on both sides. A dark wood desk takes up the corner and beside it is a door that leads into a private bathroom. A grand window with a cushioned seat looks out over green and rolling hills. But it's what's above the bed that draws my attention.

A black and white photo of an owl in flight. An owl. My sister's favorite animal. It's no coincidence that the photo is there.

Dr. DeMurr scoots past me and back toward the door. "I'll leave you to unpack." He disappears down the hall and I climb up onto the bed, staring at the owl. I lay down on my back, still staring, and I stretch my arms out wide mimicking the owl's flight.

But I'm no longer here on this bed, I'm there in the woods laying in the dirty snow...

My breaths coming slow, I stare up at the owl hovering in the sky. Nearby a fire crackles, cooking the skin our captor just peeled from my stomach.

From the change in seasons, I estimate we've been with him well over six months and closer to a year. I don't think he ever asked for a ransom. I don't think he ever planned to. I think he always knew what he wanted to do with us.

"Here, this will help with the pain," our captor rasps, feeding me an herb. Why is his voice sometimes raspy and other times not?

As I slowly suck on it, he soothes the raw patches on my abdomen with a thick paste of honey and charcoal.

I try to focus on his eyes that are visible behind the hood but everything is a blur with the herbs in my system. I don't want to eat them but the pain is too much. I need whatever it is he's giving me.

I focus back on the owl. Why isn't it moving?

My captor recaps the jar of thick paste and moves away from me. Through the trees, I hear the big black and brown dog, yelping, and whining. I used to be afraid of him but now I'm not. I like it when he comes over and licks me. I like it when he lays on the other side of the basement door, sniffing the gap where the door doesn't quite reach the bottom.

Something wet drips across my cheek and I involuntarily flinch. I keep staring at the owl. Why is it hovering in the sky? Is it looking at me?

Another drop of something wet lands on my cheek, sliding down toward my lips. My tongue comes out to grab it and I taste the distinct salty iron of blood.

Is the owl bleeding?

The sun shifts, coming out from behind the winter clouds and illuminating the woods. I blink and the owl becomes my sister.

She's hanging above me, suspended by her wrists and attached to a limb. Her bare, dirty feet dangle limp, pointing right at me. Her head lay at an odd angle, her chin touching her chest, and blood covers the entire right side of her head where her ear has been sliced free to expose fleshy meat.

I open my mouth and I scream.

"No!" I thrash across the bed. "No!" I yank at my ear. "Take mine! Take mine!"

Something heavy lands on me and, with a growl and a grunt, I shove at it. I claw at it.

"It's okay," Rachel coos. "Easy. Easy." Her warm and comforting fingertips touch my face, lightly tapping across my cheekbones, down my nose, and across my forehead. "I'm right here. I'm right here."

With my eyes still closed, I go still under her tapping, and the weight that has me pinned gradually eases. I open my eyes to see Dr. DeMurr climbing from my bed with claw marks down his cheeks and neck. I want to tell him I'm sorry but I don't.

Above me, Rachel smiles, kind and gentle, now soothing her fingertips into my tangled hair to softly massage my head. With a shiver, I reach for her and she opens her arms to accept me. I crawl into her lap and while she rocks me I cry the first tears I've had since being with our captor.

Dr. DeMurr takes a step away, giving us space.

Sometime later, I lift my head and I focus on Rachel's smooth dark skin, pretty and glossy lips, and tilted black eyes. I only just met her but there's something very different about Rachel, and though at this moment I can't quite figure out what it is, I like it. I like that she touches me without hesitation.

With a kind smile, she says, "Better?"

I nod.

"Caroline," Dr. DeMurr says but I don't take my eyes off Rachel. "Let Rachel help you get cleaned up and then I'd like to see you in my office."

Dr. DeMurr sits behind a large and gleaming dark wood desk. His lips curve upward when I walk in his office door. On a brown leather chair sits a notepad and pencil. I take them and place them in my lap as I slide up into the chair.

Looking across the desk, I note the scratches trailing his cheeks and neck, noting him taking in my ears, too. I flip the notepad open and scribble *I'm sorry* and I show it to him.

His eyes gentle. "That's quite all right, Caroline." Closing a red leather journal, he places it in a file cabinet built under his desk and I hear the sound of digits as he punches in a code to lock it.

With a quiet breath, I put the pad back down on my lap and I glance around the office. Over to the right stands an old-timey clock, its methodical ticking filling the air. In the back corner sits a round wooden table and chairs. Beyond that spans a window much like the one in my bedroom with a cushioned seat and looking out over the hills that roll down the mountain to the town below.

Shelves line every wall, filled with books and journals, and my gaze trails the spines. Reaching over, Dr. DeMurr presses the button on top of a sound machine and a slow, deep and methodical whirl emits from the speakers. For a good solid minute he doesn't speak, just lets the white noise resonate through the air. I think he's trying to lull me into a hypnotic state but I find myself blocking out the sound machine and focusing instead on the grandfather clock and its tick.

In his pleasing alto tone, Dr. DeMurr speaks. "I want you to know that our home is a safe place for you to explore yourself. If you want to scream, you scream. If you want to dance, dance. If you want to throw something, throw it."

Linking his long tan fingers, he settles them across his flat stomach and leans back in his chair. Again, he lets a good solid minute go by while the sound machine fills the air. And again, I focus instead on the tick.

Outside the window, a shadow moves, and I refocus on Rachel as she sits in a rocking chair. She must sense my eyes because she lifts her own to look at me.

"I know you have nightmares about the time that you were gone and I know those nightmares involve your sister."

I bring my attention from Rachel over to meet Dr. DeMurr's gaze. I see acceptance there and not the constant worry I always detect in others' eyes.

"Do you remember the last time you saw your sister?" He asks.

I take the pencil and the pad and I scrawl, *Yes*.

"What did you see?"

Her eyeball, I scribble.

FOURTEEN

Present Day

The following day Vincent moves Becka to his home and invites me and Fallon to dinner. I go more for the food than anything. Vincent has a way of preparing dishes that I like. Otherwise, I can take food or I can leave it. I eat only because I have to, not because I want to.

After we're all seated in the formal dining room, Vincent smiles warmly at each of us, motioning to the platters of food laid out down the center of the table. "Bon appétit." He points to the bowl of spice that he placed next to my setting. "Especially for you."

"Thank you." He knows I like my food hotter than most. Taking a helping of mango-artichoke salad, I glance to the end of the table where Rachel always sat. I'm not sure I'll ever get used to seeing that spot empty.

Becka looks straight at Vincent. "So, Dr. DeMurr, what about you? I assume you have or had, parents?"

"Anytime you're comfortable calling me Vincent, you're welcome to. But to your question, both of my parents died when I was just a little boy. I was in the foster system after that until I aged out."

As I pinch spice from the bowl and sprinkle it over my food, I consider that for a few seconds. "We're all orphans here."

"Yes," he says. "We do have various things in common, don't we? But we've done well at assembling our little family." He gives a kind glance in Becka's direction. "Now grown by one."

He's right about that. We're linked whether we want to be or not. Our little family is getting bigger, yet there's still something so foreign about the concept. Maybe because we created this family. We weren't born into it. In some ways, it makes more sense. The family you're born into is just people you don't choose. But when you make a family with others, you get to choose.

As Suzi and I have chosen. We're building a family of our own I suppose.

"Family tends to adopt the same attitudes and behaviors." Becka glances across to me and Fallon. "I'll try not to get bit by that bug."

I reel a bit from that comment, not sure if she realizes she just insulted us. Fallon doesn't seem to have heard, or if he did, he doesn't care as he dishes a generous portion of the meat skewers onto his plate. The smell wafts my way, filling my lungs with the aroma, and I hate that it smells so good.

"I think you'll find their attitude and behavior worth considering," Vincent says to Becka and it makes me smile.

"So you assemble this family and we're to burst with love for you?" she asks. "Let me guess, no one can offer the safety and understanding that you do."

I wait for Vincent to respond to her continued insults but he doesn't.

Leaning in, Becka inspects the dish. "Well, anyway, what are we eating tonight?"

"Frog," he answers.

"Should've jumped faster," Becka jokes, and Vincent smiles. She cuts her gaze across the table at me before glancing briefly to the salad on my plate. "You don't eat meat?"

"No," I say.

"Why?" She asks.

Because I can't handle the way it makes me feel. But I don't say this and I don't make eye contact with Vincent when I say, "Personal choice."

Given that Becka only recently found out her father was possibly feeding her human girls, I'm surprised she's eating meat, too.

She says, "*Cruelty to animals is a sign of sociopathic behavior*. My dad used to say that."

And cruelty to humans? I want to ask but refrain.

"Be kind to the animal and then eat it," Becka adds. "There's no need for unnecessary suffering."

Becka doesn't say anything after that as she helps herself to dinner and eats, rotating her way around the plate —frog skewers, roll, salad, then back to the skewer—it's very organized, the way she eats.

Quiet moments tick by, filled only by the sound of our eating and the soft classical music playing in the background. I wait for Becka to break the silence, curious what'll come out of her mouth next.

She doesn't disappoint when she says, "So, Fallon, you don't talk much. What haunts you, my new friend?"

Fallon sits a foot or so away from me and visibly he

tenses. I want to jump in and say something but I need to give him the right to speak first.

Becka saves him from answering by following that with a shrug. "It's okay. We all have secrets tucked away."

There is something about this girl that rubs me the wrong way. She's a little *too* comfortable. When I first arrived here to Vincent and Rachel's home I was twelve years old and anything but. I was withdrawn, in shock, and mute.

Only days ago, Becka's father was savagely gutted. And there Becka sits, eating frog skewers like it's not odd at all she's now living in a new home and eating dinner with the person who discovered her father was a cannibal.

Vincent won't like what I'm about to do but he's going to have to get over it. "Harley Laine was a killer and, as his daughter, you have a bond to him that will never go away."

Quietly Vincent clears his throat but I don't look at him and instead keep my eyes level on Becka.

She swallows her bite. "What exactly are you implying? Do you think I was involved in the things my father did?"

"I think you're a little too comfortable with the things he did."

Shaking her head, Becka lays her fork down. "What, do you think if I was all tragic over here that the whole thing would make more sense?"

"Yes, actually I do."

Becka shrugs. "Well, that's not who I am." Pushing back from the table, she stands and her indifferent look becomes cold. She turns to Vincent. "Vincent, may I be excused?"

He inclines his head and, without another look at me, Becka leaves the dining room. But she doesn't go upstairs to where the bedrooms are, she disappears through the front door to wander the grounds.

I don't look at Vincent but I can feel his disappointing stare. "She needs an anchor, Caroline, as did you. As did Fallon. She's lost and it's up to us to help her find her way."

Why? Because we discovered what her father was doing? That makes no sense to me. "All she did was insult us and you let her."

"It wasn't the right time to not let her," Vincent says.

Vincent has his ways but tonight I'm not in the mood for them. I fork up another bite of mango-artichoke salad and I try to figure out what I'm feeling, why I'm acting the way I am, but nothing makes sense.

"You're jealous, Caroline. I gave you my word that I would protect you and now I'm leaving you to your own devices so I can focus on Becka. You're feeling abandoned."

My head snaps up and I glare at Vincent. "No, I'm not."

Under the table, Fallon reaches over and lays a comforting hand on my thigh. His fingers flex into my jeans. "Why don't we call it a night," he quietly suggests.

Vincent ignores him. "Yes, you are, Caroline. But the question is, how do you plan on dealing with it?"

FIFTEEN

I lumber down the dark road, staring vacantly ahead. A chill crawls through me and I shiver, dimly aware I'm dressed in my long pajamas. A bare foot steps into my peripheral vision, its dirty skin scraping against the pavement. It draws my attention and I look down, not sure if it's my foot or someone else's.

Tilting my head back, I look up at the bright moon. My heartbeat slows, thudding deep in my ears. The blood in my veins whirls and tumbles and I stop as my body sways. The foot brushes against me and I don't react. I simply look down at it. Only now it's not my foot, it's Annabelle's. I can tell from the second toe that's longer than the others and the pinky one twisted at an odd angle.

The road stretches in front of me, winding into the night. It vibrates in and out of focus as beams of light cut through the darkness. I hold my arm up to block the light's glare and squint into the brightness to note a black Camaro coming my way.

Fallon?

He rolls to a stop, looking at me through the open window. "Caroline? What are you doing?"

"I'm...I'm not sure."

Opening his door, he swings his legs out to stand. "Were you sleepwalking?"

"I-I don't think so."

Fallon takes off his leather jacket and wraps it around my shoulders, surrounding me in his warmth and scent. "Jesus Christ, look at your feet."

As if they're detached from my body, I look down at them noting the blood and dirt. "Where am I?"

"You're about a mile from our house. We went to Vincent's for dinner, I brought you home, then I went to campus to get some lab time in. You don't remember?"

I think about that real hard but I can't seem to latch onto the details.

Leaning down, Fallon picks up Petal. "What a good girl you are, following your mommy." He rubs her little gray head before turning a slow circle to look at my surroundings.

"What time is it?" I ask, swaying again.

"Around one in the morning." Leaning down, he looks into my eyes. "Did you take something?"

"No." I look back down at my bloody and dirty feet, gradually becoming aware that they hurt. "I thought my feet were Annabelle's."

Petal wiggles out of Fallon's arms, jumping down to circle my ankles. She's worried about me.

"I need to sit down," I tell him and lower myself to the ground but he grabs me under the arm.

"No, let me take you home."

Fallon picks Petal back up, tucking her against his long sleeve Henley, and leads us both over to the passenger side.

He gets me situated before climbing back behind the wheel and setting Petal in my lap.

Closing my eyes, I lay my head back and let him take me home. Was I sleepwalking? I'm not sure. I still could be.

A few minutes later, Fallon pulls into our gravel driveway. He lets Petal out before helping me up the porch and walking through the front door, standing wide open, where Zane sits keeping watch. Fallon leads me into the bathroom and sits me on the toilet seat. While he runs a bath for me, I glance at myself in the full-length mirror. My dark hair hangs long and tattered, scrapes cover my ankles, and blood and dirt cake my feet. I turn my fingers over to see dirt under my nails as well.

With a wet rag, Fallon cleans my feet. "Let me get the majority of this cleaned off and then we'll get you in the tub."

"Is that blood?" I ask, trying hard to remember what happened but nothing comes.

"Yes, it is."

I stare at the top of his blond head as he efficiently works, gently wiping away debris, rinsing the rag, and starting over.

"It's been years since I've seen you like this," he says. "Are you sure you didn't take anything?"

"I'm sure. Where were you coming from?" I ask.

"I just told you that. We went to dinner at Vincent's, I brought you home, then I went back out to the campus. Don't you remember?"

"I...I think so."

He sits back on his haunches, studying me, and his light eyebrows draw together with worry. "I think the question is more, where were *you* coming from?"

SIXTEEN

The next morning, I sit on my porch with Suzi quietly rocking in the chair beside me. As usual, she's knitting, pausing once in a while to sip her green tea. White fingerless mittens cover her hands and idly I watch her slightly arthritic fingers as they work the white yarn and needles. I can't be sure but I think this one is a beanie.

I usually wait for her to speak first but she's not talking this morning. Maybe she knows I have a lot on my mind. Like last night and how Fallon found me, Vincent's words to me about being jealous of Becka, and all the memories of late scraping their way to the surface.

I break the silence. "How long were you a school teacher?"

If she's surprised to hear my voice, she doesn't react. "Thirty years."

"Why did you go into that field?"

"I didn't have a happy childhood and I had no one to talk to. I knew I never wanted that for others. I always want people to have someone to talk to. Someone who listens. I almost became a school counselor and chose elementary education instead."

"Is that why you sit here nearly every morning? Because you know I need someone?"

She doesn't look at me as she continues knitting but her face curves up into a smile. "No, I come over here every morning because I like the company. I like *you*."

"So it's not my brain you want to pick?" Because I'm not used to people not having an agenda with me.

Lifting her head, Suzi finally looks over at me and her smile slowly fades as she does. "No, Caroline. I don't want to pick your brain. I like you and I like Fallon, and I'm so very happy you two are my neighbors. But if you don't want me coming over here, then just say."

"No!" I shake my head. "No. I'm sorry. I like you, too. Please don't stop coming over. That's not what I want."

Her sweet face curves up into another smile and seeing it has me breathing out a sigh of relief. "Good, now why don't you tell me about the fancy dinner you had last night. Fallon said you went to Vincent's?"

As if on cue, Vincent's SUV rolls into our driveway and comes to a stop.

"Do you want me to go?" Suzi asks.

"No, please stay."

With a nod, she goes back to knitting as Vincent climbs from his SUV and crosses over to where we sit. Carefully, he takes in my tired face and I note the file he's carrying. There's been another girl found.

"Where's Becka?" I ask.

"Still in bed when I left." He moves his gaze off me and over to Suzi, clearly waiting on her to leave, but Suzi ignores him as she quietly keeps knitting.

"Shall we go inside?" I ask because I want him to know

Suzi is welcome here. They both are. Just because he shows up doesn't mean she has to leave. He needs to know this. I won't be made to feel I have to pick one over the other.

With a nod, he follows me inside and over to the rustic dining room table where Fallon sits sipping coffee and staring at me. I come to a stop, my gaze taking in all his unopened textbooks.

"You okay?" I ask.

"No, I'm not. All I can think about is last night."

Vincent slides out a chair and sits. "What happened last night?"

A few quiet seconds go by as I remain standing, trying to figure out how to tell Vincent about last night when Fallon decides to do it for me. "We think Caroline might have been sleepwalking. I found her out wandering the road and she couldn't remember how she got there."

Vincent glances between us and if he's alarmed, his expression doesn't show it. Instead, he takes his flat cap off and lays it on the table. "You walked in your sleep quite a bit when you were younger but nothing in years. Are you sure that's what you were doing?"

"I'm not sure of anything. But what else could it be?"

"Could be stress," he says.

"Stress?" Fallon huffs an unamused laugh. "Well go the hell figure. She needed more than a few months off. Now she's back doing exactly what caused her to have a nervous breakdown. Cannibalism or not, you shouldn't have asked her to come back so soon."

"He didn't make me do anything I don't want to do," I quietly say.

Fallon leans forward in his chair. "He just said it could be stress. You were walking around last night and you don't remember anything. Don't you find that alarming?"

Yes, but in reality, it's the least alarming thing about me.

Vincent keeps his voice low and calm, not reacting to Fallon's irritation. "Was there anything aggressive about her last night?"

"No." Fallon drags his gaze off me and over to Vincent. "You're pushing her too far, too soon."

Vincent nods. "If that's the case, then Caroline, you need to tell me that. Your health is more important than what's inside this folder."

Fallon visibly tenses as I slide into a chair and I reach for the folder. A photo lay inside. It's the girl from the garage, the one found in chains, still clothed and sprawled on the garage floor right where I found Harley.

The girl is now dead.

Tears press my eyes as I stare at the horrifying scene. At the deep and choppy slices that try to run the length of her torso but don't quite make it. At the profound gap where someone thrust his hand in inelegantly to remove organs but left them mangled and sitting inside instead.

Without taking my eyes off the photo, I say, "Detective Uzzo said that she was going to talk to this girl again. Do you know if that happened?"

"It was supposed to happen later today," Vincent answers.

"And now she's dead. Who found her?"

"The mother," Vincent says. "She went into her bedroom to check on her, discovered she was missing and traced her cell to Harley's cabin and garage."

I blink my eyes to clear the blur and I focus on the cavernous somewhat-haphazard slicing. "Whoever killed Harley, their cuts had been vicious slices, yes, but expertly done. The girl found in the dorm and the one found in the park had been done cleanly and with a practiced hand, as well. This girl is a copycat. It's done by someone who wanted it to look like The Organ Ripper but didn't quite do it."

Vincent clears his throat. "I thought we were working on the hypothesis that The Organ Ripper is a team, as in two. But now you're saying there might be three?"

I don't answer him and instead, look at the speculated time of death. This girl was killed last night around midnight. At the same time, I was out sleepwalking. I don't want my mind to go there but it does. Harley's cabin is only thirty miles from here. I could've easily driven there and back. It's been years since I had a bout of sleepwalking but I clearly remember waking up behind the wheel of Vincent's SUV. I had driven nearly five miles from his home before I awoke and realized what had happened.

Fallon found me last night with scrapes and dirt and blood.

Something uneasy twists through my stomach and, pushing back from the table, I stand. "I need to see the scene."

SEVENTEEN

Police cars fill the area and I stand on this side of the barricade beside Fallon, taking in the scene at Harley's cabin and the detached garage. I could cross over the barricade but I don't want to. I want to observe from this distance.

My gaze tracks across the investigators moving in and around the yard and the garage. Two cops unroll yet another spool of yellow tape.

Detective Uzzo steps out of the garage with Vincent close behind. Swiping my finger across my phone, I bring up the photo of the girl's body sprawled across the floor. Her midsection split open and her stomach laying in an odd clump as if someone yanked it out and then shoved it back in.

Fallon glances over at my screen and if the scene bothers him, he doesn't show it. Like me, he's seen a lot worse. Powering down my phone, I say, "Something is off. As I told Vincent, the girl in the park and the girl in the dorm were done by the same person. There is no doubt in my mind about that. Whoever did Harley had a similar practiced hand but not the same mentality. Harley's killer wanted violence. This new girl was done by somebody else. Somebody who wanted to shut her up and at the same time make it look like it was The Organ Ripper."

"So possibly back to two killers versus Vincent's mention of three?" Fallon asks.

"All I know is that I'm not ready to buy into the fact there are three killers. Something is off." But more importantly, I don't feel the connection I thought I might be coming here. Yeah, something is off.

Sliding my phone into my back pocket, I glance through the woods back toward the garage. "Yes, whoever killed this girl was trying to shut her up. The last time I saw her was in Harley's cabin. She thought she recognized Becka, then got spooked and ran."

"I thought bringing you in was supposed to help." A cop standing on the other side of the barricade glances at me over his shoulder. "Some help. Now another girl is dead."

Fallon opens his mouth to say something and I grasp his forearm, shaking my head. The cop's frustrated. I get it. So am I.

The cop turns his back to me. "Why don't you do whatever it is you do and figure this shit out."

A shadow over to my right shifts and I glance over to see a reporter approaching with a camera following behind. Touching Fallon's arm again, I nod for us to go and that just spurs her on. "Caroline, is it true Harley Laine was feeding the girls to his daughter and his clients?"

The reporter pushes in closer and Fallon turns around to shield me from her and the camera. "Why do you guys always have to be such a pain in the ass?"

She gasps, recognizing Fallon now, I'm sure thinking what a jackpot she just hit. A commotion behind us draws her attention away from both of us and I turn to see a woman pushing through the barricade. She's sobbing, so wracked with grief she can barely stand. She must be the dead girl's mother.

And as I think this, I realize that I haven't bothered to know any of their names. When did I become so detached? When I first started helping Vincent and Detective Uzzo, I made sure to always know everyone's name.

Now though, they are "girl from the dorm" or "girl from the park" or "girl in chains".

EIGHTEEN

I sit in the dark field that separates our little rental house from Suzi's home. The trail she takes nearly every morning lies a few yards away from me with her home an acre or so behind me. Another acre in front of me sits our place and I stare at the dot of yellow light glowing from inside our home.

I like sitting here and doing this. It makes me feel like I'm with Grandpa again, night fishing, floating quietly in the middle of the lake. We would look at the houses in the distance and wonder what they were doing inside.

It makes me feel safe like my mind can't be breached by grotesque images and noise. Like the madness I often sense is at a safe distance. I try so hard to know the killers' Vincent brings me. I try to see past their acts and beneath the surface of their deeds. Sometimes I help, then other times there are things like the girl in chains that happen.

Girl from the dorm, girl from the park, girl in chains.

Irene. Yasmine. Nadia.

I need to always know their names. I can't ever be so

detached that I don't take the time to know names. I have to stay connected.

Irene. Yasmine. Nadia.

Nadia, the girl in chains.

Her death is on me. Not because I couldn't save her but because I feel like I killed her. I got too close. My involvement with this attracted the attention of whoever killed her.

Irene and Yasmine were done with clean, almost reverent, cuts and that does not match the savagery with which Harley Laine was done. And neither match the hesitancy with which Nadia was done. Yet the practiced hand of Irene and Yasmine match that of Harley. It's the motivation that is different.

Irene and Yasmine were special, they were needed. Harley was violent, retribution. Nadia was a last-minute thing gone wrong and made to look like The Organ Ripper. A copycat.

I hate even thinking this but I hope there's another body. I'll be curious to see if it's special, if it's violent, or if it's a copycat.

I finish off the last of the homemade seed bar that I brought out here with me and, grasping my sister's necklace, I lay back in the field and I stare up at the star-filled winter sky. A crisp breeze blows past and I catch the scent of embers. Suzi must have started a fire.

My thoughts drift and I allow them, sinking into them. When next I open my eyes, I'm no longer on my back. I'm curled on my side in the field and a shiver runs through me. I must have fallen asleep.

I sense, more than see, a presence beside me and I turn over to see a girl with dark red hair, though I don't recognize her. It's not any of the recently dead girls. I don't know who it is.

Wait, I do. It's the girl from all those years ago. The one our captor made me—I shake my head. I don't want my mind to go there.

She's sitting in the dry grass, staring across the field at mine and Fallon's home. She's older now, the age she would naturally be if she had lived. I'm imagining her but I go with it, sitting up and waiting. I wish I knew her name. I never learned it.

She doesn't look at me and I tilt a little to see the front of her naked body, expecting to find it raw and sliced open but it's not. She's whole and perfect. But I wouldn't be seeing this if she wasn't somehow connected to everything going on right now.

She looks over at me then, her dark eyes staring into mine, and her fear ripples through me with such power that I cringe. Yet, I'm not afraid. I'm more curious than anything.

Hold still. Still. It'll all be over in a second. Second.

My lips quiver. "I'm sorry," I tell her. "I'm sorry I—"

"Caroline!" Fallon yells and I turn away from the girl. Fallon and Zane run toward me across the dark field. I glance back, hoping to still see her, and find the spot empty.

"Jesus Christ," Fallon pants, coming down in front of me.

Wiping my eyes, I sniff.

"What's wrong?"

"Memories. Horrible memories." I look at his striped pajama bottoms and the leather jacket that he threw on over his tee. "What time is it?"

"Four in the morning." Fallon reaches for Zane. "I fell asleep waiting for you. His whining woke me up. I had no clue you were still out here."

Four in the morning. I came out here around nine at night. The last thing I remember, I was laying and looking up at the stars, hoping for another body. "I must've fallen asleep."

Tugging me close, Fallon searches my face, probably trying to ascertain if I'm truly awake.

"I feel fine," I assure him. "I fell asleep and woke up just a few minutes ago." I look again to where the girl was and I see nothing but a dry, winter field.

"I yelled out for you," Fallon says. "When you didn't answer, I let Zane out the front door and he took off over here."

Reaching up, I rub Zane's big head and panting, he drops with exhaustion, reminding me he's not a young pup anymore.

Fallon rubs his hands up and down my sweater-covered arms, warming me. Oddly though, I'm not as cold as I should be for thirty-degree weather. Cradling my cheeks, Fallon presses a kiss to my forehead. "Let's get inside."

"Do you mind if we sit here for a few minutes?"

Fallon doesn't immediately answer that, then with a nod, he settles in behind me, opening his leather jacket and wrapping it around me. I rest my head against his shoulder, staring idly across the field at our home. Just like I was doing hours ago before I drifted off.

"I never like what the cases do to you but this one is different. You're even more connected to the victims and the killer than usual."

"I know. Perhaps my 'talent' is maturing. Or perhaps it's solely to do with the cannibalistic side of it." I snuggle further into his warmth. "Either way, just keep being in my corner."

He caresses his cheek over mine, scraping my skin softly with his stubble. "Always."

"I can handle more than you think I can."

Fallon doesn't respond to that, then, "You're the strongest person I know, Caroline."

"Same goes."

"Then why don't you start by telling me who was here with you? Because I heard you talking to someone."

Slowly, I circle that question and the subsequent answer around in my brain. I think of Vincent's cautionary words about keeping Fallon in the dark. I would never tell Fallon that though. His and Vincent's relationship always seems to teeter on a fine thread.

"I saw the girl held captive with me and Annabelle."

"Makes sense, considering the case."

"Hm," I say, though my gut tells me it's more than that. This case, Annabelle, and now the other girl—it's my brain's way of telling me it's all connected. If I didn't know for sure what happened to our captor, I'd be ready to think he'd come back and was now The Organ Ripper. But that's impossible and nobody but Vincent and I know that. "What I do know is that I need some normalcy in all of this horror. I need you to be that normal."

In my periphery I see Fallon searching the side of my face in that thorough and purposeful way that he has. Then with a quiet sigh, he says, "Okay, I'll be your normal. How about we just sit here? We won't talk unless you want to. And when you're ready to go, you just stand up and I'll follow. Deal?"

With a little smile, I close my eyes. "Deal."

"Just promise me one thing, keep talking to me. Don't shut me out. Okay?"

"Okay," I say but somewhere way deep inside I'm pretty sure I just lied.

NINETEEN

Early the next afternoon, Vincent and Uzzo arrive at my front door. Their unannounced arrival, coupled with the fact Uzzo is carrying a folder, can't be good. Last night I was curious to see if there would be another girl and that folder contains one.

"Good afternoon," Vincent greets me, noting Fallon's Camaro is gone. "Is Fallon gone to class?"

"No, the grocery," I answer, glad for that. I don't want Fallon to see whatever is in the folder. I don't want him to tell Vincent and Uzzo about finding me in the field last night talking to a dead girl.

Stepping aside, I gesture them in but my gaze doesn't leave the manila folder gripped in Uzzo's fingers. As Vincent always does when he comes here, he goes straight into our dining room and, after settling his long coat over the back of a wood chair, he takes a seat.

"Coffee? Water? Tea?" I ask them.

"Water," Uzzo says.

"Nothing for me," Vincent replies.

While I go about getting Uzzo her water, she says, "Suzi tells me you two are becoming good friends."

Despite the fact I'm about to see pictures of another victim, I smile a little. "Yes, Suzi is 'good people'."

Something sweet and loving glints through Uzzo's eyes and it makes me think of Fallon. Or rather how I feel about Fallon. Is it possible Suzi and Detective Uzzo are more than just friends? I love that thought so very much.

Vincent clears his throat. "Shall we?"

Sliding Uzzo her water, I take the chair at the head of the table with Uzzo on the right and Vincent on the left. Looking again at the folder, queasiness churns through my stomach. "What happened?"

Uzzo speaks, not taking her fingers off the folder. "The body was found in a motel just up the road at two this morning."

I don't like that whatever I'm about to see happened so close to where I live. "Odd time to find a body."

"The owner was walking the property and saw the body through a slit in the curtains. Sixteen. Caucasian. Strangled. Split open with a hunting knife. Organs removed."

"Security cameras?" I ask.

"It's a mom-and-pop place. Old. So no cameras. The room wasn't registered to anybody. Whoever killed her broke into the room. Also traces of honey and charcoal."

"Just like the others. For healing." This one was special, not violent, and not a copycat.

Vincent nods to the folder. "Are you sure? We don't want to push you."

"I'm more than sure." Sliding the folder across the rustic table, I take a second to breathe, then I open the flap and slide out the first picture.

It's of a naked girl, sprawled face-up on the motel bed,

her arms and legs extended and secured at the wrists and ankles. I focus on her face. "Name?" I ask.

"Gaby."

Irene, the girl from the dorm. Yasmine, the girl from the park. Nadia, the girl in chains. And now Gaby, the girl from the motel. Add to that the first two still undiscovered bodies and our count's now up to six. Including Harley, seven.

With a nod, I look back down at the photo that perfectly matches Yasmine from the park. At the dark splotches on her throat from being strangled, at the redness around her wrists and ankles from the struggle, and at the practiced and sure way she's been split open and fileted with her organs removed. At the wildflowers that, instead of outlining her body, are placed inside to fill the void.

Closing my eyes, I take a deep breath, exhale, and I step into the darkness of my mind. My heart slows and with each deep thud, I settle into the scene. Everything rewinds in quick motion as the blood washes clean, the flaps of skin seal together, and Gaby lays alive on the bed.

I become The Organ Ripper, straddling her, my gloved fingers around her throat. She struggles, thrashes, then she loses consciousness far quicker than the others. Not dead though. Never dead. I take the organs while they are still alive and being pumped with hormones.

With rope, I secure her wrists and ankles to the four corners of the bed, ready for when she wakes up. I cut away her clothes and stuff her shirt into her mouth to muffle the screams that will come.

She wakes up then, her eyes wide with fear, and I smile down at her. I wait for a connection but nothing comes.

With a resigned sigh, I take the hunting knife and I split her open quickly, as painlessly as possible, then I expertly remove the organs. With great care, I treat her raw skin with honey and charcoal because I'm not an animal. I do care. Then I gently layer wildflowers inside of her.

Opening my eyes, I come out of the scene and look right at Vincent. "The killer has given us some presents."

Vincent shifts forward. "And they are?"

"He was looking for a connection and he didn't find it."

"That was your original thought," Vincent says. "A replacement of something gone wrong. A reliving of something going right."

"Yes," I agree. "Also, the wildflowers, the honey, and charcoal. He's allowing us to connect all the girls. He wants us to know Harley didn't work alone. They help each other. Probably have been helping each other for years."

With a nod, Uzzo makes a few notes on her pad.

I continue, more to myself than them, "Harley developed his methods with someone else. He taught his methods. Harley wanted to pass The Organ Ripper legacy down." I sit up with a surge. "The legacy wants us to know they are better. They are different. They are artistic. The student surpasses the master."

"Or Harley was the student and the master got sick of his ways," Vincent says.

I look at Vincent. "Interesting take."

Uzzo says, "The girl in chains though. She doesn't match."

"Nadia." I make sure to say her name. "Not done with the skilled hand of the others. Someone wanted to shut her up in a bad copycat attempt."

Vincent says, "Our original thought was that Harley was killing the girls and feeding them to Becka or his clients. But now with this new girl—"

"Gaby." I make sure he knows her name.

"Gaby," Vincent says. "Harley didn't kill Gaby, so what

is the killer doing with the organs? Eating them himself? Is he taking over Harley's client list?"

"Speaking of—" I glance at Uzzo.

"Yes." She nods. "Of the clients who voluntarily came forward, we got the samples back and there were no traces of human organs."

"And the clients who haven't come forward?" I ask.

"We're still looking for the complete list," Uzzo says.

I think about that for a few seconds. "It's almost like Harley suspected all of this was going to happen so he hid important documents. Like the client list and possibly other properties that he owns."

Vincent sits up. "You think so?"

"It makes sense."

Uzzo says, "There's a black market out there for everything. Organs included. If you're right in the legacy idea, perhaps the legacy was greedy and wanted to keep all the money. Perhaps the legacy hasn't consumed any of the organs."

I slide the pictures back into the folder. "Well, I guess you'll have to ask the reigning Organ Ripper that question."

"We're asking you," Vincent says.

His abrupt tone catches me off guard and my eyes snap to his. "In case you forgot, you're the official profiler. I'm only helping."

A stillness washes over the small dining room as Vincent regards me with both guilt and irritation that I suspect has everything to do with him and not me. Sometimes I think my "talent" for this frustrates him. He wishes it came easy for him as it does me and I wish I didn't have it at all.

"My apologies," he mumbles.

Uzzo clears her throat. "Why don't I step outside and

let you two have a moment?" Quietly she gathers her things and makes her way outside.

When the door closes behind her, Vincent says, "You should know that she's curious why you haven't made connections between your captor and The Organ Ripper. She's ready to believe your captor has come back and is on a new killing spree."

"You know why I haven't made the connection."

"Yes, of course. But if this case doesn't wrap soon, we're going to need to figure out how to close that door. We don't need Uzzo probing into your past."

He's right and I don't have a response to that. Not even Fallon knows that secret.

With that, Vincent gathers his things and makes his way over to the door. Grasping the handle, he turns to me. "I know you're hiding something from me. When you're ready, my door is open. No judgment. We're not supposed to keep secrets from each other, Caroline."

TWENTY

A few hours later I find myself standing in Vincent's office, staring at him across the expanse of his gleaming, dark wood desk. *I know you're hiding something from me.* His parting words are all that I have thought about since he left my home. I need to tell him that in addition to my recent hallucinations/dreams/nightmares/visions—whatever you want to call them—of Annabelle, that I saw the other girl, too.

This is a new territory for me and I need Vincent to help me through it. To understand it.

Taking my unsteady gaze off him, I fish inside my front jeans pocket for my headache pills.

"You seem to be taking a lot of those lately. Have your headaches gotten worse?" He asks.

By way of answer, I put two caplets in my mouth and grab Vincent's mug of herbal tea to wash them down.

Carefully, he eyes me. "Caroline, what's going on?"

"Are we okay?" I ask.

"Of course."

Turning, I pace the perimeter of his office, my gaze trailing over his books, journals, and historical maps framed and hung on the walls. I wander over to the French doors and see Becka sitting on the back porch, wrapped in a blanket, sewing on the same doll. So safe.

Without looking away from Becka, I say, "I think I need to sleep handcuffed to my bed."

"I take it you had another sleepwalking episode."

"Sort of." Turning away from the window, I trail back over to his bookshelves, idly looking at the framed photographs. There's one of Vincent and Rachel, much like I remember them when I first arrived here. There's one of Fallon with Zane sitting proudly beside him. There's also one of me taken by the fountain with my dark hair blowing in the breeze.

My eyes trace back to Rachel. It's my fault she left. Vincent chose me over her.

I turn to look at him. "Do you miss Rachel?"

"Of course. I love Rachel very much."

"Do you ever talk with her?"

"No, she's never once returned my phone calls or emails. But I have to respect that. She wanted to move on and sometimes that's what people need."

"Where does she live now?"

"I don't know, Caroline." A muscle flexes in his jaw and I can tell this subject is too close to his heart.

Still, I ask one last question. "Do you think she'll come back now that I'm gone?"

He shifts in his leather chair, crossing one leg over the other. "Her leaving had to do with a lot of things. You aren't to blame."

Vincent has said as much before but I still don't believe him. She left the morning after they found me in their room beside their bed. It's the last time I remember sleepwalking, until recently.

I turn away from the photos to look at Vincent. "Why am I the one who walked out from the woods that day? Why not Annabelle? Why did our captor torture her more than me?"

If Vincent finds the change in topic odd, he doesn't say so. "He tortured you, too, Caroline."

"But not to the extent he did Annabelle and the other girl." It's not often I talk about the other girl and what he made me do to her.

"Perhaps he saw something in you he didn't see in the other two."

I in no way take that as a compliment. "Why did he just leave me? Why didn't he kill me?"

"We'll never know for sure but in the state you were found, it's likely he thought you were already dead."

"Where do you think my captor went after I was found?"

"I think he was long gone before you ever stumbled from those woods."

"Do you think he did to other kids what he did to us?"

"Yes, which is all the more reason why it is a good thing you—"

Turning away, I shake my head, not wanting him to say the words. I don't want to remember what I did. Vincent respects that and doesn't finish the sentence.

Idly, I pace again.

"You did what you had to survive," Vincent says. "You know that."

I nod.

"The recent killings have you thinking about your past," Vincent says. "More than usual."

"Yes, of course. The use of a hunting knife. The choking. The removal of organs. The traces of honey and charcoal. Cannibalism. No stripping of skin though, but the parallels are there." Except the honey and charcoal are being applied to a corpse, not to promote healing as it was done to me.

Running a long finger over his bottom lip, Vincent thinks through everything I just said. "You're not unlike this killer."

That comment stops me cold. "How so?"

"You said yourself he's looking for peace. You are, too, in helping me with profiles."

With a sigh, I turn away to look out his French doors and down the mountain to the town below. "As I do with most of the cases, I've been trying to think like Harley and the legacy."

"But instead you find yourself in old patterns, like this development of sleepwalking again."

"And hallucinations. I saw the other girl, the one our captor brought in after taking us. I saw her last night in the field."

Still gazing out the French doors, I hear him sit up in his chair. "Interesting. That's never happened to you before. You've dreamt about her, just like you have Annabelle, but not this."

"I know."

"Did she speak to you?"

I almost tell him yes. I almost tell him exactly what she said but something makes me stop. I'm not sure what but perhaps it's simply because I don't want to remember what I did to her. "No," I say.

"I knew you were keeping something from me. I can tell when you do. Tell me, where were you when it happened?"

"I'd gone out to the field across from our house to think. I fell asleep thinking about how I wished another body would should up so that I could make better connections. And then when I woke up, she was sitting beside me."

"It's like your long-buried memories are trying to surface. It's like something in your brain is trying to connect your captor to the recent killings."

I turn away from the French doors to see him carefully studying me. "Yes, those were my thoughts, too." But again, there is no way that can be.

"Interesting." Vincent takes a breath, holding it for a second and then releases it. "This happened about the time the murder was taking place in the motel down the road from your house?"

"What are you trying to say?"

"Nothing. Just mapping timelines." He sits back in his chair. "You're still grounding yourself with time and place, aren't you?"

"Here and there I do."

"Do it several times a day now. You can't let this push you over the edge. We need you."

"I can make myself do this," I tell him. "But something is going on this time. My body is reacting differently. It's not like three months ago when I had a nervous breakdown. It's different. It's consuming, yes, but in a more personal way."

"You can walk out of here and never look at another file again but you and I both know the guilt will eat at you."

He's right about that.

I keep standing for a few moments, looking down at him still seated behind his desk, waiting for him to say more but he doesn't. He doesn't seem alarmed that I'm connecting so deeply with this case, the victims, my sister, and our captor. Maybe I'm making more of this than there is. Maybe this is simply the next phase of my "talent."

Quietly, I turn away. "Well, I guess I'm going to go."

"Okay," he says, still eyeing me with deeper scrutiny than he usually does.

I'm regretting telling him now. I don't want to be on his petri dish again.

I turn to leave and nearly run smack into Becka. I don't like that she just overheard us. She's standing close, too close, and I hear her inhale.

"Did you just smell me?" I ask.

Chuckling, she takes a nervous step back. "Of course not."

"What are you doing standing there? Are you eaves-dropping?"

"Caroline," Vincent sighs, "I'll see you later."

Smiling now, Becka steps around me, heading into the office. Without a glance back, I cross the foyer and let myself out.

There is something about Becka that's not right.

TWENTY-ONE

Winter settles across the mountain, blanketing everything with snow and ice. Dressed in my winter coat and gloves, I descend the curving stairs to meet Dr. DeMurr at the front door. As always, he hands me a spiral pad and a sharpened pencil.

This is our morning routine, strolling the ground, him talking about math and science, asking questions, and me scribbling my thoughts. It reminds me of all the times Grandpa and I would sit and read or go outside and explore the world.

With the usual welcoming curve to his lips, Dr. DeMurr glances down to my wrist where I wear the new woven and beaded bracelet Rachel and I made. "Pretty," he says and I smile.

He opens the door and I step through ahead of him onto the wide porch. Something over to the left catches my attention and I glance over to see a man carrying firewood. With a dark hood over his head, he walks toward us.

My entire body goes numb. "Captor," I rasp, not recognizing my voice.

I fly across the snow-covered ground, my sharpened pencil up and ready. I leap into the air, coming down with a wide arc of the pencil, driving the sharpened point straight into his collar bone.

With a scream, he goes down, the firewood tumbling, and I follow his movement. Grabbing a piece of the wood, I climb on top of him and I pummel his head with the blunt end of the wood. I toss it aside, stretch open my mouth and I sink my teeth into his neck right where his coat meets the hood over his head. With a holler, he thrashes, the sound and movement fuel my rage.

Strong hands clamp onto my shoulders, dragging me off, and I fight against their vise grip as my teeth release their hold. "Uncover your head," Dr. DeMurr commands the man, struggling to hold me back.

Scrambling away, the man takes his hood off and breathing heavy, he stares at me through wide, terrified eyes. I stare back, slowly realizing it's Timothy, the maintenance man. His gloved hand comes up, yanking the pencil from his neck, and blood trickles out to dot the snow.

"Do you see?" Dr. DeMurr asks me, for the first time his voice not calm but instead authoritative. "That is why you always have to be sure before you make a move." He squeezes my shoulders, forcing me to look up into his face. "Do you see?"

With a swallow, I nod.

Rachel appears, going straight to Timothy, and with soft murmurs, she helps him to his feet. Dr. DeMurr releases me and I stand in the snow watching Rachel lead Timothy away. When he's inside the mansion, I look down to where I attacked him and I see the pencil, the wood, and the disheveled snow, all splattered in blood.

My tongue comes out and I lick the corner of my mouth, tasting Timothy's blood. It brings me an odd sense of comfort.

Dr. DeMurr tracks my movement before nodding to where Timothy just was. "Now, clean it up."

As I sit next to Suzi thinking through the nine-year-old memory, I question if the whole thing with Timothy was staged. Did Vincent ask him to wear the hood to see how I would respond? Or did Vincent know he would be walking across the grounds at that exact moment? Was the whole thing some progressive way of making me face my fears?

It sounds like something Vincent would do. He's nothing if not unconventional in dealing with patients. The fact is, I've always trusted him to have my best interest. I've always trusted his guidance. I wouldn't be the person I am today without him. I would likely be an animal.

Still, though, I find myself questioning those ways.

And I likely wouldn't be reliving these old memories if it wasn't for my involvement with The Organ Ripper and the connection I feel must be there between him and my captor.

With a contemplative breath, I glance over to Suzi who is rocking quietly, her eyes closed, a pleasant smile curling her tinted lips. A slight breeze stirs the air, lifting strands of her creamsicle hair to float in the winter sunshine warming her face.

"Suzi, how would you help someone overcome their fears?"

She keeps rocking, still with her eyes closed. "It takes time but eventually I would try to help the person confront that fear."

"As in someone afraid of flying might work up to one day skydiving?"

"That would be a great success, yes."

"What about a child who has been brutally abused by a man wearing a hood. Would you want that child to face another hooded man?"

Suzi's rocking comes to an abrupt stop and, opening her eyes, she looks directly at me. The fierceness in her gaze unsettles me. "Absolutely not."

An uneasy swallow works its way down my throat. Yes, I'm questioning Vincent's ways.

TWENTY-TWO

The next morning Vincent picks me up and we drive in silence for almost fifteen minutes before he asks, "Everything okay? You're very quiet."

"Do you remember that time Timothy was wearing a hood and I attacked him?" I ask.

"Of course."

Turning in the passenger seat, I look directly at the side of Vincent's familiar face. "Did you plan that?"

Vincent doesn't answer as he debates his words. Like a chess match, he's strategizing several moves ahead—lie versus the truth and the fallout of each. It takes him a few more seconds before he glances over at me. "Yes, Caroline, I did."

"Wow, I was hoping that would not be the answer."

He looks back at the road. "Were you expecting me to lie?"

"Yes, I think maybe I was."

"It bothers me to hear that from you. I'm the one person who you should be able to trust. Think about all that we've shared. Think about the breakthrough that you had after that. For one, you finally spoke, but most importantly, you began to feel strong and not like a victim."

Well, he's right about that. I turn away to look back out the front window. "Thank you for not lying."

"You're welcome. Now it's my turn. Did you come to this by yourself?"

"I was sitting with Suzi on the porch when I remembered things. I laid the scenario out to her in a hypothetical situation and she adamantly did not agree."

"What you and I do together is private, Caroline. I would appreciate, even in a hypothetical situation, that you keep Suzi out of it."

"Okay."

We don't speak after that as he continues driving. He is right—I did have a breakthrough after the scene with Timothy. Yet I can't help wondering how I would have responded if Suzi was the one who had been caring for me all those years and not Vincent.

Roughly thirty minutes later we arrive at our destination. As his SUV approaches the very grim-looking brick building, I read the plaque affixed above the entrance. HOSPITAL FOR THE INSANE.

Dad's words from so long ago slink through my mind. *I can't do it anymore. I don't know how to help you. It's time to take you someplace else.*

"Erwin is the guy's name," Vincent says as he pulls the SUV into a guest spot and parks. "He's claiming to be The Organ Ripper. He walked right in the door and introduced himself to the night guard. Then when the guard didn't believe him, Erwin bit his ear off."

The word "ear" doesn't sit well with me. "Trying to prove a point?" I ask.

"That's why I brought you. I want to get your take on the guy."

Opening the passenger side, I climb out and as I round the hood, my gaze takes in the sign again, gluing onto the word "insane". The institution where Dad took me had the same word. At least one good thing came out of that. It's where I met Vincent.

Or actually, that's not true. I met him before that.

"What is it?" He asks.

Looking away from the sign, I follow him up the steps, more nervous about stepping inside than seeing this Erwin man. "When did we meet?"

"The first time you were nine and had just been found. I was called in for an evaluation. Why?"

"I always think we met in the institution where Dad put me."

"No. I kept up with your case though. So when you were institutionalized, I felt I already knew you very well."

I stop walking. "What do you mean you kept up with my case?"

Vincent gives me a quizzical look. "I used to meet with your father. I thought you knew."

"No." No one ever told me or if they did, I don't remember.

Vincent puts a gentle hand around the back of my neck. "You're past all of that. Never again. Okay, Caroline? Never again."

I appreciate his words but still, uneasiness crawls through me.

Detective Uzzo is already here waiting inside and we exchange a few pleasant hellos. A well-groomed, older gentleman emerges from down the hall to meet us all at the door. Something about him seems familiar and it takes me a few seconds to place him as Dr. Gray. He came to Vincent and Rachel's home for dinner a few times years ago.

Shaking hands with Vincent first, he says, "Been too long. How have you been?"

"So very good. Thank you for asking." Vincent turns to us. "You already know Detective Uzzo and you remember Caroline, I'm sure?"

Dr. Gray and Uzzo say hello before he turns to me with a big warm smile. "Of course, I remember Caroline." We exchange handshakes and he leads us down a gleaming tile hall and through a door already standing open.

Closing the door, he motions for us to sit in the black leather chairs situated in front of his desk. While he pours us all glasses of water from a cart, I take a few seconds to look around.

My gaze traces across the glass-topped mahogany desk, the leather chairs, the bookshelves, and I note there are no family pictures on display. If he sees patients in here, then I imagine he doesn't want them glimpsing into his personal life. I sure wouldn't.

With a smile, Dr. Gray hands us the glasses before taking a seat behind the desk. "This Erwin fella walked right in here last night and turned himself into the night guard. The night guard said Erwin came across behaved, well-spoken, and cooperative. So much so that the night guard thought he was joking. That's when Erwin bit his ear off."

"To make a point," I say again.

"Exactly. We have the whole thing on film if you want to see it."

With a glance at Vincent and Uzzo, I nod. I do want to see it.

Reclining back in his chair, Dr. Gray studies me for a

moment. "You have been quite the topic of many a conversation."

"Oh?"

"Surviving what you did and now this curious talent you have at connecting with killers. You are certainly unique."

I recognize that look in his eyes. Vincent gets it, too, when he's eager to explore my mind. "I'm not here to be analyzed," I politely say and Dr. Gray chuckles.

"The video?" Uzzo reminds him.

Dr. Gray takes a minute to open the laptop on his desk and bring up the video, then he turns it around on pause. "I have to warn you, it's brutal."

Uzzo looks at me and with a nod, I say, "Go ahead."

Erwin, a chubby dark-haired man in his late forties, wearing dress pants and a tucked-in shirt with no tie, walks through the front door we just did. Overhead industrial florescent bulbs streak the hall with harsh light. An elderly night guard sees him coming and approaches.

Holding out his hand, Erwin introduces himself. The guard reluctantly and with great confusion shakes his hand. Then Erwin tells the guard he's The Organ Ripper, here to turn himself in, and for a second the guard just stares. Then he chuckles and looks around as if he's being punked or something.

In a brutal, startling blow, Erwin punches the guard straight in the Adam's apple. He stumbles back, coming up against the wall. Eyes wide with a mixture of pain and fear, the guard gurgles and grapples for his throat.

Slowly, Erwin approaches and the guard's body slumps to the floor as the gurgling turns into desperate coughing. Erwin must have injured his esophagus with the blow.

Staring wide-eyed up at Erwin, the guard scoots away and for a few seconds, Erwin doesn't move, just tracks the guard's feeble retreat with his eyes.

Then, as if making a decision, Erwin follows. Reaching down, he grabs the front of the guard's uniform, lifts him, and with bared teeth, he sinks into his ear with a violent thrust.

Other guards rush in, Erwin is pulled off and the screen goes blank. Closing the laptop, Dr. Gray takes a second to clear his throat before looking at me across his massive desk. "What do you think?"

"What do we know about Erwin?" I ask.

Dr. Gray smiles as if he was waiting for that question. "A psychology teacher who splits his time between two different private schools. One where the body was returned to her bed and the other school where the girl from the park attended."

"Irene and Yasmine," I say their names. "Any connection to Nadia and Gaby, the other two dead girls?"

"I'm looking into that," Uzzo says. "As well as the first two missing girls whose bodies have yet to be discovered."

"Okay, so Erwin is involved," I agree. "But this was impulsive, walking in and biting off an ear. The Organ Ripper is meticulous and wouldn't have done it that way. This was an act of a scared man."

A small smile plays across Dr. Gray's lips and I don't like that he's pleased with my observations. I'm not here to impress him. "There's certainly a peculiar cleverness about you, Caroline."

I resist the urge to roll my eyes. I'm beyond sick of hearing those types of comments.

Vincent glances over at me, reading my mind. "After

what happened to Harley, Erwin is scared he's next. He's in here hiding."

"Yes, I believe so." Sliding forward, I come out of my seat. "I'd like to meet this Erwin."

TWENTY-THREE

The steel door of the maximum-security section closes behind us and when the bolt slides into place, I can't stop the flinch that hunches my shoulders.

Vincent puts his hand on my forearm. "I'll do all the talking and remember—"

"No expression. I know."

Our footsteps echo through the hall and my gaze tracks up to the camera mounted in the corner where Dr. Gray and Uzzo are watching. Cells run to the left of us, some padded, some not, all with glass walls versus bars, some with occupants and others vacant. I wait for the occupants to look at us, to speak, but none of them do. Are they drugged?

We approach the last cell and come to stand several feet away, side-by-side, looking in. Dressed in all white, Erwin is lying on a bolted-down cot staring right at us. Holding my expression blank, I study him, waiting for a sense of this man but nothing comes.

"Hello," he politely greets us.

Vincent says, "My name is Dr. Vincent—"

"I know who you are." Erwin sits up in bed, his legs folded, still staring at us. "I've heard you speak. I've read your articles. I'm a total fan." Erwin looks at me. "And I know you're Caroline." Leaning forward, he studies me.

Still holding my expression blank, nothing comes. I have no sense of this man.

"You claim to be The Organ Ripper," Vincent says.

Erwin shrugs. "I don't care much for that title. I mean, who can compete with the infamous Jack, right?"

"Is that why you're coming forward?" Vincent asks. "You didn't like the title?"

Pushing off the bed, Erwin stands, and carefully, I look him up and down. Dark hair, beady eyes, cocky expression, about five-eight, chubby in the middle. Those beady eyes twinkle as if he just thought of something clever to say. "Are we going to do all those tests now? Checklists, Rorschach, IQ..." He grabs his genitals, almost as an afterthought. "Or maybe you should just show me the pictures of all my victims. You know, the ones no one else sees."

"Does murder arouse you, Erwin?" Vincent asks.

His face lights up. "Oh, yes."

"And what were you hoping to accomplish by biting the ear off that guard? Did that arouse you as well?"

Thankfully, Erwin lets go of his genitals. "No, that was just to prove a point."

"And do you often prove points?"

Erwin's eyes narrow in on Vincent. "It's not my job to prove I'm The Organ Ripper."

"That's where you're wrong, Erwin. It is your job."

Erwin spins away, clearly irritated, and quietly I wait. Out of the corner of my eye, I catch Vincent watching me as I watch Erwin. He paces his cell and I study his movement, then abruptly he turns and gazes right at me.

Erwin's tongue comes out to lick his bottom lip like he just tasted something particularly savory. He rasps, "We can talk about how delicious human meat is. You would know that. Right, Caroline?"

All sound dulls and I hear only the noise of my circulatory system humming. I stare numbly at Erwin and gradually I am no longer here in this hall, I am...

He's just over there, whistling those three slow notes as he lays intestines out, getting ready to wash them. They lie across a flat rock, baking in the winter sun like an eerie pile of pasta. Nearby a fire crackles around the skewers of meat.

Annabelle's tongue comes out, lapping at the grease dribbling over her hands and wrists. She won't look at me.

I can't look at her.

"It'll be a week before we eat again." She sucks her pinky. "Don't think about it. Just eat it."

Our captor is in front of us now but I'm not sure how that can be. He's over there, too, whistling near the pile of pasta.

He leers down at me through the dark hood. "Maybe you'd like it better if it was your sister, huh?" This time the sometimes rasp is present.

Annabelle goes still. Though she doesn't speak a word, I hear her internal pleading. Please, Caroline, please.

And so, without looking at the gutted red-haired girl swaying from a hook some twenty feet away, I lift the hunk of organ and I open my mouth.

I don't remember leaving Erwin's cell but I'm now back in Dr. Gray's office. He and Vincent are speaking with Uzzo but their voices trail in and out of my head in fuzzy traces.

The rasp and the memory it sparked. For the first time, I remember two captors.

Not one.

There were two of them.

TWENTY-FOUR

The ringing of my phone jars me awake and I sit straight up in bed. Zane and Petal share the empty spot beside me and Fallon is sprawled in the chair in the corner, having fallen asleep reading.

My phone rings again and I look around, trying to figure out where I left it. Zane stirs, his big head perking up, and I mumble a quiet, "Sorry," as I feel around in the covers.

It rings again and Fallon shoots straight up, looking through the darkness at me.

"It's okay," I murmur. "Just the phone."

He gives a groggy nod and I slide from the bed, feeling around in the dark, locating the phone under my jeans. "Hello?"

An eerily long pause follows, then a brief crackle of static.

"Hello?" I say again.

The voice hitches. "Caroline?"

I don't breathe. I don't move.

Fallon comes down in front of me. "Who is it?"

I shake my head. It can't be.

"Caroline?" Fallon smooths my hair from my face. "Talk to me. You're scaring me. Who is it?"

I shake my head. It can't be.

"Caroline?" the voice in my ear whispers. "Is it you?"

I lick my lips. "Annabelle?"

TWENTY-FIVE

One phone rings, then another, and then another in over-lapping and intertwining twills. On the screen, relay points and trunk lines blink and strobe across a digital map. A list of telephone numbers scrolls the right margin as they run through the tracing software.

To the right of me stands Fallon and to the left Vincent. Detective Uzzo sits at the computer station, studying the scrolling data while we hover behind her.

Uzzo shakes her head. "I'm hooked into every telephone provider and I'm finding nothing."

"Then look some more," I snap.

Detective Uzzo pushes away from her home computer and slowly comes to her feet. In the dim-lit interior of her home office, she turns to look at me. "You come to me at two-thirty in the morning, to *my home* I might add, claiming your sister contacted you. It is now nearly daybreak and all I have been doing for the past three-plus hours is looking. And looking. And looking. There is nothing there. There is no trace of a call made to your cell at one-thirty-seven this morning."

"But it rang." I look at Fallon for confirmation and he nods. "I answered. The voice was Annabelle. I'm telling you. It was Annabelle."

With a sigh, Detective Uzzo scrubs her fingers through her short gray hair, making it stand out in a million directions. She glances at Vincent and he must take that as his cue to step in. "You haven't heard her voice in many, many years. Are you sure?"

I nod. "I'm sure." There is no way I would ever forget her voice.

"A voice as a little girl or as it would be now?" Detective Uzzo asks.

That stops me in my tracks. The voice did seem young.

Detective Uzzo turns away, glancing once again at her computer. "You were dead asleep when that call came in. You could have been disoriented."

"I wasn't." Or at least I don't think I was.

She rotates back, this time looking at Fallon. "Did you hear the voice or just the ring?"

Fallon casts me a helpless look. "Just the ring."

"Caroline," Vincent quietly speaks. "You know Annabelle is dead."

My jaw tightens at the turn this is taking. "I'm not crazy. I know what I heard." But even as I say this, doubt niggles around inside of me. Given the hallucinations I've been having, it is plausible.

Fallon turns toward the door. "Let's get you home. You're tired."

I don't follow Fallon. "The fact is, Annabelle's body was never found and until I lay eyes on my sister's remains, I'll never fully believe she's dead."

All three of them fall silent.

I straighten up, determined not to look unstable. "Now

as long as we're all here, let's talk about The Organ Ripper." I look at Detective Uzzo. "Anything on the human hair rug?"

"Yes, we've been getting DNA hits to cold cases that track nearly thirty years."

"How horrible," Fallon mumbles.

"Yes, but at least now those families can have closure." Something my family never had. "Thirty years. That means Harley was practicing cannibalism before Becka was even born, which means her illness is not the catalyst for this. Something else is."

"Plus, not all the cold cases are girls. Some are men and others are women," Uzzo says.

"Which plays more into dominant cannibalism versus medicinal," I say. "Anything on the first two local girls that have yet to be found?"

"No DNA match with the rug," Uzzo answers.

"Thoughts on Erwin?" I ask. Because I sure have some.

Uzzo shakes her head. "After you two left, I had a conversation with him. He seemed more interested in you, Caroline, and Vincent."

"There's a reason for that," I say.

Vincent folds his arms. "Oh?"

"Do you remember the last words Erwin said to me? They had a rasp to them that triggered a memory." I look between the three of them. "I think he may have been in the woods with me all those years ago. I think there were two."

"Oh my God," Fallon whispers.

"Why are you just now telling me this?" Vincent asks.

"I was numb. I needed time to think. I had planned on talking to you today about it." And I get it. He'd rather we spoke privately about this.

Uzzo blows out a breath as she rubs her palms into her

eyes. "Thank God the FBI will be here tomorrow." She stops rubbing her eyes. "I'm so sorry, Caroline. You say you *think* Erwin may have been in those woods? You're not sure?"

I shake my head. "My memories from that period are still very fuzzy, choppy at best."

"That's okay, it gives me new questions to ask." Uzzo glances at her screen.

Vincent says, "Given this new information, I'd like to speak with him, too. Privately. I don't want Caroline to see him again."

"Agreed." Seeing him again would emotionally crumble me. "But *if* Annabelle is dead, then he may know where her body is."

Uzzo nods. "We'll get what we can from him. Know that we will."

"He may have been in the woods with me all those years ago but this claim that he's The Organ Ripper isn't connecting with me. Vincent pegged it when he said Erwin's hiding. He knows something and is afraid for his life."

"What are you thinking?" Uzzo asks.

My gaze goes to Vincent and I find his dark eyes focused solely on me. I think he knows what I'm about to suggest and, as if reading my mind, his jaw tightens in a silent message not to.

"I say we go public about Erwin. Don't announce that he claims to be the Organ Ripper but do let everyone know he has verifiable information on the killer. Then use him as bait. Come up with reasons to transport him publicly to various places. Make a big to-do about it. We may get lucky and lure the real killer out."

"That's not a bad idea," comes a voice from behind me

and I turn to see Suzi standing in the doorway to Uzzo's office.

My jaw drops. "Hey!"

She winks at me and Fallon. "Hey, there."

"I'm sorry," Uzzo says. "Did we wake you?"

Suzi waves that off. "It's all good." She takes a step forward into the room. "I'm just a retired school teacher but Caroline's idea does sound decent. Leak details on Erwin and then use him as bait."

Still with a tight jaw, Vincent turns away. He excuses himself and leaves Uzzo's home. He is not happy with this plan and I'm not entirely sure why. If there's one thing about Vincent, he will push a boundary. He will cross a line. He is known for his unorthodox ways.

Or maybe he's not happy because it wasn't his idea. We're taking his spotlight away.

PART THREE

Eight Years Ago

The church bell gongs and slowly I walk down the aisle with Rachel right beside me, gripping my hand. People pack the pews, sniffling and crying, and I want to scream at them to shut up. Who are all these people anyway?

I don't look at their faces. I already know what I'll see.

Oh, the poor thing. First her sister, then her mom, and now her dad.

So many deaths and all because of me.

They found Dad's body much like they found Mom's, lying in bed as if asleep with an empty pill bottle on the nightstand. Unlike Mom, Dad left a note and it said simply, *I'm sorry.*

No, I'm the one who is sorry. Why then am I the only one still alive?

We make it to the end of the aisle and Rachel guides me into a pew where Dr. DeMurr and Fallon already sit. My new family.

The preacher speaks but I don't listen and instead stare at the giant framed photograph of my dad with his dark hair and blue eyes, smiling kindly for the camera.

When did he lose that smile? When did he become so sad? I don't know why I ask myself these questions because I already know the answer.

The day my twin and I were taken.

Behind me someone sobs, loud and uncontrollable, and I turn in the pew to glare at the person. I don't know her. Shouldn't I be the one who is sobbing? What gives her the right?

Rachel slides her arm around me, silently telling me to turn back around.

My gaze goes to the framed photo again and I tune into myself, trying to figure out what I feel. Sadness, yes, and confusion. Anger, too. But mostly relief. Now I won't feel guilty about staying with Dr. DeMurr and Rachel.

When the whole thing is over and we are back in Dr. DeMurr's car, Rachel hands a pad and pencil over the front seat in case I want to communicate.

I flip it open, my pencil poised, but nothing comes. Instead, I think of what Dr. DeMurr said a year ago when I first arrived at their home. He said to not filter myself—to scream if I wanted to scream, to dance if I wanted to dance, to throw something if I wanted to throw—but right now I want...

My hand takes on a life of its own as I crudely draw exactly what I want. I'm aware of Fallon sitting beside me watching my every stroke but I don't care. My pencil moves over the paper, scratching and digging in. When I'm done, I breathe out and I slide the pencil into the spiral.

A fly buzzes past and Fallon reaches out to grab it. As he does, I snag his wrist. "No," I say and his brown eyes widen. It's the first time I've ever spoken to him. Pressing the down button on the window, the fly catches the wind and is gone. "There you go. Be free, little fly."

The warm air whirls in, rustling the pages of my pad, drawing my attention back down to it. Now that I'm not in the moment and a few seconds have gone by, I cock my head and study it, seeing it new.

It's my captor, sprawled and hanging from a tree, and in the bottom corner sits a fire pit with skewers full of his organs and skin.

My vision turns sharp and tinged with red as I keep staring at the drawing. My captor's whistle echoes through my mind in its slow three-tone eeriness...

That whistle plays in a maddening loop the whole way home.

As soon as Vincent parks the vehicle, I'm out of it and go straight to my room. Sitting at my desk, I push the sleeves up on my funeral dress to feel the breeze move across my arms as I continue to sketch. This one a memory...

A blur of movement flashes out of the corner of my eye and our captor loops a thin rope around my head. I raise both arms, reaching up to grab the rope but it cuts into my neck. From where she sits chained to the tree, Annabelle makes eye contact with me, then she opens her mouth and she screams.

The sound coming from her lips shrills through the trees, so high-pitched it deafens me. Or maybe my dark and muddy hearing is more from the rope tightening, cutting off circulation to my head.

Through strained eyes, I watch Annabelle's hands come up to cover her ears like her own scream is too much to hear.

My body arcs off the ground as our captor lifts me, putting his weight behind the choking. But I keep my eyes on my sister as he turns me from her.

Over to the left, something scurries and I'm not sure if it's an animal or human. If it's a human, why aren't they helping us?

Our captor releases his chokehold and I drop to the ground. I breathe, eagerly gulping in shaky breaths. My ears ring and slowly the ringing becomes Annabelle's scream again.

This is a game he plays. Choking us, then giving breath back.

I finish sketching the memory and, ripping the page from the pad, I lay it aside and begin another one. I love the sound the thick page makes when I rip it from its spiral. There's a cleansing finality to the sound.

At my feet lays Zane. I didn't realize he'd come in.

Behind me, the floor creaks and I don't have to look to know it's either Rachel or Vincent. I can tell by the weight of the creak.

I continue sketching, aware the person is moving across my room. It's Rachel. I recognize her scent—a mixture of lemongrass and ginger from the homemade soap she prefers.

Zane lifts his heavy head from my feet to glance at Rachel, then with a sigh, he settles his big skull back down.

The shadows around me shift, catching in the late afternoon sun streaming in my window, and Rachel comes to stand beside me. Quietly, she stares down at the pencil sketch I just did, and then she looks at the one I did in the car.

I don't look up at her, I simply keep drawing, this one of a fantasy of our captor nailed to a tree with his stomach fileted open and guts curling out.

Rachel swallows and the gurgle echoes through my otherwise silent room. "Is this what you want to do to him?"

"Yes," I simply respond.

I wet my finger and smudge a little bit of the pencil lead to blur it and fill in the guts, then I draw his black and brown dog. I think I'll have the dog eat the guts, all while our captor is still alive. It is possible to gut someone and have them remain alive. I know this for a fact.

The air around me shifts, becoming alive with a slight pulse. It's enough to make me stop sketching and I shift only my eyes to glance over to Rachel. "You're trembling," I say, not looking up at her. "Do I scare you?"

"Of course not." She's lying. I can tell by the tone in her voice.

"I would never hurt you." Turning in my chair, I look up at her. "Nor Vincent, or Fallon. None of you."

Her lips curve into a gentle and accepting smile and it brings me relief. "I've never seen you draw before."

"I know. Annabelle was always the artist, not me. I guess I'm channeling her."

Rachel places a warm, but hesitant, hand on my shoulder. "It's because you carry her with you. She's inside of you."

Slowly, I turn back to my sketches and my brain is now a muddled fog. *She's inside of you.* "Yes, I suppose she is."

TWENTY-SIX

Present Day

The look on Vincent's face when I suggested leaking Erwin has been bothering me all day. Yes, Detective Uzzo is crossing a line by leaking information to the press but Vincent is typically on board with things that teeter lines.

That night, I drive the fifteen miles or so up the mountain to Vincent's home. When I walk in the grand double doors, I run straight into Becka. It's almost like she was staring out the window waiting on me.

"I'm here to see Vincent," I tell her, stepping around and heading straight into his study.

She hurries behind. "He's not here."

I slide into a leather seat across from his desk. "Then I'll wait."

"Are you eating dinner with us? Its venison, beets, and mushrooms." She flings a dismissive hand in the air. "You can have the beets and mushrooms."

"Maybe I'll have the venison instead," I say, solely to provoke her.

"Good," she responds, unfazed by my words. "Eating means life. You put life in your belly and you live. At least that's what my dad always told me."

Boldly, Becka slides into Vincent's high back chair and I simply stare at her audacity. Not even I have sat in his office chair. Reaching underneath, she gives a tug on the handle of his locked, built-in file cabinet. "What do you suppose he keeps in here?"

"Private things and I would suggest you respect that."

With a shrug, she kicks her feet up on his shiny desk. "Vincent had to go down the mountain. Could be a while before he's back."

As if not on cue, Vincent strolls in through the open office door and Becka scrambles to stand. I hide my smirk. I've known Vincent for a long time and he doesn't share his desk and chair.

Mumbling apologies, Becka goes to stand in the corner and, with first a look of warning in her direction, he glances down at me. "Did I know you were coming?"

"No."

I glance at Becka. "Can we have a moment?"

Ducking her head, she shuffles across the floor and out of the office, leaving the door wide open. She's lingering to listen and I'm sure Vincent suspects so, too. Still, I say, "I got the impression you weren't on board with my suggestion about going public with Erwin."

"Not initially but I've got things covered now."

"What does that mean?"

"It means I went to see Erwin. Given this new plan to go public with him, then I figure he needs to know the details of the crimes."

My jaw drops. "You're planting his mind with evidence."

A smile creeps into Vincent's lips. "There's nothing wrong with a little coercive persuasion. It's perfectly reasonable in certain situations."

"And what situations are those?"

He slides around his desk to sit in the chair Becka vacated. "Are you going to question my alternative ways? Do you not trust that I know what I'm doing by now?"

He may be justified in his mind but he's crossing too many lines for my comfort. "What about Annabelle? Did he have information on her?"

Vincent sighs. "I thoroughly dug around in his brain. He was messing with you. I'm sure he read my articles on you and knew the exact words to say."

"What does Uzzo think?"

"She agrees."

Well, I don't. I now want to talk to Erwin.

TWENTY-SEVEN

When I arrive home, Fallon's car is gone and I assume he's doing one of his late-night lab things on campus. I let Zane out to do his thing. When he's done, I lock the door and scooping Petal up, I make my way into the kitchen.

I give them both treats and then I put a kettle on to boil. Turning toward the cabinet, I open it to grab a pack of herbal tea and I freeze when I see the note taped to the microwave.

im alive.are you?

IT'S WRITTEN on white paper in a red pencil. But it's the star above the "i" used instead of a dot that makes me stumble back.

Annabelle always drew stars above her i's.

TWENTY-EIGHT

Detective Uzzo supervises the people moving in and out of my house, dusting for prints, scanning everything with a UV light, and using transparent tape to collect evidence. I sit at the dining room table with Fallon right beside me, staring at the giant zip lock Evidence bag that now contains my sister's letter.

"Getting a lot of usable prints," I hear a tech say. "Probably belong to Caroline and Fallon, though. I can't imagine whoever left that note would be so stupid to leave a print."

"What do they mean 'whoever left that note'?" I turn to Fallon. "Do they not think Annabelle was here?"

Taking my hand, he folds it warmly between his but he doesn't respond to me. I stare at the blond bristle covering his cheeks, trying to read his mind, but he's not even looking at me. He's watching everyone move around our home.

Is he thinking The Organ Ripper is playing a trick on me? I don't see how that can be. No one, not even Vincent, knows about the stars Annabelle used to dot her i's with. For that matter, I haven't thought about it in years.

"Found something!" Someone yells from the guest bedroom.

My pulse elevates as a tech comes down the hall carrying a red pencil. The note was done in red pencil. He comes into the kitchen where the light is best and I barely breathe as he opens a case and performs a quick analysis of the pencil and the lead. He then feeds the information into a computer and a few minutes later looks up at Detective Uzzo with a nod.

"You just nodded." Letting go of Fallon's hand, I stand up. "What does that nod mean?"

Detective Uzzo doesn't answer me like she's both absorbing the information and rejecting it at the same time.

I raise my voice. "What's going on?"

Someone walks through my front door and I turn to see Vincent coming in. Detective Uzzo must have called him because I sure didn't. My gaze goes back to Uzzo, waiting.

"It means—" Her gaze goes from me to Vincent, back to me. "It means, that note was written with that pencil."

"Okay." I nod. "And?"

"It only has your prints," Uzzo answers.

"Which means whoever wrote it used a glove," I surmise.

Detective Uzzo casts a hesitant look in Vincent's direction and, with a nod, he steps toward me. Vincent says, "Sometimes when we want something to be true, we go to any length to make it so."

My gaze goes between Uzzo and Vincent and I harden my resolve as realization dawns on me. "You think I wrote that?"

Neither one of them responds and I look down at Fallon, hoping to see him just as shocked as me but instead, I see concern. He thinks I may have written that note, too.

"No. Annabelle has to be alive." But even as I say it, doubt and frustration root inside of me, and my throat rolls with a swallow.

Uncomfortable long seconds go by, and with each one, my brain clicks back through the years...

I pace the length of Vincent's office. "You recently spoke at a conference. Did you mention me?"

"Yes, but I did not mention you by name. Merely your case."

Amused, I pace back the other way. "And what do people think of me?"

"One person asked an interesting question if you had developed the ability to mirror people's actions and speech."

I think about that a second. "No, I don't think so."

Vincent chuckles. "Well, we'll have to watch out if you do."

My butt lands hard into the kitchen chair as I stare down at the note inside of the clear zip-lock bag. I want to be outraged but the truth is, with all that has been happening, I'm not entirely sure. Am I mirroring Annabelle?

TWENTY-NINE

I stand in our bedroom, staring out at the dark field that separates our home from Suzi's up on the hill. Her greenhouse glows faintly, reminding me of Harley's greenhouse and Vincent's.

Harley's had a multitude of vegetables, fruits, and herbs that he cooked with. As does Vincent's. I've never been to Suzi's. I don't know what she grows in there.

Fallon stands underneath the willow tree in our side yard, sipping a beer and staring out into the night. He's probably thinking about what happened earlier.

Shifting slightly, I lift my tee and glance at the strips of misshapen tissue crisscrossing my abdomen. I run my finger over the rippled area near my ribs before lowering the hem of my shirt back into place. Bitter saliva gathers in the back of my jaw and, with a wince, I swallow down the nauseating taste.

From behind me a shadow shifts and my gaze moves to the reflection of Suzi standing in our open bedroom door. I didn't hear her come in. Her lips curl into a soft smile. "I heard what happened and came to check on you." She nods to my stomach. "Everything that's been happening has you reliving things, doesn't it?"

I don't bother asking her how she knows about my stomach. It's no secret what happened to me in those woods all those many years ago. "Do you think I'll ever be normal?"

"You are normal. Why would you ask that?"

With one last glance at Fallon, I turn away from the window. "I'm not like Fallon. He had his childhood trauma and seems way more adjusted to life than I do."

"Trauma affects people in different ways."

Adjusting my tee-shirt, I cross over to my bedside table and pick up the bracelet I've been working on over the last few days. It's a patterned weave that Rachel taught me many years ago. Running it through my fingers, I take a seat on the edge of our bed. "Do you know what happened with Fallon?"

"Yes, he's shared some things with me." Suzi crosses our room to sit beside me on the bed. "You're different than Fallon. Don't compare yourself to him."

With a nod, I glance again out our window to where he stands, still sipping his beer. It makes me think of home and how Dad used to do that. He used to stand outside with Grandpa, sipping beer, and silently taking in the night.

"What are you thinking of?" Suzi asks.

"Home." I sigh, my mood dipping. "When I was a little girl."

"Good memories, I hope."

"The best. But it still makes me sad. Sad for all that could have been." I glance over at her sweet face surrounded by her creamsicle hair, lit on one side from the light spilling in from the hall, dark on the other from our bedroom and the night outside. "Maybe the difference is that Fallon had closure. He saw the dead bodies of his family. I've never had that with Annabelle."

"I know." Shifting, Suzi crosses her leg. "And then things like the phone call happen and the letter. It makes your mind crazy with 'what ifs'."

"It does. The thought that my sister might be alive both excites me and sucks the life out of me. I'm not sure how it can be so." But if she *is* alive then it means I didn't do what I've always feared. Something so horrible, I can't even silently say the words.

"Isolating yourself isn't helping. Why don't you go outside and be with Fallon? You need to relate to someone in all of this. He may seem strong and 'normal' but I would wager that he could use a hug from you right now."

I like that Suzi has suggested I go to Fallon. Vincent never does.

Yes, I like it, but for some reason those words have me not thinking of Fallon but instead of the sketchpad I filled years ago with pages after pages of horrific scenes. I had become obsessed with different ways to kill my captor. The dark pull of that obsession is taking root in me again.

With a sigh, I glance down at the bracelet I'm still holding. That darkness is exactly why Rachel started teaching me jewelry making. She wanted a way to connect with me and show me a lighter side to life.

"Yes, Fallon shares things with me," Suzi says a moment later, cycling the conversation back around. "I hope you know that you can as well."

My gaze shifts from the bracelet back to Suzi and as I think through her words, I study her round features that offer a source of comfort and familiarity. "I worry that if I show you too much of myself that I'll scare you off. That you'll leave."

A frown flashes across her face. "I've taken a personal interest in both you and Fallon. I don't intend on ending our friendship over your honest thoughts and actions. You still have a lot to work through and you need a safe environment to do so. I'm here for whatever you need, Caroline. I mean that."

With a nod, I look back down at the bracelet. Rachel said similar words to me years ago but she ended up leaving. I tend to run people off.

Shifting forward, Suzi surprises me when she places her hand on my forearm. It reminds me of when I first came to live with Vincent and Rachel. She did the same thing, placed her hand on my forearm. And then I lifted my forearm and kissed her hand. I tasted her skin, my tongue flittering across, and Rachel went cold underneath me. I frightened her that day.

I won't frighten Suzi.

"Can I ask you a question?" She asks.

Lifting my eyes, I look at her. "Yes."

"Did Vincent ever try to desensitize you with the scent of honey?"

The question takes me totally off guard. She must be asking me this because of our previous conversation regarding my memory of Timothy and the dark hood.

It was seven years ago...

I walk through the open office door and into Vincent's study. His large and gleaming desk sits unoccupied and I stand for a second, listening to the grandfather clock tick-tick-tick.

My nostrils flare slightly with the newness of his scent. There's a sweetness to it that hasn't been there before. Turning, I see him sitting at the small round table in the back corner. Watching me.

Giving me the usual tranquil smile, he motions for me to sit beside him at the table. One single file sits closed with his hands linked on top of it and I give it a cursory glance as I pull a chair out and sit down.

"Do you know why we're sitting here today?" He asks.

I think about that a second. "Because you want there to be a sense of comradery. Equality. Comfortableness. Sitting beside each other accomplishes that. Sitting across from each other alludes to power."

"Very good, Caroline." His hands unclasp and he lays them side by side, palms down on the folder. "I'm going to show you a few pictures and I want you to tell me how they make you feel. If at any time you're uncomfortable, just tell me and I'll put them away."

I nod.

Vincent reaches his fingers toward my wrist. "May I feel your pulse?"

"Sure." I hold out my wrist and he presses two fingers to the pulse point.

With his other hand, he opens the folder and takes out the first photograph. It is of a woman who I would guess is in her forties, half-clothed, with her throat slit. Vincent turns over the next picture and it is of an older man with a single gunshot to his head.

He taps the first picture. "A prostitute who was murdered by one of her johns." He taps the second picture. "A man who was shot by someone he embezzled money from." His fingers on my wrist press in just a little. "How do you feel looking at those two pictures?"

"Indifferent," I say. "Detached."

"Why?"

"They died of stupidity."

With a nod, Vincent turns over the last picture. It is a boy *a few years younger than me who has been beaten to near death. I zero in on the face, looking past the lumps and bruises. It's a young Fallon.*

I move back in my chair, away from Vincent's touch, and he responds by sliding the photos back into the folder.

"And how does that last one make you feel?" He asks.

My fingers curl into the armrests of the chair. "Furious."

"What do you want to do right now?"

"Kill whoever did that to Fallon."

"What if I told you I did that to Fallon?"

"Then I would kill you," I say without a second of hesitation.

"But you told Rachel that you would never hurt me."

I give Vincent a sharp look and my nostrils flare with the sweetness that is new to his usual scent. "Don't play word games with me. And don't you ever mix honey with your soap again."

He doesn't answer me and instead silently studies my face. Then with a quiet sigh, he says, "It was just an experiment, Caroline. I apologize if I stepped over a line."

"Caroline?" Suzi prompts, bringing me from the memory. "Did he?"

I swallow. "Yes."

With a quiet sigh, she moves to grasp my hand warmly between both of hers. But she doesn't say anything, she simply nods.

"You don't agree?"

"Well, I'm not certified in mental health but if I was, it's not how I would've handled things. If it worked for you though, then who am I to agree or disagree?"

Yet, it didn't work for me. It only served to aggravate me that day. Maybe he did it too soon. Or maybe he shouldn't have done it all.

As I think through other times he experimented with me and my recovery, some successful and others not, my gaze drifts back over to the window and Suzi's greenhouse glowing calmly in the distance. An unwelcome thought niggles its way in. "What do you grow in your greenhouse?"

"Flowers mostly. Why?"

Then I gently layer wildflowers inside of her, letting her know I care. "Wildflowers?"

She doesn't hesitate one single second with her response, "I know there were wildflowers found on the victims. I also know there were traces of honey and charcoal. Herbs, too."

I keep looking at the greenhouse. "The herbs were traced to Harley's greenhouse. But we've yet to trace the wildflowers."

"I have nothing to hide."

With a sigh, I look back into her eyes. "I'm sorry."

"You don't trust easily. I get it. Take all the samples you want." She lets go of my hand and I miss it.

"Can I show you something?" I ask, wanting the connection back.

"Of course."

Pushing up off my bed, I cross over to our closet and lifting on my toes, I slide my mom's jewelry case down off the top shelf. I bring it back over to the bed and open it. Inside lays Mom's wedding band. Dad's too. I also have a silver bookmark that belonged to my grandfather and a few other miscellaneous items. But in the secret compartment underneath lays what I'm looking for.

I take everything out, open up the hidden compartment, and carefully lift out the worn swatch of the sundress I wore the day I was taken. Gently, I unfold the white material to reveal the tiny pile of bones within.

"No one knows about these but Fallon. Not Vincent, nor Rachel. No one."

"What are they?"

"Six years ago, I went back to that horrible house in the woods and I found these buried beneath the tree he used to chain us to. I don't know if they are Annabelle's or the other girl who was there. I'm afraid to know. I'm afraid that if they are my sister's, then she really is dead." I'm afraid that means I—

Reaching over, Suzi takes my hand again and the contact relaxes me. "Thank you for showing them to me," she says. "For trusting me with this. I will keep your secret. But when you're ready, you should have them analyzed. Knowing if they are your sister's will help you put closure on your past. It will allow you to properly grieve your twin."

Suzi's right but I'm not sure I can. I like thinking she's alive and that one day we'll be reunited. "Do you think it's possible Erwin was there in the woods with us or do you think he's messing with me?"

"I think Erwin is safely behind bars and no longer a threat to society. He may have been there and he may not have. I do think it's smart that you don't want to see him again. You don't need him toying with you."

I don't tell her that I had decided *to* speak to Erwin.

"May I make a suggestion?" She asks.

"Yes."

"Create a light and colorful place in your brain to store pleasant thoughts of your sister. Make it a safe place to visit as often as you like. Don't allow it to butt up to the darkness. Then when you're ready, find out the truth about those bones."

THIRTY

Hold still. Still. It'll all be over in a second. Second.

With a deep breath, I come from the dream, sitting up in bed. Those words and their cadence. Those three notes our captor always whistled. Annabelle. The other girl. Harley. Our captor. Why is my mind connecting them? What is the link?

Is it Erwin?

Fallon's hand touches my back, rubbing a slow circle. "Everything's okay," he murmurs.

Over my shoulder, I glance down at him stretched out on his back, his eyes still closed. The dim light of our salt lamp casts an amber glow across his handsome face. My gaze goes to the digital clock on his nightstand. 3:26 in the morning. It's hard to believe just hours ago our house was filled with Uzzo's team.

Leaning down, I press a kiss to his cheek. "I'll be in the living room."

"Are you awake?" He mumbles. "You're not sleepwalking, are you?"

Caressing a finger over his brow I assure him, "I'm awake. I'll be in the living room. Go back to sleep."

He gives a slight nod and I quietly climb out of bed and head into the kitchen. After making a cup of herbal tea, I cross over to our floor to ceiling bookshelf and I slide my childhood sketchpad out. I haven't looked at this thing in years and my earlier recollection of it when I was talking with Suzi makes me think of it now.

Taking a seat on the couch, I stare at the white cardboard cover with *CAROLINE* embossed in silver. When Vincent and Rachel gave this to me, did they know I would draw such horror? Vincent probably did but Rachel always seemed uneasy with my sketches.

I place my mug on a coaster and with a deep breath, I open the cover.

Torn from its seam and laying face up is the one I drew with our captor nailed to a tree, his stomach filleted open. Next is the one I did of the big dog eating his guts. After that, is one of my sister chained up and screaming. The one behind that is of the other girl...

On and on I sift through the pages, studying each one with a new eye. In the one I drew of my sister, our captor is approaching from the left and there's a shadow moving through the woods behind her. Could that shadow have been another person?

Erwin?

I don't know.

In the back of the pad lays one of our captor. Not with a hood as I always saw him, not with the blurry face that came later with the drugs. But after that, years later in fact, when I knew what he looked like.

I take in the thick dark bristle on his cheeks, his thin

lips, and his green wide-set eyes. I can almost hear his fingers scratching through that bristle.

I try to see Erwin in that face but I don't. Is it possible I merged two people into one? Or maybe Vincent's right, in that Erwin has read the research on me and is just toying with my memories.

In my periphery, something moves, and I glance up to see Fallon standing in the bedroom door looking out at me. His gaze tracks down to the sketch I'm looking at. He's seen this pad before. I've got nothing to hide, at least where the sketches are concerned.

"Is the light bothering you?" I ask.

He shakes his head. "Just checking on you." He nods to the pad, saying what he always does. "One day he will be found. He will pay for what he did. And now that Erwin is a possible link, perhaps that day will come sooner than later."

With a nod, I close the sketchpad. One day I'll tell Fallon that my captor has already paid but today is not the day. Instead, I ask, "Do you revisit your past?"

"I do," he says. "But I have a fear of finding a memory I don't want to be wedged into my brain."

"Me, too," I whisper. "I fear remembering exactly what happened." Maybe that's why I don't want to know about those tiny bones hidden in my mother's jewelry box. Because if Annabelle truly is dead then I have to face how she most likely died. No, I want that memory foggy and lost. Always lost.

Fallon shuffles into the kitchen after that and, flicking on the overhead dimmer light, he opens the freezer door. A cool fog spills out as he takes out a frozen bag of okra and places it on the counter. "I'm not tired. I think I'll prep a crockpot for later."

"Okay," I say, grabbing my mug and going to stand at the kitchen island.

For several minutes he moves around the kitchen, selecting spices, grabbing a cutting board, and slicing vegetables with a skilled technique I envy. Watching him work reminds me of all the times he cooked with Vincent back at the house on the mountain. Fallon told me once that cooking was the only time he could get lost and not have thoughts of the past. I suspect it had more to do with Vincent. It seemed like cooking was the only time the two of them bonded.

Cooking was to them what profiling has always been to me and Vincent. A way to connect, to relate. A shared interest. A commonality.

Sliding his eyes over to mine, Fallon smiles at me and something soft vibrates in the air. It reminds me of all the times we caught each other staring when we were younger.

"You're not my brother, Fallon, no matter how many times Vincent and Rachel suggest it."

With a tiny grin, Fallon gives me a shy glance. "Why do you think we've never kissed?"

I shrug. "Maybe I'm too broken."

"You're not broken. If you're broken then I'm broken, too."

"Okay, then what's our excuse?"

His brows come down in amusement. "The whole kissing thing sounds like something other people do. Not us."

"Like normal people, you mean?"

Fallon glances away. "Yeah, I guess."

I clasp my hands on both sides of his face, making him look at me. "Then let's give it a try."

For several seconds, our gazes search each other's, then we lean forward and our lips meet for the very first time.

"What are you smiling at?" Fallon asks.

"I was just remembering our first kiss."

Fallon chuckles. "Neither one of us had a clue what we were doing."

"No, but it was super cute."

"That it was. Thank God our technique has improved."

"Thank God," I agree and we share another smile.

He dives into the refrigerator and my attention drifts over to the files scattered across the dining room table, filled with all the parts and pieces of The Organ Ripper's case.

"Want a suggestion?" Fallon asks.

"Sure." I bring my attention back to him.

"Focus on one thing and when you have exhausted all resources on that one thing, move to the next. Also, use me as a sounding board. I know Vincent is always your sounding board in these types of situations but use me. I'm here."

Fallon's right. I'm trying to juggle all the pieces of the puzzle when I should be focusing on one thing. "Okay, sounding board, from your medical student viewpoint, could The Organ Ripper be selling some of what he takes on a transplant black market?"

From the cabinet, Fallon grabs the crockpot and places it on top of the counter. "No. If he were removing for black market purposes, he would need to leave certain things attached—veins and whatnot—for the organ to be placed inside the paying customer."

"Which leads back to cannibalism." My thoughts drift to the legacy idea again. Harley's legacy. Becka is Harley's daughter, and yes, she is odd but that doesn't mean she's out ripping people's organs. "What do you think of Becka?"

Fallon opens the bag of okra and dumps it into the crockpot and expertly chops several roman tomatoes. "Honestly, I don't care for her and I think she might know more than she's letting on."

"Like?"

"She was raised by a serial killer. She had to, at a minimum, have felt something was off." Lifting the cutting board, Fallon slides the chopped tomatoes into the pot. "Vincent's very protective of her."

"As he was with us."

"True," Fallon agrees.

"When Nadia saw Becka in the cabin, she thought she recognized her. Nadia said something about Becka having black hair."

"And then Nadia turns up dead."

"Are you saying Becka killed Nadia to shut her up?" I ask.

"No, I'm just stating facts."

I try to imagine Becka savagely slicing Nadia open and yanking out her organs in a fumbled attempt to make it look like The Organ Ripper and the image doesn't seem so far-fetched. I'd love to get Becka in a room with Nadia's corpse to see her reaction but there is no way Vincent would agree to that. Plus, I'm not even sure Uzzo would allow it.

Fallon peels an onion under a stream of water. "What about Erwin?"

"Uzzo is still digging in. We do have a viable connection between Erwin and two of the girls. Though now that Uzzo went public with Erwin's identity, maybe we'll get more of a connection."

"No, I mean to you."

I sigh. "I don't know. My brain is so foggy."

"I get that. I do. He mentioned that he read Vincent's articles, heard him speak, and whatever else. He's read about you and me in Vincent's work. Perhaps, he truly just wanted to meet you."

I take a sip of my tea. "Vincent's first impression was that Erwin gave himself up to be safe from whoever killed Harley. That does feel right to me, in that somehow he's connected to Harley. But it also feels right that he may have been there in the woods with us all those years ago. I could have easily merged two people into one—my captor."

"Or your captor bragged to him about what he was doing with you, Annabelle and the other girl."

I breathe out. "Who the hell brags about that?"

"I'm sorry. You and I both know how many monsters are out there."

True. "One thing I do know, my thoughts are working differently. They used to come to me while looking at photos or visiting crime scenes. Now they're coming to me all the time and my brain is weaving Annabelle into them, the other girl, too, and our captor." Or captors as it may be.

Fallon stops with the food prep to look at me. "Caroline, save for the stripping of skin, the parallels are there. You said from the start you felt The Organ Ripper was a team, two people, Harley and someone else. Erwin aside, why have you not hypothesized that your captor is part of that team?"

I don't answer that because I don't want to keep lying to Fallon. There is no way Harley and my captor are a team. But somehow things are connected. I don't know how though. It seems to go deeper than Erwin, the man who turned himself in and bit off an ear.

Perhaps our captor knew Harley and they both knew Erwin. That's why my brain keeps making connections. They share the same methods.

Methods.

Methods.

Methods are developed over years. Even going back to childhood.

With a surge of thought, I scoot over to the dining room table and look through Harley's file. He's lived in Tennessee his entire life. Raised by a single mother. Public educated. Started working in a kitchen as a teen. Went to culinary school. Eventually became a private chef. According to the file, Becka's mother died from complications during the delivery.

I back up, focusing again on Harley's childhood. He was raised by a single mom who died of breast cancer when Harley was in culinary school. He has no other family. He attended camp every summer. A camp for "troubled boys".

Interesting.

A possible place he could've met someone like my captor and Erwin?

Though according to Vincent, my captor was a drifter. But I think Vincent's off on that.

Harley wasn't doing the girls on his property. That garage was merely a holding place. I thought from the start Harley might own another property but Uzzo has yet to find anything. There's someplace else. A place that he's familiar with, where he feels comfortable, and perhaps holds a sense of nostalgia. It's where he honed his methods.

At this hour, Uzzo won't answer but I still send her a quick text. I NEED EVERYTHING YOU CAN GET ME ON HARLEY'S CHILDHOOD. SCHOOL. CAMP. WHAT ELSE? I NEED LOCATIONS. AND FRIENDS, TOO.

Laying the phone down, I close the file and look back in the kitchen at Fallon. He glances up from stirring the vegetables and when he sees I'm no longer looking at the file, he says, "Okay, bear with me here and my train of thought."

I nod. "Shoot."

"So, Harley has been hacking up teen girls, women, men, and probably even young children for the better part of thirty years. Harley eats some. He possibly sells some. He feeds some to Becka. Becka's been in and out of remission and that possibly drove Harley's victim list as he picked girls that were Becka's age. This coincides with your thoughts that the killer was motivated by loss or the thought of loss. Harley has either been working with someone all along or possibly alone and only recently began training the legacy.

Somewhere along the way though, Harley and this other person had a disagreement resulting in Harley's stabbing. All the victims, except Nadia, have been done by similar and/or the same practiced hand in which two killers who work together would have. Meanwhile, with the honey, charcoal, and the wildflowers, it's some twisted way of caring for the victim, just like your captor did with you. That, along with the choking aspect, is causing you to feel even more of a personal connection than you usually do, and to surmise this is all somehow connected to what happened to you in those woods when you were eight years old." Fallon takes a breath. "Does that all sound about right?"

I stare at Fallon across the kitchen. "Listening to you say it like that sounds crazy."

"Are you kidding me? Given your past and mine and all the cases you've helped with over the years, nothing is too crazy. Your captor has never been found and Erwin may, or may not, know who it is. That aside, and asking you again, why are you not fully on board that your captor could be the person who has been working with Harley?"

Now is the time to tell Fallon what happened to our captor. He'll understand. All I have to do is open my mouth and speak the words. All I have to do is open my mouth.

And so I do and right as I'm about to speak, a thought drifts in. *Does he have secrets he's not telling me?*

"What?" Fallon asks.

Unexpected nerves flare through me.

"What?" He asks again.

I swallow. "Do you have any secrets you're keeping from me?"

He opens his mouth. He closes it. He opens it again. "Why would you ask me that?"

"Why aren't you answering?"

For a few tense seconds, neither one of us says anything as we keep looking at each other in the dimly lit kitchen with the crockpot on the counter beside us. He turns away first, flipping the switch to low and turning the faucet on to rinse his hands.

I keep staring at him, waiting for him to answer but he doesn't. He simply rotates the faucet off, dries his hands on a paper towel, tosses it into the garbage, then says, "I'm going to close my eyes for a while."

Then he's gone, leaving me standing dumbfounded. Holy shit, Fallon's keeping something from me.

THIRTY-ONE

I pinch a bit of spice across my last few bites of oatmeal, spoon it into my mouth, and let it melt across my tongue. I've tried copying Vincent's homemade spice concoction but I never seem to get it right.

Create a light and colorful place in my mind to put memories of Annabelle. That's what Suzi said and I do that now. Or at least I try but the fatigue from being up for so many hours off-balances my efforts.

After rinsing my bowl out, I settle down on the couch, sliding my legs under Zane's big body and enjoying the warmth and weight of him. Petal jumps up on the armrest, casually strolling across, then turns a few circles before settling into a cushion and giving Zane his space.

I glance at my watch. "My name is Caroline Christianson. It's 6:45 in the morning. I'm at my home. I'm alive and well."

After I ground myself, I allow my eyes to drift close, listening to Fallon in the shower and telling myself when he gets out, we'll talk. I need to know what he's keeping from me, or perhaps, it's more that I have to be okay with the fact he has secrets just like I do.

I check my phone but Uzzo hasn't texted back yet. After I talk with Fallon, I'll give Uzzo a call. I'll ask about getting Becka in a room with Nadia's corpse, even though I'm pretty sure that won't fly. I'll inquire about the cold cases. I'll schedule a time to talk with Erwin. I'll ask about Harley's childhood. I'll . . .

A distant, nearly imperceptible cry drifts through the air and my hand pauses mid-stroke on Zane's head but the sound slowly dissipates. Opening my eyes, I look at Zane and then Petal, neither of them reacts. I must be hearing things.

With a deep sigh, I close my eyes and stroke Zane's head again and there it is—a distant, faint cry. I look at Zane and Petal and, again, neither of them reacts.

I scoot up on the couch, listening closely, and another cry, or more like a whimper, filters in, just as far but a little louder now, like an animal in distress. I glance over to the bathroom door, ready to ask Fallon if he hears anything, but the fan is going and he won't hear me.

Sliding out from underneath Zane, I grab my jacket off the hook by the door and I step outside onto our porch. My gaze tracks across our front yard and the field that spans between us and Suzi's house, everything covered in morning dew and glistening with the rising sun.

The cry comes, sounding more frantic now, from the trees that border the side of our property. I hurry over and the whimpering rises and falls, growing louder on my approach. The desperation and fear woven through it make me wince.

"Where are you?" I search the trees, trying to figure out where the sound is coming from.

All goes quiet and I hold my breath, hoping to hear it again. Above my head, the clouds shift, covering the morning sun, and for a moment dots swim in my vision. I blink several times, refocus, and there in the woods lay Harley with Gaby, the girl from the motel, beside him. Both are fully clothed and with their eyes closed, they look like they're simply resting.

Quietly, I approach and neither of them opens their eyes as I come to sit beside them. A brisk wind blows through, creaking the frozen tree limbs. The clouds shift and one beam of sunlight snakes through to illuminate another area a few yards away.

Irene, the girl from the dorm, lays there with Yasmine, the girl from the park. Like Harley and Gaby, both are fully clothed and with their eyes closed, they simply look like they're resting.

Wildflowers surround Harley and Gaby only but not Irene and Yasmine.

Irene and Yasmine, done before Harley died.

Gaby, done after Harley.

Wildflowers around Harley and Gaby.

Harley did Irene and Yasmine. That's why they are laying together. Whoever killed Harley also did Gaby, that's why they are laying together.

Then I gently layer wildflowers inside of her, letting her know I care.

The wildflowers are telling me that I'm connected to whoever did Harley and Gaby. The flowers aren't meant to thank or show appreciation to the victim. The flowers are for me. This is all about me.

Beside me Harley shifts, opening his eyes. He looks at me and a sad smile curls through his lips. "I messed up."

"Caroline." A distant whispering draws my glance to

the right and away from what I'm looking at. Across my yard walks Vincent with Becka right beside him. "Caroline?"

I blink a few times and glance around to find myself alone, sitting in the woods among the sparse trees.

Vincent comes to a stop at the edge of the trees. "What are you doing sitting in there?"

With a frown, I look around. "What time is it?"

"A bit past nine."

It was 6:45 the last time I grounded myself.

Vincent steps into the woods, coming to a stop in front of me. Squatting down, he scrutinizes my eyes. "Perhaps you were sleepwalking again. Where's Fallon?"

"Inside." I glance beyond Vincent to see Becka hovering in the side yard, watching us. "What is she doing here?"

"Well, considering you asked Detective Uzzo to have her followed, I figured taking her with me everywhere would be a better alternative."

"I did..." I was planning on talking to Uzzo about getting Becka in a room with Nadia's corpse but I don't remember asking Uzzo to have Becka followed. That thought hadn't even occurred to me but it must have been buried in my brain somewhere otherwise I wouldn't have asked Uzzo.

In a conversation, I don't remember.

"Perhaps you're the one who needs to be followed." Vincent holds a gloved hand out to me. "Come on, let's get you up."

I take his hand. "Were my eyes open or closed just now?"

"They were open."

"It feels like I just woke up."

He helps me to my feet. "What were you seeing?"

I look at Becka, not wanting to talk in front of her, and Vincent glances over his shoulder at her. "Please wait for me in the car," he says and she quietly does as instructed. Her compliance surprises me. Every time I've been around her, she's been anything but. She's on her best behavior. Smart girl, given I placed a call to Uzzo that I don't remember.

When Becka is back inside of Vincent's SUV, I say, "Harley was here, lying with Gaby. Over to the side were the other two girls, Irene and Yasmine. Harley looked at me and he said, 'I messed up.'"

Vincent thinks about that a second. "Separation of bodies telling us that one killer, Harley, did the first two girls and another killer, the legacy, did Harley and Gaby."

"Yes, and Harley's words of 'I messed up' coincide with our thoughts that he and his partner/legacy/protégé, whatever you want to call it, disagreed. The partner returned the bodies and led us to Harley. What's new here though, is that I also saw wildflowers around Harley and Gaby only."

"And this tells you?" Vincent walks from the woods.

"'Then I gently lay wildflowers inside of her, letting her know I care.' It's what I thought when I visited the motel scene. '...letting her know I care.' I thought it was the killer caring for the victim but it's me. The killer wants me to know I'm the driving force behind this. When Annabelle and I were taken, we were wearing wildflower crowns. We always wore them. They were our favorites. They still are. This is about me. The killer isn't thanking the victims by decorating them, he's letting me know that he's thinking of me. He knows me and he's somehow connected to my past. You said my captor was a drifter. What if you're wrong?

There could be more to him. We've been discounting Erwin's involvement but he might be the link."

"Let me do some more digging on your captor's identity."

I nod, already thinking about the sketch from my pad and facial recognition. I've never thought to scan it. My captor was a drifter and I accepted that. Frankly I never really cared about his identity because he got what he deserved. But now, there is something there. I need to scan the sketch into the program. I may get something, or I may get nothing, but I can certainly try.

Vincent stops walking and turns to face me. "I know I've said it before but now would be a good time to say it again. I do not advise that you ever tell Fallon what happened to your captor."

The conversation I had with Fallon a few hours ago filters back into my thoughts. I don't like that Fallon and I have secrets, and I don't like even more that Vincent keeps reminding me to keep them. It makes me wonder if Vincent is having a similar conversation with Fallon.

I choose not to respond to his cautionary words. Instead, I glance beyond Vincent to the SUV where Becka sits inside, staring straight at me. "Why do you take in strays? Me, Fallon, Becka. Why?"

The change in topic catches Vincent off guard and it takes a second for him to respond. "I became frustrated at the number of patients I couldn't help. I became frustrated at how tied my hands were with policy. I wanted full reign to try my methods." Reaching out, he gently cups my shoulder. "I'm glad I did because you and Fallon are two great successes."

I keep staring at Becka. "And you're hoping she'll be one, too."

"Yes, I am."

"What other great successes have you had?"

Vincent doesn't answer me and I turn away from the SUV to look into his dark eyes. My head tilts as I try to read his thoughts but I can tell he's keeping them neutral. Something tells me his successes have been few and far between. Interesting.

Either way, I say, "I have a lot of respect for what you do. I used to try and see others through your eyes. Sometimes I still do. Did you know that?"

His lips twitch. "Dime store psychoanalysis?"

"You've helped me over the years. I hesitate to think about what I would've become without your guidance. You taught me how to channel my dark thoughts into something positive. When I first started assisting you with profiles, I began researching psychopaths. I even printed off a checklist and went down it, not surprised to find how many little boxes I checked about myself. I also did a checklist for Fallon and one on you. According to the internet, we're all crazy."

Vincent chuckles. "Psychopaths aren't crazy. They are aware of what they're doing and also the consequences surrounding those actions."

"Then how would you diagnose me?" In all the years I've known him, I've never thought to ask him that question.

"I would diagnose you with an antisocial personality disorder."

I give a nod because that about sums up it up. "Do you think psychopaths can be attracted to each other?"

Vincent considers that and I think he detects the underlying question: Are Fallon and I attracted to each other because we're both internet-checklist psychopaths? "I think some people are naturally pulled in by psychopaths," Vincent says.

With a sigh I glance away, looking now at our house. Fallon stands in the kitchen, peering out at me and Vincent in the side yard. I give him a small smile to let him know I'm okay.

That spot above my left brow pangs and reaching up I press my fingertips into it. "So why are you here? Is it about the Uzzo/Becka thing?"

"Yes, I do wish you would have talked to me first before calling Uzzo. You seem to be making a lot of independent decisions these days. You used to include me in your processes."

That's funny because to me my independent decisions are few and far between. Or rather my ability to tell him about them. "We have to cut the umbilical cord sometime," I try to make a joke.

He doesn't find it funny.

Now is probably not the time to broach the subject of getting Becka in a room with Nadia's corpse. Though if I called Uzzo about having her followed, I did probably mention the corpse idea, too. What I want to know is, when exactly did I call Uzzo? While I was sleepwalking?

The sound of footsteps has me glancing over to see Fallon approaching. Without a glance at Vincent, he comes right up to me and hands me my pill bottle before turning to Vincent. "What did you just say to her? Why is her head hurting?"

I love Fallon, I do, but sometimes he gets way too protective. "I'm okay. It's my fault. I had another sleep-walking episode."

"What?" Fallon reaches for me. "When? Just now? Jesus Christ, Caroline. I thought you were asleep on the couch this whole time. I got out of the shower and saw Zane cuddled with a pile of blankets that I thought was you. I'm sorry."

"It's okay. I'm okay."

"No, you're not." Fallon touches that spot above my left brow. "If you were okay, you wouldn't be getting so many headaches and tossing back so many pills."

Well, he's right about that.

A sudden high-pitched sound pierces through my head and I wince as I try to keep my focus on Fallon. Taking the bottle from my fingers, he shakes out two and hands them to me.

"I'll take them when I get inside."

From his inside coat pocket, Vincent pulls out an aluminum-wrapped square item and hands it to me. "Some more of those seed bars you like." He backs away. "I'm going to head out. Make sure you eat something with those pills."

"See you later," I say.

He walks to the SUV, staring at Suzi's home in the distance and the greenhouse beside it.

"I know finding killers is your job but perhaps it's time for you to work with someone else," Fallon says. "Vincent isn't the only profiler."

On this, it does no good to argue with Fallon. He's never understood the connection I share with Vincent. Instead, I take a step toward him, wrapping my arms around his middle and laying my cheek on his chest. "Thank you for always being so protective of me."

With a sigh, he hugs me to him. "But?"

"But I am okay. Okay?"

Pulling back a little, Fallon levels those warm brown eyes on mine. For a long moment, he considers me. I make sure he sees in my eyes that I am, indeed, okay.

With a little smile, he presses a kiss to my cheek. "You'll tell me if you're not?"

"I will." I inhale a deep breath, letting it out slowly, still looking into his familiar eyes. "Fallon, we need to talk."

He nods. "I know. But I also need to get to class. Let's talk when I get home."

THIRTY-TWO

When I get back inside the house, I've got an email from Uzzo:

Caroline, I have got a lot on my plate (as you know) and luckily with the FBI's arrival, I'm getting some much-needed assistance. I wanted to give you a quick update. First, Erwin has refused your request to speak with him. I'm sorry, but please know we are beginning to connect the dots.

We were finally able to open Harley's password-protected client list only to find the lists encrypted. I'll let you know as soon as I know more about that.

Second, we found a connection between Erwin and Harley that goes back to childhood. Thanks to your text, that got me looking and digging. Though Erwin is originally from Kentucky, apparently he attended the same camp for troubled boys that Harley did. And though the camp is no longer operational, the grounds and vacated cabins are still there. A logging company owns the property now. The same logging company that owns the property where you and Annabelle were held captive. A coincidence? I don't think so. I've already dispatched a team to check out the vacant camp. It could very well be where Harley performed his acts.

I want to discuss your comments about Becka, too. Let's plan on talking later...

I recall thinking that I wanted to speak with Erwin but I don't recall asking to. I didn't expect him to refuse my request and I'm more than curious as to why. He talked to Vincent. Why not me? And there's no telling what all I said to Uzzo about Becka. I don't want Uzzo to know I'm having issues remembering things. For now, I'll let her take the lead in bringing that back up.

I re-read the lines about the logging company. I knew it. I knew there was a connection between my captor and Harley, which now apparently *does* include Erwin.

Picking up my phone, I shoot Detective Uzzo a quick text: WHAT IS THE NAME OF THE SUMMER CAMP?

CAMP DESONK, she types back. THE NAME OF THE LOGGING COMPANY IS EMERSON LOGGING.

I already knew that one. Years ago when I found that out, I researched the company but found nothing odd. Uzzo's right though, this isn't a coincidence.

I type CAMP DESONK into a search bar and 23,400 results pop up. That's a lot of results.

With a sigh, I grab one of Vincent's homemade seed bars and click on the first one.

THIRTY-THREE

Becka's face curls into a sneaky smile. "You're sleepwalking right now."

"Am I?"

She leans in a little. "I've been following you."

I go still.

"Why are you here?" she asks.

I turn a slow circle, taking in Harley's cabin and the surrounding woods. I don't know why I'm here. I think I was following Becka but I'm not sure.

"You're confused, aren't you?" She asks.

"Yes..."

She studies me for a few seconds like she's trying to figure out what to do with me. Then, as if figuring it out, she smirks. "You've been a very naughty girl. Do you know what you've done?"

I'm caught between the curiosity of wanting to know and the denial of whatever it is.

"Don't worry, I won't tell anyone. Not even Vincent."

I turn another circle, looking for Vincent. If Becka is

here, shouldn't he be here, too? "I thought Vincent was keeping an eye on you."

"And you believe that?" Amusement glints through her eyes. "That's what he tells people so they'll leave me alone."

Snow falls around us and I lift my head in an automatic gesture, just like Annabelle used to do. She loved the flakes on her face. Her laughter rises in my ears in a haunting strain and I bring my attention back down to Becka to see that she's moved closer still.

"Someone wants to meet you," she whispers, nodding toward the line of trees before turning and strolling back toward Harley's cabin.

I walk in the direction she nodded, searching through the nighttime. But I see no one. For a brief moment, I think perhaps Becka is messing with me but then footsteps emerge, leading through the dusting of snow further into the woods. I'm careful to step on top of the other person's snow prints, just like Annabelle and I used to do when we were kids.

I move further into the trees and as I do, the area slowly darkens, cutting out all moonlight, and I'm swallowed into the woods.

Hugging a tree, I wait for my eyes to adjust and when they do, I see it up ahead. It's a mushroom patch, thick with a variety of fungi, the ground dug through and the mushrooms upended. It's what's underneath though, that catches my eye.

Body parts.

My gaze freezes on the chunks of meat and bones. A scream slices through the air, then another, and another, weaving together, overlapping, becoming a chorus of horrific harmonizing.

I put my hands over my ears and I close my eyes and all I hear now is the beat that comes with silence.

"Caroline?"

My eyes snap open but I'm not in the woods. I'm now in Vincent's living room.

"Caroline?"

I glance up to find him standing in the open archway, dressed in his blue and green checkered robe. I gave him that robe a few Christmases ago.

"What are you doing here?" He asks.

"I..." I look around. "I don't know."

Vincent moves into the room, taking a seat in a leather sitting chair. His gaze goes out the bank of windows to where my Mini Cooper sits in his circular drive. I glance at the oversized round clock hanging on the wall. It's after midnight.

"What's the last thing you remember?" He asks.

"Fallon went to class, we were going to talk later. I got an email from Uzzo. Then I started researching a few things. I must have drifted off. But then I was having a conversation with Becka out at Harley's cabin. Or at least I think I was..." I don't tell him what I saw under the mushrooms. I want to see for myself if it's real or not. Because if it is, then I was not dreaming.

"You mean you were dreaming of a conversation with Becka?"

I think about everything for a few seconds, trying to decide what to say. I end up repeating, "Fallon went to class, we were going to talk later. An email came in from Uzzo. I started researching a few things. I must have drifted off. But then I had the dream I was out at Harley's cabin and when I woke, I was here instead." I pace Vincent's living room. "Something is wrong with me."

"No, nothing is wrong with you. You're disassociating. It's a survival technique. The things you have been feeling surrounding this case are overwhelming you."

I sigh. "They are."

"You save lives," Vincent says. "That has always been your motivation. Saving lives makes you feel good and worthy. At the expense of your own life though, it's not worth it."

"Are you telling me that you agree with Fallon in that I need to step back from this all together?"

Vincent doesn't have an answer. He doesn't want me to stop helping. He wants me to do a better job of balancing.

"Between my sleepwalking and my hallucinations, do you think it might be medical? As in a brain tumor?"

"Caroline." Vincent sighs. "You don't have a brain tumor but we can get you checked out if you need that peace of mind. Did you say something about researching? What were you researching?"

For some reason I don't tell him the specifics, instead, I say, "Just stuff about Harley. All things you already know."

Vincent runs a long finger across his bottom lip as he studies me. "I am worried about you."

I stop pacing. "I'm worried about me, too. I'm afraid—"

"Afraid of what, Caroline?"

My throat closes together with what I'm about to admit. "I'm afraid—" I swallow. "I'm afraid that I'm going to wake up from sleepwalking and realize that I did something really bad."

"Perhaps you should consider moving back in here so that I can keep an eye on you."

The words roll from his mouth quickly, as if he's been waiting for the exact moment to say them.

Becka strolls in, saving me from a response and carrying a glass of milk. "I thought I heard voices."

I wait for Vincent to tell her now is not the time but he remains silently contemplating me as Becka slides onto the leather couch and curls her legs up and under. The doll that she's been working on sits in the corner of the couch and she pulls it onto her lap. "What are you two talking about?"

Quietly, I take her in, going through the details of the dream I just had. Is it possible Becka and I were at Harley's cabin tonight?

With a shrug, Becka takes a sip of milk and then sits it on a gold coaster. "So, I was thinking about my future and how to make money. What are your thoughts on a book? Don't you think people will want to read about what it was like to grow up with my father? I mean, they already think I'm warped coming from who I did. I might as well give them a front-row seat to my crazy."

With a quiet sigh, Vincent moves his gaze off me and over to Becka. "You would be forfeiting your privacy and ours."

She shrugs. "So, my privacy is already forfeited."

Vincent waves his hand around the room. "All of this would change."

"Trust me," I say. "Whatever you're feeling now won't last. Don't be eager to do a tell-all."

Becka's dark green eyes trace from Vincent over to me. "And why would you care? I'm not important to you."

True, she's not. But I do feel an unwelcome responsibility for her.

"Or am I important now that I want to do a tell-all?" Becka snides.

"Becka," Vincent quietly speaks. "You've been through a traumatic event and it's making you say out of character things. Why don't we talk about this in the morning when we're all well-rested?"

She picks her milk up, sips, then sets it back down. "I don't need anyone's permission to do a tell-all."

"No," he agrees. "But I would hope I, *we*, mean something to you that will warrant consideration of our feelings. Because once you open this door, you can't control what comes through it."

Becka considers that and her defiance visibly softens. I take that as my cue it's time to leave. "I'm heading out then."

"Do you want me to follow you?" Vincent asks. "Do you want me to call Fallon?"

"No," I say. "I'll be fine."

"Bye." Becka gives me a two-finger wave and the movement stops me in my tracks. I've seen that exact wave before.

THIRTY-FOUR

"How'd it go with Vincent?" Fallon asks the next morning.

I glance up from my toasted seed bar. "Huh?"

"You called me and told me you were going to Vincent's place. Don't you remember?"

"Oh..." No, I don't remember. I do remember Fallon went to class. I remember we said we would talk when he got home. I remember researching on the internet. The dream of discovering the mushroom patch. Standing in Vincent's living room after apparently sleepwalking my way there. Arriving home to find Fallon asleep in bed. But I do not remember calling Fallon.

I'm having entire conversations and not even realizing it. What's worse is that Fallon doesn't realize it either. "How did I seem when I told you I was going?"

"You seemed fine." Fallon frowns. "Why?"

I don't respond and instead, think about that for a few seconds. Having conversations, driving around, not remembering details. Vincent's right, I did sleepwalk quite a bit when I was younger but it wasn't until I snuck Rachel's

medicinal herbs that the sleepwalking turned into more
unusual behavior.

"Anything you want to tell me?" Fallon prompts.

"Do you remember when I was sneaking Rachel's hallu-
cinogenic herbs?"

"Please tell me you're not doing that again. Do I need to
remind you what happened?"

"No, I'm not. I promise." I wouldn't chance it.

Crossing behind me, Fallon opens the blinds and the
morning sun pours in. I'm not going to tell him I sleepwalked my way to Vincent's home last night. Fallon is
already worried about me. I don't need him more so.

A few moments pass while he makes coffee and
buttered toast before moving to the table and taking the seat
beside me. Idly I sip my coffee, thinking about ending up at
Vincent's, following sounds into the woods, and of the
internet search on Camp Desonk.

That last thought has me grabbing the laptop and
opening the lid. My search is still up and paused on an old
photo. Moving the cursor, I zoom in and see a group of
teenage boys standing with their arms looped around each
other. I study each of their faces but it's been thirty-some
years since this photo was taken and so it's hard to tell. But I
paused on this photo for a reason.

"I don't know why we think we can hide things from
each other." It's a simple statement Fallon makes, not a
question, just a statement, and a deafening silence follows.

I move my attention from the laptop and over to Fallon
and for a moment I simply look at him. I don't know why we
think we can either.

Reaching across the short distance, he weaves his fingers
through mine. "I want to be so much for you. And I am here
for you but I won't watch you fall apart. Not again."

My heart nearly stops. "What are you saying?"

"I'm saying that we should be beyond this. Why don't we know everything about each other? What or *who* is making us keep secrets?"

By "who" he means Vincent.

Outside tires crunch over our gravel yard and I glance over my shoulder to see Detective Uzzo's old Chevy truck pull in.

"Of course, someone is here." With a sigh, Fallon pushes back from the table. "I'm leaving."

I reach for him. "Fallon."

He shakes his head, gives me a chaste kiss, and leaves his breakfast right where it is as he heads out and Detective Uzzo comes in.

Uzzo's got her phone to her ear. "Vincent," she tells me, before putting the phone on speaker. Obviously, Uzzo has already told Vincent whatever it is because she quickly catches me up. "An anonymous tip led us back out to Harley's cabin. The first two missing girls have been found, or rather what's left of them, buried some fifty yards away right under a patch of wild mushrooms."

I wasn't dreaming. I was there. I sleepwalked my way to Harley's cabin, which means my DNA is probably there at the mushroom patch. I need to tell them both right now.

"The team is out there as we speak, dissecting the scene," Uzzo says.

"And the FBI?" Vincent asks.

"Even with their help, we're spread thin. Especially now with the Camp Desonk lead."

"The what?" Vincent asks.

"A connection between Erwin and Harley," Uzzo says. "They attended the same summer camp. One for troubled boys. I dispatched a team to check it out and ended up calling them back because of the mushroom patch. Now I've got a patrolman watching the deserted area until I can get CSI out there. Right now, we're up to our hairline with the mushroom patch discovery. We've also managed to wrap up several of the cold cases from the hair found in the rug. The body count linked to Harley is well in the dozens now. I just wish we had the actual bodies and not just hair. I want closure for the grieving families."

"Given that Harley is dead, you'll likely never find those bodies," Vincent says. "Or be able to verify if they were killed in the same manner as the recent murders."

That rug and Becka's discovery of it goes through my mind, followed by her words last night regarding a tell-all. "What if Becka intentionally led us to that rug? She knew or suspected there was hair in it. She wanted it known that Harley had such an enormous body count. The more bodies, the more infamous Harley becomes. The more infamous Becka becomes as the daughter of a cannibalistic serial killer." The more money her tell-all novel makes.

Uzzo says, "We all know Becka is a link, but to what end is unclear. I agree with Caroline. I want to see Becka in a room with Nadia. Unfortunately, Nadia's body has been claimed by her parents and they won't agree to it. However, now we have the first two girls. I want to see how Becka reacts to them and I want Caroline in that room, too, to gauge Becka's response."

Uzzo looks at me and I keep my expression passive. Apparently, when I called her about having Becka followed, I did indeed ask if we could put her in a room with Nadia. Entire conversations and not even remembering it. Not good.

Vincent says, "You can't put Becka in a room with

butchered girls. Caroline, why would you suggest such a thing?"

"Uzzo's right," I say. "Becka is a link, but to what end is unclear. If you want me to get a true picture of her, then I do need to see her reaction to a corpse her father has butchered. Vincent, it'll give you a clearer picture, too. You know it will."

Vincent sighs and if Detective Uzzo wasn't here, Vincent would have words with me over this idea. It's exactly why I didn't run it by him in the first place. These are the independent decisions I'm making that bother him.

Uzzo says, "I think she's a common thread that needs to come unraveled."

"I want to go on record that I do not agree with this," Vincent says.

"Noted. I want her at the morgue in a few hours. By then we'll have one of the bodies currently being dug up." Detective Uzzo clicks off, looking right at me. I start to tell her about being at the mushroom patch, about talking to Becka while I was there, but Uzzo's phone rings again. "I'll see you in a few hours," she says before answering her phone and leaving my house.

I'm not sure how much of my visit to the mushroom patch was a dream, reality, or hallucination. Even if I do tell Uzzo, I don't know exactly what to say because I'm not sure. Either way, I'd rather be ahead of it before they find my DNA and I'm forced to tell.

Moving my mouse, I unfreeze my laptop and pull up the photo of the teenage boys again. Normally, I would send something like this to Uzzo but with everything going on right now, the photo would likely be put on her already enormous and continually growing list of things to do surrounding this case.

Instead, I launch facial recognition software and let it do its thing.

THIRTY-FIVE

A few hours later, I stand in the morgue with Becka beside me and Vincent beside her, staring down at a body covered by a sheet. Across from us, on the other side of the body, stands Detective Uzzo and a woman from the FBI. Uzzo introduced her as Agent Tanaka.

A dark and earthy, death-like smell permeates the room, and both Vincent and Becka press handkerchiefs to their noses but I don't. To me, the scent of rotting flesh has always been more sweet and acrid than most people describe. Yet as I breathe through my mouth, I have to force my thoughts to stay in the here and now.

"Becka," Detective Uzzo says. "I want you to look at this body and tell me if you recognize her."

My gaze cuts over to Becka to see her body tense, every sense tuned, and her fists clenched around the handkerchief as if she wants to flee. Looking at her anxious body language right now, I'm not sure she was there at the mushroom patch. Maybe I sleepwalked my way there and hallucinated my conversation with her.

Or maybe I'm so far inside this killer's head, that I saw

where he went last night. He may have been the one who uncovered the bodies. For whatever reason, he wanted them found.

Or maybe not. Hell, I don't know.

Detective Uzzo puts her hands on the sheet that covers the body, ready to pull it back, but on a last thought glances at me. She's cognizant of the break down I had and is checking to make sure I'm all right.

Bracing myself, I give her the go-ahead.

She pulls back the sheet to reveal a partially exposed skeleton with soft tissue still clinging in liquid and putrefied dark clumps. Insects, maggots, and worms have burrowed in and around, tunneling through. Though the hair and nails have fallen out, traces of them remain. Through the decomposition, I make out a long wound that runs the length of her torso, tattered and wide from the decomposition but done with a similar expert hand as all the others.

Not Nadia, though. And to my knowledge, she's the only body to have been released. I find that a little coincidental but I keep that to myself for now.

I am hyper-aware of everything around me. The silence. The ticking of the clock. My breathing. I freeze in place as I stare down at the girl who months ago would have been laughing with her friends or eating pizza and watching a movie.

The detective's voice echoes in the room. "Have you seen this girl before?"

Becka looks up at Detective Uzzo, holding her gaze. Her eyes shine with alertness but her voice is flat when she answers, "No." She looks back down at the corpse. "Can we cover her up please?"

Vincent moves to do just that at the same time Agent Tanaka shakes her head. "This girl was gutted and her organs removed. Becka, I've seen the pictures of you and your father with the animals you killed and gutted."

"We're done here," Vincent says, grasping Becka's arm.

Detective Uzzo levels him with a steely stare. "You can be done but Becka isn't done until Tanaka and I say so."

Vincent's jaw tightens but he nods for Becka to keep going.

"Did you ever meet this girl? Did you see this girl in your garage? Did you help your father get this girl? Was that your role in things? Two girls have died after Harley's death, Nadia and Gaby. Are you carrying on your father's legacy? Did you kill those two girls?" Uzzo asks, surprising me. I didn't expect her to go down this route.

"No," Becka says. "No to it all."

"Let's talk about Nadia, the girl found in chains in your garage," Uzzo says. "I find it peculiar that she dies the day after you two 'met' in your cabin. She died conveniently on the same day her parents were bringing her in to talk with me. Don't you find that peculiar, too?"

Becka's gaze doesn't waver. "I'm a survivor. Just like Caroline."

I don't like that she just compared herself to me. Detective Uzzo turns her attention off Becka and over to me. "Caroline, anything?"

Truthfully, I expected to envision more. Perhaps the stress of seeing an actual body after my nervous breakdown is blocking my response. Looking away from the body, I shake my head. I've disappointed Uzzo.

She covers the body and the relief of not seeing it anymore rolls through me.

"Do you believe her?" Uzzo asks.

My eyes widen a bit. I hadn't expected this either—that she would question me right in front of Vincent and Becka.

I think about my words carefully before answering. "I think Becka is keeping things to herself but Vincent took her in and he wouldn't have done that if he held reservations about Becka and her future."

I didn't exactly tell the truth but I didn't lie either. It's true, Vincent doesn't just help anyone. He's careful with his selection. I do think Becka knows things and, like Fallon, I don't care for her but I also see her as a victim in this. She was raised by a serial killer and there's no telling what she was forced to do.

A couple of odd beats go by and I can tell by the way Uzzo keeps looking at me that she doesn't like my answer. I get it, she's desperate for answers.

Finally, she dismisses us.

As we're walking from the room, Becka asks, "Have you found the greenhouse where the wildflowers were grown?"

Uzzo doesn't answer, just nods for us to leave.

Becka continues, "Because I saw that your friend, Suzi, has a greenhouse."

Vincent grasps Becka's arm, ushering her out. "Just because Suzi has a greenhouse doesn't mean she's involved in this."

It surprises me that Vincent is so quick to jump to Suzi's defense. It surprises me, even more, when Becka says, "Actually, you have a greenhouse, too."

"It doesn't take a genius to break into a greenhouse and steal samples and/or plant evidence in hopes of leading cops on a wild goose chase," Vincent responds.

Becka's lips twitch and my gaze narrows in on the movement. She enjoys winding people up.

The two of them continue down the hall and Uzzo grasps my arm. "You okay?" She quietly asks.

I appreciate her checking in. "I'm sorry I couldn't be more help."

"It's okay."

I follow after Vincent and Becka and as I push through the door that leads outside, I glance over my shoulder to see Uzzo still standing in the hall, staring at me. Unclipping her cell from a belt clip, she dials a number and turns away for privacy. I'll bet anything she's calling Suzi to ask for her to voluntarily bring samples in. And I bet Suzi's going to think I'm the reason why. I'll have to make sure I tell her I'm not.

Outside the morgue, Vincent stops walking and turns Becka to face him. "You are extremely close to losing your privileges. I am the sole reason why you have a home right now. One word from me and Uzzo will place you anywhere I say. And that doesn't mean a foster home where you have the freedom to roam. That means a facility under lock and key. Is that what you want? Because your actions tell me you do."

With a sigh, Becka doesn't answer his question and instead says, "It can be a comfort to see a corpse, especially to the family who needed closure."

Vincent's jaw hardens as he fishes his keys from his front pocket. "Is that why you dug up the mushroom patch?"

Woah. My gaze snaps to Becka and she averts her eyes but Vincent doesn't move as he stares hard at her. He's really angry.

Vincent takes a step forward, still staring hard at her. "Let me tell you something, you may think you're clever but you are not."

It occurs to me then. "You did this to create more drama. You're trying to add to the plot of your book. Just like how you led us to the rug."

Becka's chin hikes up a notch. "I'm not afraid to face my past. The detective wanted the first two bodies. Now she has them."

"And what about all the cold cases? There are a lot of families that need closure—"

Vincent holds his hand up, stopping me. "Becka, you've betrayed my trust. After all, I've done for you, I deserve more than this."

After all he's done for her...something tells me that's more than simply providing her a home. Becka glances away then, she could be faking it but Vincent's harshness does seem to bother her.

"Trust goes both ways." He aims the key fob at the SUV and unlocks it. "Get in. Caroline and I will be back in a few minutes. And, so help me God, if you are not here when I get back, you will regret it. Do you understand me?"

With a genuinely nervous swallow, Becka nods.

"I need to say something first." I look between them. "Last night before I found my way to your living room, Vincent, I was at Harley's cabin. Or at least I think I was. Becka, you were there. You talked to me. Then you pointed me to the mushroom patch so that I would find the bodies that you uncovered."

Becka shakes her head. "I don't know what you're talking about. I did uncover the bodies to help out the investigation. Yes, I was there but you weren't." Then she turns and climbs in the SUV, leaving me standing outside with Vincent.

I look up at him. "I knew about the mushroom patch before Uzzo came to my house. How can that be?"

Vincent shakes his head. "I don't know. Either you were indeed sleepwalking and Becka is being sly, or—"

"I'm so far inside the killer's head that I'm seeing what

he's seeing, which means he was there last night with Becka. Either that or you're right, she's lying. I was there and she's messing with me."

With an irritable sigh, Vincent walks back toward the morgue and I follow silently. I don't think I've ever seen him quite this agitated and I experience true relief his irritation is aimed at Becka and not me. Though I've never admitted it out loud, I've always held a healthy fear of Vincent. Not like he'd-kill-me type of fear but more of what he would do if I double-crossed him.

I think Rachel felt the same way.

The room we were just in sits dimly lit now with the body still there on the gurney and covered by a sheet. Vincent walks straight in and over to the gurney. Unlike Uzzo, he doesn't check to see I'm okay, he takes hold of the sheet and lowers it back down.

Stepping back, he waves me forward. He wants me to try again and dig deep. To see more than I did with Detective Uzzo here. Like her, he's frustrated and I get it.

I can do this. With a deep breath, I look down at the remains, eyeing the rotting flesh, and spying a rib poking through an area of decomposition. My gaze trails up to her skeleton face and I close my eyes.

The room darkens and what light was here shifts to illuminate the girl's body. I take in a shallow breath and step into the blackness of my mind. The skeleton sits up, the sheet falls completely away, and her legs swing over the table. Her feet touch the floor and, as they do, all the skin on her body returns and she is a girl again, fully clothed in running gear. She stands to face me.

Her face goes from a look of pleasant curiosity to one full of agony. She looks down and I follow her movement to see a hunting knife now sticking from her stomach. Slowly I blink and we've now reversed positions with the knife sticking out of my stomach, not hers. I am now the girl. Bloody fingers hold the hilt and I look up to see Becka belongs to those bloody fingers, her wide-eyed expression is one of shocked curiosity.

Then Harley moves in, roughly pushing her aside, and Becka races away to be gobbled up by the black. Harley puts his fingers around the hilt and the nearly dead girl gasps for breath as something else moves in. A shadow. Darkness. A familiar evil that scrapes down my neck. I both want to see and I don't and I shake my head, taking a step back, telling myself to return.

Harley's lips move. *Hold still. Still. It'll all be over in a second. Second.*

A deep breath sucks into my lungs and when I open my eyes, I am back here in the morgue standing beside Vincent with the skeleton laying on the table. Those three eerie notes float through the air...

I whirl away from the body and I race from the room. The door slams behind me and I fall back against the wall. Something ominous tingles my spine and briskly I run my hands up and down my arms. A dark undercurrent tightens around my throat and I open my mouth for breath.

"You okay?" Vincent asks, his voice coming from far away. But he's right beside me now and I don't remember him stepping from the room. "Breathe," he says.

I do. In. Out. In. And words tumble from my lips. "Becka stabbed that girl. Not Harley. Becka. She stabbed that girl."

My pulse thumps in my eardrums. *My name is Caroline Christianson and I am okay. I'm alive.* In. Out. In.

"Was Harley there?" he asks.

I need to hear him say I'm okay. Why isn't he telling me I'm okay?

Behind my eyes, fiery ache flares, and I scramble in my pockets for pills. Where are they? Where are they?

"Was Harley there?" Vincent repeats.

"Yes! God, give me a minute!" I find my pills and toss them back. Pushing away from the wall, I pace down the hall straight to the water fountain. After gulping several mouthfuls, I duck my entire face in the soft stream.

My body flashes hot then cold and I let go of the spindle and straighten up. Vincent appears beside me, pressing a soft cotton handkerchief to my face and gently grasping my shoulder.

"I'm sorry," he murmurs.

For several long seconds, I stand with my face buried in the handkerchief breathing. In. Out. In.

My name is Caroline Christianson and I'm okay. I'm alive.

Finally, when my pulse has slowed and my body temperature has leveled out, I slide the handkerchief away and look up into Vincent's face.

"I'm sorry," he says again. "I pushed too hard."

I hand him back the handkerchief. "It's okay." I step away, taking a few more seconds to breathe and get my thoughts collected. "Vincent, it was so vivid what I saw, almost like I was there, too. With everything going on with me, I'm not sure what's real and what's being created by my brain."

"I understand. Talk through it."

"Becka stabbed the girl. Harley was there. But he simply put his fingers around the hilt, almost as if he was taking the blame. Then Becka disappeared and someone else arrived. A blackness. An existence. A presence." My throat rolls on a dry swallow. "It was a familiar evil. I know this evil. It was there in the woods with me all those years ago."

Vincent runs a long finger over his bottom lip but he doesn't respond to what I just said.

"I got the feeling Becka was in shock that she did this," I say. "She was afraid she was going to be found. But her expression also held curiosity, like she wanted to experience the stabbing. She wanted to know what it felt like."

I scrub my fingers over my scalp, truly not sure what my mind made up in all of this. "You suspected this, didn't you? That she might be involved in the actual killing? Do you think Harley made her?"

After all I've done for you. Those were Vincent's words to Becka. "You encouraged Nadia's parents to pick up the body, didn't you? You didn't want Becka in a room with Nadia's corpse because you suspect Becka killed Nadia in an attempt to shut her up."

With a sigh, Vincent finally turns away from me and paces down the hall. He thinks through everything before turning and pacing back. "Becka hasn't admitted anything to me. She's hard to crack. She's lived her entire life with a monster. There's no telling the extent of things she's been made to do. I want you to keep all of this to yourself. I need to think through everything. I need to know the circumstances before I take the next steps. Whether you want to admit or not, you can relate to Becka better than anybody. For now, it is your responsibility to keep her secrets. Just like I have yours."

I hate when he brings that up. My secrets. But he's right, I can relate to Becka. I was made to do things I never want to put a voice to. "What about the other thing I said? The evil that I sensed was there in the woods with me all those years ago. What if Harley was there? My captor, Erwin, Harley...is it possible all three of them tortured us? It would explain why my mind is making so many connections between all of this and my past."

Desperately, I search Vincent's eyes. "Is that possible?"

"Yes, I think so."

PART FOUR

Six Years Ago

Vincent travels a lot with work, oftentimes he's gone for days on end, leaving Fallon and I alone with Rachel. I don't like it when he travels because Rachel spends more time with Fallon than me.

When Vincent's in town though, he lets me go down the mountain with him. Some days he travels to the private college to teach a class. Other times to the mental institution where I once resided to visit patients. Sometimes he goes to the police station to consult with profiling. And other times he goes to the county hospital, too. Vincent has many jobs.

I stay far away when he visits the mental institution.

On the days he goes to college, I like to listen to him lecture on criminal profiling. Other times I lose myself in the library, my favorite section being the scientific one and specifically anatomy. I sit for hours flipping through pages, drawn to the details of the body's inner workings. Consumed by how everything works together.

Often a man in his early twenties occupies the table next to mine, always scribbling with a pen, nodding and murmuring to himself. Every so often when he stretches his neck, I play a game of gauging the length of it. But what I find most interesting about this man is how the artery in his forehead swells with concentration at the same time the jugular in his neck presses out against his skin.

On the days' Vincent goes to the county hospital, I go with him and I roam the halls, taking note of the smells and playing a game, too, of finding the dying ones. Sometimes when no one is looking, I wander into their rooms and stare at their faces, seeing death moving in.

On this particular day though, we don't go to any of those places.

"I want to see our family home," I had told him last week, to which he simply nodded and responded, "We'll go over the weekend."

Situated on top of a peak, our family home used to overlook rolling hills that Grandpa grew up on. In the years I've been gone, a company bought all the land, sold off lots, and subdivisions are going in.

By my request, Vincent takes the back way, coming up on the train tracks where my whole life changed. He stops his SUV and stays seated while I climb out. Thick trees line the area between the tracks and where our home used to be, blocking the view. Grandpa planted them for that exact reason. If only he hadn't planted them, would someone have seen us that day?

Giving Vincent a nod that I'm okay to go alone, I step into the quiet woods and come upon the backside of what used to be our home. The above-ground pool that Dad erected is gone, to be replaced by a giant sandpit. My sister would have loved that sandpit.

The house was sold as-is. How many of my things are still in there? How many of Grandpa's things? Of my parents'? Of my sister's?

I step closer, not into view, but hovering in the shadows. I continue staring at the two-story log home, wanting to feel something but remaining curiously flat. Perhaps my lack of reaction means I'm not broken anymore. Or maybe it means I *am* broken. I bet Vincent would have an opinion on that.

A clatter draws my attention, coming from the side of the house. My eyes turn to see a little boy picking up stones and placing them in a pail. The sound of humming has my gaze shifting to the open kitchen window and to a woman standing at the sink, doing dishes. In the window hangs a hand-painted piece of stained glass. There used to not be anything in that window.

Clouds move in, covering the sun and casting the area in odd shadows. That day there had been odd shadows, too.

I move back through the woods, coming to the tracks and seeing Vincent now outside of the SUV, leaning up against it. From under his flat cap, he watches me and I turn away to stroll down the tracks.

My gaze wanders up and down them. On the right stretches the new construction sites and on the left woods, woods, and more woods. I stare at those woods, willing my mind to go back. Somewhere deep and burrowed in, I draw on a new sound. A rumbling engine, not cared for, and in need of work.

Overhead a crow caws and a chill creeps across my neck. Glancing up, I see one that merges with others, wavering in and out. They look down at me through their dark eyes. *Several beaks yank at the flesh, dragging the bone through the leaves.*

I move forward, over the tracks and into the woods. The clouds shift and the sun beams down, its rays spreading through the branches. Silence presses in on me and I don't like it. Reaching up, I grasp my sister's necklace and I hum "This Little Light of Mine" to cut the quiet.

Something over to my left sparkles in the sun and I turn toward it. As I crunch over the dry ground, I realize it's a memorial for us. Everyone thought we were dead.

Tacked to a tree is a picture of me and my sister in a waterproof casing. A plaque beneath that reads BELOVED SISTERS. DAUGHTERS. And lacquered to the plaque, the matching rings that we wore on our pinkies when we were just babies.

Reaching out, I touch those rings but my hand is no longer mine. It's Annabelle's hand. I recognize the freckle on her index finger. The area around me swims and I latch onto the tree.

For several minutes I remain standing, my eyes closed, and finally, I kneel at the base of the trunk. From behind me comes Vincent's voice. "Would you like to see the rest?"

Sunny rain patters on us now as we weave our way through the mountain town. I roll the window down a few inches to feel the cool breeze on my cheeks. The lingering scent of Honeysuckle clings to the air, soon to be gone with the change of weather.

I rest my head against the back of the seat, letting it lull with the sway of the SUV. We take a turn down a dirt road, weaving through more trees, and finally slowing to a stop.

I immediately recognize the scene. It's where I stumbled from the trees all those years ago...

My bare feet drag through the leaves and twigs and I stare hard at their movement, telling my right foot to move, then my left. A loud horn echoes through my head and I sway with vertigo. My left arm lifts and my fingers latch onto a skinny tree trunk. For a few seconds, I don't move.

"Oh my God!" Footsteps pound toward me and I lift my head to see a woman, her eyes wide, nearly tripping over her own feet as she runs through the thick trees toward me.

Behind her stretches a thin and winding road, covered in gravel and pine needles. A truck sits there, its lights directed right on me through the dusk.

My body sways and I tighten my legs, making myself stay upright. I lift my face to the overcast sky and the tree limbs curling over me, blocking out the entire view.

The woman comes to a stop a few feet from me. She scrambles to unbutton her lightweight sweater. "I'm not going to hurt you," she assures me. "Let me put this around you."

My sundress is so thin and worn, it's barely staying on my body. I try hard to remember anything but the effort to think exhausts me.

With great care and caution, the woman wraps her thin sweater around me and buttons it together. She scrambles in the back pocket of her jeans and brings out a phone. With a shaky finger, she dials some numbers, and a voice filters through the speaker. "Nine-one-one. What is your emergency?"

"Hello? Hello? I need help. I just found a little girl in the woods and, from the looks of her, she's been badly mistreated." The woman listens to whoever is on the phone before saying to me, "What's your name sweetheart?"

My eyes close and I inhale the woodsy scent of her sweater. It reminds me of Grandpa and how I used to help him and my parents cut and carry wood for our fire. My body sways again and I give in to the momentum, letting my limbs crumble into the ground of twigs, leaves, and dry dirt.

The woman reaches for me. "I-I don't think she can talk. Should I put her in my truck? What should I do?"

My fingers curl around a worm and I bring it to my lips. It slides down my swollen tongue and throat and I let out an audible groan.

The woman gasps, staring at me in horror.

"Caroline," I whisper. "My name is Caroline Christianson."

I come from the memory, looking up and down the dirt road. Sixty miles separates where my sister and I were taken from right here where I emerged from the trees. Only sixty miles. We weren't moved over state lines like many thought, we were right here. Right here.

I wanted to see the rest and here we are.

Pulling over, Vincent cuts the engine and reaches under his seat to retrieve something.

"Who owns this?" I ask.

"A logging company. Emerson Logging, to be exact. They own numerous similar properties all over the south."

Hundreds of acres of deserted woods. *A good place to hide and torture children*, I silently add.

Vincent lays a medium-sized hunting knife on the seat between us. It's similar to the one in all my drawings. "I want you to carry this with you."

I eye the sheathed knife, hesitant to pick it up. "Why?"

"Hopefully, it will allow you to build associations, step beyond your fears, and achieve clarity with buried memories."

"Hopefully?"

His lips twitch. "I never know with you."

Quickly, before I have time to give it much thought, I reach over and grab the hilt, then just as quickly, I open my door and climb out. I grip the object in my hand, telling myself that's all it is—an object—and I take off walking through the trees. I want to look down at the knife, to unsheathe it and look at the serrated backside, to see if any long-buried memories come barreling forward, but instead, I put all my energy into ignoring it.

Vincent leads the way as if he's been here many times before. I'm sure he has, as was every investigator and reporter in the weeks and months following my emergence from these trees.

There is no identifiable path, just trees, bushes, and the thick pine needles covering the ground.

About fifteen minutes later, we come to a stop and he points through the maze of tree trunks to a crudely erected white-washed house some twenty yards away. "Just there. I'm not going to go with you. This is something you need to do alone."

I don't question that because it's exactly what I want, so I step toward it, noting Vincent is stepping away, fading back into the trees to give me privacy.

Dark water stains trail the walls where no gutters exist. The house is smaller than I remember and I stand a few feet from it, studying its weathered boards and makeshift construction and eyeing the cobwebs covering the interior of the windows.

I take a deep breath, wanting to step forward, to grasp the doorknob and go inside, to see the basement where he kept us, but something stops me. Maybe I'm not ready to be here.

Instead, I move away, turning my back on it, and staring at the fire pit where our captor cooked. A circle of stone surrounds it, each one weathered by the elements. The iron grate he used to place the meat on still sits balanced across the stones.

Beer bottles, miscellaneous food wrappers, and other various trash litter the area. I'm sure looky-loos (as my grandpa used to call them) come here to see where we were tortured. Morbid curiosity.

My eyes track across all the trash, following the ground over to the large oak tree that sits several paces from the fire pit. The tree where the other girl was hung. The tree where my sister eventually dangled by her wrists.

My feet shuffle through the dirt and twigs as I make my way around the stone pit, coming to stand at the tree. Carefully I take it in, looking for any traces my sister was here but everything is weathered from years gone by.

Without conscious thought, I move closer to the base of the trunk and as I do, I see myself years ago, barely clothed, the bones jutting out along my spine as I dig into the ground, burying something.

I come down on my knees, placing the knife aside, and my fingers claw at the ground as I dig around the base of the trunk through the dirt and pine needles. It doesn't take me long to find it. I recognize the material of the white sundress I wore that day at the train tracks. Here now, dirty and worn where I ripped a section off and bundled it around some lightweight items.

Lifting it out of the hole, I hold the bundle to my nose, inhaling, catching the intertwined scents of me and my sister. Then carefully, I lay it down and unfold the material, finding a clump of tiny bones inside.

I'm not sure if they belong to Annabelle or the other girl

but seeing them brings me an odd comfort. For several long moments, I close my eyes, my hand resting on top of the bones, and for the first time since I was a little girl, I say a prayer.

Those three eerie notes drift by and the air around me shifts.

I'm no longer alone.

Footsteps crunch across leaves. The scent of day-old sweat fills the air. I know that ripe scent.

Tucking the wrapped bones into the pocket of my jacket, I pick the knife back up and I turn to see a man rounding the corner of the ramshackle house. He catches sight of me and comes to an immediate stop. I take in his red flannel shirt, his blue beanie, and his brown bushy beard.

He steps closer and closer still. Reaching up, he scratches his neck. "I didn't realize someone was here," the rusty twang of his voice creeps down my spine. Not quite the rasp I remember but close.

With a frown, he looks around. "Were you just whistling?"

He knows full well he was the one who was whistling.

He scratches his neck again and the bristly sound reverberates through my brain.

Holding the hunting knife in front of me, I unsheathe it, noting the serrated prongs running along the back. Perfect to disembowel someone with. I look up into his wide-set familiar green eyes. The whistle, the scratchy beard. This is him.

This is him.

A surge of adrenaline pumps through my veins and I lunge forward. His face warbles in and out, becoming two, three, then four.

There's a tear of fabric. A wet crunch. A pulse of blood.

He stiffens, his eyes going wide as I plunge the hunting knife into the right side of his abdomen and yank it straight across to the left. Beneath him, his legs crumble and he looks up at me in mesmerized shock as his hands come up to grip the knife seated in his gut.

His eyes glass over and his guts make a familiar wet sound when they curl out of him and through the torn material of his flannel.

"No," I whisper, watching him fall to his knees and the life fade from his eyes. "No." I reach for him, shoving the guts back inside. What have I done?

What have I done?

Over to the left, a shadow moves, and I jerk away from it before realizing it's Vincent. He holds his hands up, palms out. "It's okay."

I open my mouth to speak but nothing comes out.

Vincent steps around the fire pit, moving toward me, not even looking at the man. "Is that your captor?"

"Y-yes." My gaze moves off Vincent's familiar face and back to my captor. Blood seeps from his mouth and he chokes on it, coughing, his body trembling, his lips moving like he's trying to talk.

My entire body involuntarily shakes. *What have I done? What have I done?*

"I thought this was what you wanted," Vincent says, his voice calm.

Yes. No. I don't know. It all happened so quickly.

With one last gasp, the man falls still.

I don't move. Neither does Vincent. We both just stare at my captor's disemboweled body.

A bird chirps.

Something scurries through the woods.

My heartbeat thumps in my ears.

Hold still. Still. It'll all be over in a second. Second. That's what he always said and he's right. It is all over in a second. Quick. Really quick, and I didn't even mean it to be.

A wave of nausea washes over me. "I murdered him," I mumble.

"It was justified. What would be the alternative, that he kill you?"

"You knew he was going to be here, didn't you?"

Vincent nods. "I did."

"That's why you gave me the knife. You wanted me to kill him."

"No, I wanted you to have the option."

My gaze drags off the man that I *just killed* and back over to Vincent. I see acceptance and an understanding in his eyes that releases the tension crunching my shoulders. I try to think. To feel. But everything is dull. I think I'm in shock.

"Who was he?" I ask.

"I don't know. Just a drifter."

"But how...?"

"I visit this place every so often, trying to get a true understanding of what happened here all those many years ago, trying to help you get an understanding, too. A few months ago, I saw him here and I hid and watched him. I knew from that whistle who he was." Vincent points to the corner of the house where I now see a tiny camera. "I installed that to see if he would come back. And he did. Once a week he walks through here and just looks around, likely remembering what happened or planning the next one."

"So, bringing me here today was timed."

"Yes."

I should be angry but I'm not. I should feel manipulated but I don't. Instead, I reach into my pocket and I grasp hold of the bones. The blood in my neck throbs and I ask a question that has been simmering just beneath my skin. "He fed me my sister, didn't he?"

"Yes, Caroline. I think so."

My eyelids squeeze closed. No, I will never believe that.

"Let me help you," he simply says.

Neither one of us says anything after that as I follow Vincent's instructions of how to dispose of the body—digging a grave, dumping the body in, treating it with lye, covering it back up with dirt and leaves and limbs.

If I think it's odd that Vincent knows how to do this, I don't ask. I don't say a word. I just do what he says.

When we're done, he simply says, "I will always keep your secrets, Caroline. Remember that."

THIRTY-SIX

Present Day

After the morgue visit, I go straight home to check my laptop and the facial recognition software. In the picture, there are four teenage boys. As expected, one comes back as Harley Laine and another as Erwin Myers. A third is identified as Teagan Raye. The fourth comes back as unidentified.

Who is taking the picture, though?

I grab my sketchpad from its spot on our bookshelf and I don't hesitate one more second to scan the photo of the man I gutted into the recognition software, as well. This is something I should have done years ago and have always been too scared.

Not anymore.

I would lay a solid bet this man was not a drifter. He's got an identity and I would lay another solid bet that he's connected to these four boys.

After I scan the sketch, I hold it up to the laptop screen

and my eyes go back and forth between my sketch and the picture of the four teenage boys. To be honest, they all look fairly similar in the grainy photo. Average height. Average weight. Brownish hair. Though Erwin seems small for his age and the way he's standing off a bit makes me think the other three perhaps excluded him from things.

I stare at the recognition software as it spins and spins. Sketches are hard and this one may come back with nothing. Then again it may come back with something.

For a second, I stare at the unidentified boy and something about him seems familiar, though I can't quite peg it. "Who are you?" I whisper. "Are you who we're looking for?"

While the software keeps spinning, I settle back and close my eyes. I want to check in with Uzzo about Camp Desonk and if they've combed it yet. I could go out there myself but, honestly, if that is where Harley was doing the kills, I don't want to go there. The screams, the torture, the deaths, it will smother me. My emotions can't handle that right now.

I want to also see if there is anything new on the encrypted client list. I want to ask Uzzo if they have anything else on Emerson Logging. But I want to wait to do all of it until I know for sure if my captor was a drifter or not. I need to know if he is connected to these four boys.

Vincent said there might have been multiple people in the woods, which means my mind merged them into one. And this could be it right here. This picture could be the key to everything. And if the man I gutted is one of these boys, then I've got to figure out how to explain to Uzzo that he's dead. That I killed him.

My eyes open back up and I glance through our dining room and into the hall where our bedroom sits. Where the closet is with the wrapped bones. I need to test them and find out if they are Annabelle's or not but I'm still not ready.

I'm not sure if I ever will be ready for that question to be answered. For that fear to be faced.

I open up a new screen on my laptop, type in EMERSON LOGGING, and get 2,110,000 results. Jesus Christ. I click on the first one and my phone twerps with a text.

Vincent: DID YOU FORGET DINNER?

"Shit."

My brain scrambles for an excuse but, honestly, I want to go. I'm curious to see Becka's demeanor now that several hours have gone by since the morgue visit. I also want to name drop Camp Desonk and see what kind of response it elicits.

Does she know her father was possibly one of my captors?

She has to at least suspect it.

Did he feed her parts of us?

THIRTY-SEVEN

Thirty minutes later, the three of us sit silently around Vincent's table—him at the head, me to his right, and Becka to his left. She's barely spoken a word since everything that went down earlier and I'm not sure what Vincent has and has not told her about what happened when we went back into the morgue.

I stare at the top of her light brown head as she keeps her face low, picking at her food. I'm picking at mine, too. It's not near as tasty as usual. The vegan meat he put in here has a smoky flavor that I don't care for.

I dig deep, trying to find that empathy Vincent speaks of but coming up with nothing. Absolutely nothing. Everyone has something to hide, Vincent has said that repeatedly but I think that's just an excuse for disturbing behavior.

"We care about you, Caroline, and want only to protect you." Rachel touches my arm and I lift my gaze to meet hers.

"Your silence is riddled with guilt," Vincent speaks. "We want you to have a future. We believe in you but you must talk to us."

The first few weeks I lived here, they said those words

to me and they come back to me now, filtering through my thoughts. I stare at Becka, trying to rephrase those words in my head. Perhaps that's what she needs to hear from me, not Vincent. I'm about to open my mouth and try when she lifts her head and looks right at me.

"You know, don't you?" She speaks so quietly I almost don't make out her words. "When you went back inside the morgue with Vincent, you saw more than you did with me there. Or maybe you didn't. Either way, I'm going to tell you." She clears her throat and her gaze moves off me and over to Vincent. "I stabbed that girl."

"We suspected so," Vincent says.

"Why didn't you tell Detective Uzzo?" Becka speaks, again very quietly.

"Because that's not the way we work," he says. "We keep secrets until it no longer makes sense to keep them."

Silent tears fall as if all the tension and façade Becka's been maintaining is leaving her body.

"You're safe," Vincent says. "No one will know the truth, at least not by us. But you need to tell us all of it and you need to tell us now. You need to admit to yourself what you did."

I barely take a breath as I wait for her words.

Still crying, her head lowers again and she wipes her nose with her fingers. "I helped," she whispers. "I have for years." A sudden sob erupts from her and her silent tears transition into a storm of self-loathing and fear.

Her mourning moves through the room and the empathy Vincent has wanted me to find for this girl courses over me in an ominous, unwelcome wave.

"I knew what he was doing," Becka whispers. "Sometimes I helped. I was the lure." She covers her face with her hands, breaking further down as the horror of what she's done hits her hard. "I didn't know how to say no." She snivels. "I didn't know any other way. I was scared." She lifts her face, pleading and raw, and broken. "But that girl was the only one I ever stabbed. She was about to get away and I was scared. Scared of what Dad would do."

"Can you tell us about Erwin?" Vincent calmly asks.

"I don't know. Dad had help. I never knew who though." Becka looks between us, pleading some more. "Maybe Erwin was that help. Because no other murders have happened since he came forward, right? He killed my dad and Nadia, too, don't you think? To shut her up?"

I ask, "Did you know Erwin and your father knew each other as teens? Did you know they both attended a program for troubled boys at Camp Desonk?"

Shaking her head, Becka's breath hitches.

I keep going. "What about your father? Did he torture me as a little girl?"

She casts a desperate look in Vincent's direction and I clench my jaw. She's not going to answer.

Vincent pushes back from the table, he goes to wrap her in his arms. "There you go. I've got you."

"My father was a monster," she sobs into his chest. "I am, too."

I know that feeling all too well but I was eight when I was made to do the horrible things I did. Granted, Becka has spent her entire life being raised by Harley but she's sixteen now and the fact is, if Harley hadn't been murdered, Becka would still be helping. Though to what extent, I'm not sure.

From Vincent's chest, she lifts her head to look at me. She gives me a hesitant, wobbly smile and my nerves click like the cogs on a roller coaster, pulling me up-up-up, then with the inevitable plunge, I am shot back to that day thir-teen years ago that changed my whole life...

I close my eyes, arch my back, and lift on my toes, and I swear I'm flying. My sundress suctions to my body and my cheeks wobble as I laugh. I stretch my arms longer, cupping my hands, and almost stumble back with the weighted wind.

Another horn, the train now saying goodbye, and then it's gone. Hopefully, the one tomorrow will be longer.

Laughing, my sister turns to me, flicking her long dark hair over her shoulder. "I hope we—" Her voice fades away as her gaze moves beyond me and her smile gradually dies.

I turn, too, and for the first time I don't see black, I see a little girl standing at the edge of the woods. With a wobbly smile, she gives us a two-finger wave.

Becka was there.

THIRTY-EIGHT

Back home from Vincent's, I drive through the rain. My brain circles the most recent memory. In the thirteen years since we were taken, that is the first time I have ever recalled that day with another person involved, and a child at that. Becka would have been two or three then. She likely doesn't remember but now she at least suspects.

She'll dig around in her memory tonight and try to remember.

Annabelle and I saw her at the edge of the woods and went to help. Then when we stepped into the woods, we were completely out of eyesight of our home and easier to snatch. We knew better than to cross the railroad tracks to the other side. It would have taken something like a little girl to make us do that.

To lure us in.

Vincent won't like it but I need to tell Uzzo.

My car peaks the last hill before our house. Down to the right, it sits, looking very cozy and warm with a few lights on inside and the surrounding yard and trees glistening in the rain.

A week ago, and going off my suggestion, Detective Uzzo went public with Erwin in hopes it would bring more information and viable leads but my idea has yet to deliver anything. Becka's right—ever since Erwin turned himself in, there have been no other bodies.

Why then, do I not feel the satisfaction that comes with wrapping things up?

It's because of the fourth unknown boy.

In the picture, Erwin seemed off to himself, wanting to be included but not quite there. Maybe his coming forward was his way of proving he's worthy of the inclusion. He's not afraid, as Vincent thought. Erwin is trying to impress. He wants to be part of the clique.

Assuming the fourth unknown boy is who we're looking for, then that's who Erwin is trying to impress.

Okay, going with that train of thought, I fear Erwin is sadly mistaken because he's playing right into the killer's game. Erwin is taking the fall.

I ease my car into our driveway and make a mad dash through the rain and up onto the porch. A few years ago, Zane would've barked at my arrival but now he's too old to care.

Over to the left sits our small tool shed and behind it looms a row of pine trees lit by the moon struggling through the storm. Their needles swish on a gust of wind, scraping against the shed's roof. Beyond that sits Suzi's house. After the storm dies down I'll see if she's up. I want to make sure she knows I'm not the one who suggested her greenhouse is connected to this.

On the rocking chair beside the door sits a large envelope encased in a plastic bag to keep out the water. CAROLINE is printed across it. As if on cue, my phone buzzes with a text from Uzzo. LEFT AN ENVELOPE ON

YOUR PORCH. LET ME KNOW WHAT YOU THINK.

GOT IT, I text back.

I take out my key and slog my way in, stopping to strip my soaked jacket and shoes. Zane lays in front of the fireplace and I whistle, indicating the open door for a pee break. He lifts his massive head, eyes the rain, and goes right back to snoozing.

I don't blame him. I'd hold my pee too.

Rain splatters the windows as I track into the kitchen. A note laying on the counter reads, *Ran to the grocery. Be back in a few.* He needs his morning milk—rain, snow, or shine.

Grabbing Petal off the kitchen counter, I rub her little gray head and make my way over to the dining room table. I take the large envelope from the plastic bag and slide out the contents.

They are printed pages of cold cases connected to the rug taken from Harley's home. A note attached under the binder clip from Uzzo reads, *What we've found so far.*

I sift through the multiple pages dating back as far as thirty years, more evidence that Harley was doing this before Becka was even born. Men, women, children—their hair is woven into Harley's trophy rug. A timeline has been included of Becka's illness with its direct connection to girls her age that Harley killed and fed her, like the recent high school-aged girls. Other than that, Harley's type was driven by something else that I'm sure has everything to do with the client list.

I note the locations of the missing people, all within hours of driving distance from here, some in Tennessee, others in the surrounding states. So, Harley would leave from here, drive out to find the next victim, transport the victim back here, and then take their organs out.

Some he perhaps kept himself and others were by order. Harley's home chef services included "special" menus.

I pull a spreadsheet from the stack next. A note attached says: *The client list contains two tabs. We decrypted one tab which is quickly matching up to the cold cases in that it is the kill list. The other tab we believe contains those who paid for the meat.*

My gaze rolls quickly down the list of kills and I don't recognize any of the names. But I see a pattern. Each name ends with a letter in parenthesis. Alana Idalgo (h). Carl Kerr (e). Eleanor League (t). Xavier Nubers (w).

What would that letter represent? The way they were killed? The city where they were taken? Is the letter connected to the person who bought their meat?

h-e-t-w.

There are more h's than the other three. The t's stop occurring six years ago and the w's stop occurring thirteen years ago. The e's are sporadic.

Four letters.

Next, I pick up a sheet with photographs taken just in the past hour at Camp Desonk. In the photos everything is lit with giant spotlights and CSI is just beginning to work in the rain. As expected, the deserted camp is overgrown and unkempt with cabins old and retired.

The inside of one of the cabins draws my attention and I lean in to get a better look. It's clean. Too clean with freshly scrubbed walls and floors. But the tools to skin and gut are lined up and tacked to the wall. A hook hangs from the ceiling and quick flashes of bodies that once hung there strobe through my brain.

In the corner of the room sits what looks like a butcher counter in a grocery store with a grinder, a scale, a prepping slab, a sink, several high-end knives, and freezers. In another corner sits a shower and a drain where the bodies are washed either before or after, or maybe both. Several clean buckets line the walls and more images strobe through my head of blood filling and spilling over. This is where the victims were taken to be processed.

It has a very clinical feel to it as if someone knew we were coming and scrubbed the place.

My gaze rolls across the pictures of the other cabins and I quickly text Uzzo. NEED INTERIOR PICS OF THE OTHER CABINS WHEN YOU GET A CHANCE.

I spread everything out on the table. Uzzo wants me to make connections so I close my eyes, breathing deep and tuning into my heartbeat. Faces flash through my mind in a rapid-fire staccato, followed by an echo of screams. I try to grab onto just one but my brain won't let me.

After several long minutes, I open my eyes and my thoughts redirect to what I was doing before I left for Vincent's. At the same time, I think, h-e-t-w. Four letters.

Four boys.

I pick up the photo taken at Camp Desonk thirty years ago. Harley, Erwin, Teagan, and the unidentified boy: h-e-t-w. If the boys are fifteen to seventeen in this photo, they would be the mid to late forties now. Something, or some-one, brought them together, which makes me think again of who took the photo.

Yes, something brought them together. A shared dark desire. They likely honed their skills with animals first, then moved onto humans.

The letter represents who killed them. Harley the most. Erwin sporadic. Teagan stopping six years ago. And the "w" unidentified boy stopping thirteen years ago.

Thirteen years ago. That's when Annabelle and I were taken.

Six years ago. That's when I killed the man I thought was our captor.

But Erwin was sporadic and that doesn't click in my mind. In the picture, he seems outside of the clique in more of an "errand boy" role.

I wake my laptop up, launch the recognition software and my heart kicks in when I see the sketch of my captor has a match. The wind and rain pick up and I scroll the cursor over at the exact second the electricity goes out.

THIRTY-NINE

"No!" I bang on the keyboard but with a long-dead battery, I need the electricity.

A small thud comes from the back of the house and I listen for a second. Maybe Fallon's coming through the back door. Though I didn't hear his engine.

Something thuds again and I stand up.

Outside the rain and wind kick up another notch and I feel my way into the kitchen where we keep the flashlights. I find one in the junk drawer and flick it on, it casts an eerie yellow glow around the room.

"Fallon?" I call out but am met with silence.

Flashlight in hand, I navigate across the kitchen and into the hall. Outside the wind swirls and howls and as I pass by the guest room, a blast of cold damp air hits me across the face. I turn, the flashlight beam swiveling, and move into the room. The yellow beam casts odd shadows off the made bed, dresser, and the chest sitting in the corner.

I shiver against the cold, noting the water trailing across the wood floor and leading to a window standing wide open. With a sigh, I pick my way across the floor and close and lock it. I grab a throw blanket off the bed and use it to wipe up the water before tossing it in the laundry room.

Flashlight still in hand, I enter the hall again and I freeze when the beam glints off more water, this time trailing down the hall, following the path I just came from. Weird. I shine my light up to the ceiling, looking for possible roof leaks, then back down to the hall.

"Fallon?" I call out but am again met with silence.

Hovering along the wall, I follow the trail. Something is leaking. This house is old and it could be any number of things. I track the water as it changes from a trail to puddles to wet imprints, all the way into my room until it finally dries out.

I turn a slow circle, still not sure where it's coming from. I look at the ceiling again, then shine the light across my empty bed. As I do, the hairs on my neck prick to alertness. I'm not alone.

I whip around, my light following my movement. It flicks across the window, the desk, and the old yellow wallpaper, before coming to a stop on a person standing in the dark corner.

I open my mouth to scream but nothing comes out. The person shifts, or more like sways, and the beam from my light plays off the shadows gathered in the corner. Something wet moves beneath my feet and I glance down. Even in the darkness of my room, I recognize the thick liquid is blood. Slowly I lift my head, my gaze following its trail leading straight back to the corner.

The person falls forward and I lunge to catch whoever it is. As I do, I slip on the blood and come down hard. My head bangs off the hardwood floor and I blackout for a second. When I come to, I'm on my knees holding a hunting knife in one hand and staring down at a woman that I don't recognize.

The rain pattering outside takes on a swoony sound and dark specks swarm in my eyes. I'm no longer here in my bedroom hallucinating a bloody woman. I'm standing in dark woods, staring at an old trailer.

The wind moans faintly through the trees and a few insects click-click as I consider the trailer where the woman lives. Inside she moves from one window to the next and I track her progress. She walks beneath a ceiling light and I get a good look at her weathered face, estimating she's younger than she looks.

She turns away, lighting a cigarette and at the same time answering the phone. If a person smokes, does it affect the way they taste? Yes, I think so.

Somewhere in the recesses of my mind, that thought should disturb me but it doesn't. I find it only a curious one.

Up above, the dark clouds shift and the rain picks up as thunder cracks across the sky.

As the woman talks on the phone, her arm waves around the room, and her cigarette ash flies. She's arguing with whoever is on the other end.

Wet hair sticks to my cheeks and I smooth it away as I creep from the trees and closer to the trailer. I move along the bedraggled bushes lining the side of her house, pausing to listen, to glance in the windows, making sure she's alone. Bit by bit, I check each window, seeing her from different angles. She's no longer on the phone and is putting on makeup now, getting ready to go out.

My nostrils open wide as I get a scent of the cigarette coming through one of the open screens. She goes out of sight and I duck to another window, peering in. The sound of her cough, riddled with smoke, rattles through the air.

The electricity goes out and she curses. Another rumble of thunder vibrates the air and I open the window and crawl through. In long strides, I cross the room, sliding my hunting knife from its sheath, and I come to a stop in her living room. I turn a slow circle, looking for her, my ears keen in the darkness.

Down the hall, something shuffles, and I turn away to follow the sound. I stride straight into a bedroom, turning another slow circle. Outside, lightning flickers across the sky and now I see the woman illuminated in the corner, bent over a dresser, trying to light a candle.

She has no clue I'm here.

I come up right behind her and, on a last-second change of plans, I slide the hunting knife right into her kidney. Her legs give way and, with a smothered gasp, she falls to the stained linoleum flooring.

I flip her over like she's a piece of meat on a grill, and her eyes widen as she gazes up at me. "Please," she begs and I catch a glimpse of meth-addict-black teeth.

Sliding the knife into her lower abdomen, I listen to her gurgle and spit. She gasps and thrashes. Coughs and wheezes.

Her blood seeps out and with shaky fingers, she reaches for me while discolored spit bubbles from her mouth. I yank the knife upward with my right hand as I simultaneously thrust my left hand into her gaping flesh.

She means nothing to me. An experiment only. Let's see if she's smoky-tasting...

With a deep breath, I zoom out of the killer's mind just as quickly as I stepped in. I'm back in my bedroom, staring down at the same woman as I hover on the edges of the hallucination. Her organs lay in a glistening heap, just like Harley's had.

The woman chokes and sputters, surprising me, and fresh blood seeps from her mouth and gushes from her deep abdominal cavity. My heartbeat pounds loud as I scramble back. Frantically I look around my bedroom, trying to ground myself but the hallucination won't stop.

I look back at the woman and as her phlegmy cough fills the room, she gets to her feet.

"No!" I shout, forcing the hallucination to stop.

I scuttle further away, trying to stand, but I slip in the seeping blood and come down hard on the floor again. The blood. The body. The knife. I lift my trembling hands and turn them over to see blood there too. What the hell? What have I done?

For a horrifying few seconds, I stare at the woman. Did I kill her?

No, I'm hallucinating. I'm hallucinating.

I roll to my knees, then my feet, and in a panicked scramble, I make it to the closed bedroom door. I fling it open and I freeze when I see Fallon walking into our home. "How long has the power been out?" He stops halfway in the front door and stares at me. "Caroline?"

I don't answer. I don't think I can.

I turn around, looking back into our bedroom and everything looks normal. I look at the floor and see the water trail that initially led me in. There is no blood. No hunting knife. No dead body.

"Do we have a leak?" Fallon comes up behind me.

I don't answer and instead push past him, going straight into the bathroom. From the medicine cabinet I grab two of my headache pills and wash them down with cold water, then I wash my face, too, fully aware Fallon is watching me.

The storm dies down and I head for the front door and the porch. I need some fresh air. Now.

Once outside, I take a few calming breaths, staring through the darkness and at the trees soaked from the storm. Fallon steps out onto the porch, wrapping a blanket around my shoulders, and together we stand in silence breathing in the cold and recent rain.

"Caroline," he speaks after several quiet moments. "What happened in there?"

"I got confused."

"I've seen you confused and that wasn't confusion. That was all-out fear."

"I was disoriented. I'm fine now." With a sigh, I pull the blanket snugger around me. "I'm supposed to reconstruct the thinking of a killer, not think I'm the killer."

"And you thought you killed somebody?" Fallon asks.

"Yes, for a moment I got lost."

"Has there been another body found?"

I shake my head. "No, not that I know of. But this was different. I constructed it in my mind all on my own. I was in the killer's mind."

The wind shifts then and the coppery scent of blood fills my senses. The taste of something smoky tinges my tongue. It's not real. It's leftover from the hallucination. Still, I look at my watch. *It's 11:36. I'm at my home in Hummingbird, Tennessee. My name is Caroline Christianson.*

My mind plays back through the hallucination. There was a violence to it that felt more real than is true. I didn't kill that woman. But I held the knife. I watched her die.

"My hallucinations are becoming my reality. I'm used to reconstructing a crime scene but this was different. It's like I was there while it was occurring. Usually, I rebuild it, not witness it in real-time." I shift to look up at him. "Do you think this murder occurred or do you think I made it up?

Because whoever killed that woman also killed Harley. It was done in the same manner." That spot above my left brow pangs and I reach up to press a couple of fingers into it.

Fallon eyes the movement. "Vincent knew when he came to you that he was placing you back into a destructive environment."

Normally when Fallon says those types of things, I am quick to defend Vincent. I am quick to reiterate that I am a grown woman and make my own decisions. This time though, none of those words come. I am not inclined to defend Vincent.

Instead, I repeat what Suzi said to me when all of this started. "Did you know children are born with mirror neurons? It helps them socialize and usually, the neurons fall away. But some people, like me, keep them or they come back after a traumatic event, like what happened with me and Annabelle. Sometimes this makes it difficult to know me because I'm constantly reflecting those around me. It's also what makes me a good profiler."

"Caroline, I know you. I know you're a good person. Why are you giving me psycho-babble right now?"

"Did you know that sometimes I hear the screams in the air when I'm looking at crime scene photos? I don't reflect those around me, I absorb them."

Fallon turns fully to face me and the shadows of the porch play off the valleys of his face. "That sounds scary and very dangerous."

I glance at my watch and silently recite, *It's 11:47. I'm at my home in Hummingbird, Tennessee. My name is Caroline Christianson.*

"What are you doing?"

"Grounding myself."

Another cool breeze blows past and the rain picks back up again, pinging off the gutter and plunking onto the porch. Through the dark, my eyes focus on the large drops as they plop in a disturbing arrhythmic metronome. The drops gather, forming puddles, and my mind pulls at me again, taking me back to that room with the woman.

"You have a vivid imagination," Fallon says. "And that laced with empathy makes your visions even more terrifying. Vincent pushes you right to the edge and you push yourself over." Fallon cups my elbow. "You know what I think? I think you want to have another nervous breakdown so it will give you an excuse to stop."

I stare at Fallon, my mind racing, and a silent moment goes by. My first thought is, *That's a ridiculous statement*, but something in it rings true. If I have a nervous breakdown then Vincent won't bother me. He'll give me space. I shouldn't need a medical reason to ask for space. I should feel comfortable doing so.

With a sigh, I look down at my bare feet. "This is what I'm supposed to do for a living but how can I when I'm constantly teetering this line?"

Fallon gives that considerable thought. "I think you don't know how to gauge that line. You think you can step over it but you can't. I've seen you help Vincent over the years and you're good, no denying it. You used to be able to handle it. You used to know your line but now you don't. Or you're outright ignoring it."

"I feel like I'm not going to come back from one of my hallucinations. It's like someone crawled inside of my head and moved everything around."

"And you promise me that you're not doing those psychedelic herbs?"

"I absolutely promise. I would never chance them again.

Not with the things I did while I was taking them…" Things I don't want to think about.

I turn to go back inside. Maybe my mirror neurons are on hyperdrive.

Fallon grasps my arm. "You and I still need to talk."

"I know. First thing tomorrow morning. Emotionally, I can't handle anything else right now."

FORTY

Sweat beads along my entire body and I kick the sheet and comforter off. With an agitated sigh, I roll over in bed and Petal jumps off to find a better place to sleep. I reach for the glass of water I left on my bedside table and find it empty.

I look at my watch. *It's 7:11 in the morning. I'm at my home in Hummingbird, Tennessee. My name is Caroline Christianson.*

I slept. I actually slept. It's been so long since I've had several hours of rest that I forgot how good it feels.

My bedside clock blinks from the power outage. It must have come back on sometime during the early morning hours, which means I can finally check my laptop and the facial recognition software.

After a quick trip to the bathroom, I make my way straight into the dining room, eager for my laptop, and I come to an immediate halt. Vincent is here, seated in the living room with Fallon.

"What's going on?" I ask. "Why didn't someone wake me?"

Fallon moves into the kitchen, pouring me a cup of

coffee. "Because you rarely sleep and after last night, you needed it."

"What happened last night?" Vincent asks but I shake my head.

There's no way I'm reliving any of that right now. "Why are you here? Where's Becka?"

"I asked a colleague of mine to watch her." Vincent exchanges a look with Fallon and I get the impression he's already in the know of why Vincent is here. He says, "Last night Erwin was being transported to a new facility and he escaped. Uzzo left you a message and has already placed someone outside to keep watch."

The weight of that sinks into me and I lower myself onto a chair. I glance out our front window where a cop car sits.

Handing me my coffee, Fallon nods to the TV in the living room that I just now notice is on mute. Grabbing the remote, Vincent unmutes it. Erwin stands handcuffed and in a hospital-issued jumpsuit. The timestamp says this was filmed last night and from the dry ground, it was filmed before the heavy rains came.

Lifting his head, Erwin breathes in the cold evening air, then rolls his neck as if he has every moment in the world. I watch his movements, trying to get a sense of the boy in the photo but nothing comes. If he was on the outside as a boy, he's matured beyond that now.

Ducking his head, he steps inside the transport van. A young guard climbs up and in after him and the door closes.

I chance a quick look at Vincent to see him focused on the television. Because of my idea, Erwin was being transported in the first place.

But then Vincent went to visit Erwin. He fed him

details of the murders. Yet if he's the "e" on the kill list, he didn't need those details.

I glance over my shoulder into the dining room where all my stuff sits from last night. Nothing is face up and visible, so no one knows yet about the photo of the four boys, about the sketch of my captor, and the recognition software.

On the TV the scene changes, cutting forward an hour to the van along the side of the road. The back door sits open and two body bags lay off to the side.

A reporter is speaking, "Sources say the only way Erwin could have escaped is if the guard unlocked him. A grave mistake as the guard is now dead. The driver, too."

Fallon mutes the TV again. "Why would the guard unlock him?"

"He wouldn't," I say. "Unless Erwin talked him into it. Or someone else told the guard to. We won't know because the guard's dead."

"Why bother escaping though, if Erwin originally turned himself in?" Fallon asks.

Vincent says, "It's more common than you think. People turn themselves in and realize they made a big mistake. Erwin saw his chance and took it."

"This is my fault," I say. "I'm the one who suggested we move Erwin around, leak information on him, try and flush details out."

Vincent says, "And I hope you've learned a lesson. You should have checked with me first."

Fallon steps forward, ready to defend, and I shake my head. Now is not the time.

The light from the TV reflects through the early morning shadows of the room and I go back to looking at the screen. Vincent unmutes the TV but all sound dulls to hum as cops move in and out of the scene. The transport van sits open with no blood inside. Because Erwin choked the young guard.

Choked.

Just like our captor did to us.

My heart thumps deep and low. Buzzing noise filters in from somewhere and I wince. Sweat beads along my neck and I lift my t-shirt to wipe it away. The same reporter speaks, his voice vibrating at the same frequency as the buzz.

My blood hums as it circulates through my veins. My heart picks up pace, like footsteps fleeing, and I glance out the living room window and into the dawning morning. But I don't see my yard or the cop car stationed outside. Instead, it's the woods where my sister and I were kept and the isolated, weathered white house. The limbs on the trees grow and branch out, intertwining, and slowly filling in. Annabelle stands in the center, her long dark hair stringy and unwashed, as she would be now at twenty-one but still dressed in the sundress as if she was eight. The limbs twist around her, becoming thorny branches, and slowly pull her in.

"Caroline?" A voice cuts through the bramble and I blink back to the here and now.

My mind resets and I look at my watch. *It's 7:32 in the morning. I'm at my home in Hummingbird, Tennessee. My name is Caroline Christianson.*

I glance at Fallon and though he doesn't say anything, he registers my odd state. I turn my attention to Vincent, recalling his last words to me. "As long as we're handing out blame, you did manipulate Erwin. Leaking his name to the press is one thing but you went way beyond that in giving him details of the crimes."

My words hang heavy in the air while Vincent keeps his dark gaze leveled on mine.

After several long seconds, Fallon clears his throat. "I think we're all in agreement that it is highly likely Erwin is coming after you two. Why don't we focus on that?" Fallon pushes away from the table and comes to stand right in front of me. Like he's my father, he puts the back of his hand on my forehead. "No wonder you're sweating. You're burning up. Are you sick?"

I brush his hand away. "I'm stressed. It's making me hot."

"Well, you look like hell."

I feel like hell. Maybe I'm coming down with something.

"You're fine," Vincent assures me. "Your immune system's a little weak. You've been putting yourself through a lot lately."

Fallon scoffs. "*She's* been putting herself through a lot?"

Vincent gathers his things and as he does my thoughts drift to what I experienced last night. Given the escape, the timing adds up. Erwin could have killed that woman. But how is it that I experienced it when I'm not even sure it happened? I haven't seen a photo. I certainly didn't go to the crime scene. Detective Uzzo hasn't told me it occurred. How do I know it did?

Because it felt real, too real, even the smoky taste in my mouth. Somewhere out there last night a woman died and I tasted her.

"Have you talked to Uzzo?" I ask Vincent.

"Yes, just briefly though. You're safe inside—both of you are—with your security in place and the patrol car outside."

I glance at the safety panel mounted next to the door to find the red light solid and engaged.

With an agitated sigh, Fallon goes to the freezer and gets a frozen pack of vegetables. He wraps it in a kitchen towel and brings it back to place it gently on my neck. I don't hide the groan of welcome relief it brings me.

For several long seconds, Vincent stares at me sitting here in my chair with the cool pack on my neck. I look into his eyes seeing concern, yes, but also something I've never seen before—regret.

Fallon adjusts the pack, sliding it down onto my shoulders.

Silently, Vincent slides his arms back into his dark blue dress coat and wedges the gray flat cap on his head. His gaze moves over to the dining room table where all my files and the laptop sits, things Uzzo gave me and other items I independently accumulated.

Vincent doesn't like that Detective Uzzo is coming to me now. Uzzo used to go to Vincent with everything and it has slowly been moving in my direction. Vincent is feeling excluded and I'm not sure how to handle that.

"What about you?" I ask. "Are you staying here?"

"I'll be fine," he says, walking toward the front door.

FORTY-ONE

As I listen to Fallon in the shower, my thoughts trail to Becka. I envision her as a little girl standing in the tree line near those railroad tracks and my jaw hardens. Because of her, we walked into those woods.

She admitted to stabbing one of the two girls found in the mushroom patch. Becka was raised by a serial killer. Is she too far gone? Is she beyond help? Vincent doesn't think so because he took her in.

He took us in, too, when we had no one else and had committed unspeakable crimes, and now it's Becka. But what exactly does Vincent see in her? What is her redeeming quality?

While Fallon moves from the bathroom over into our bedroom, I mentally tuck Becka away for now and I make myself comfortable at our dining room table, ready to dig in.

As I munch on a seed bar, I bring up the facial recognition software. From the sketch that I scanned and fed in, I receive a few possible matches. But only one catches my eye —Teagan Ray, one of the four boys from the photo taken at Camp Desonk for troubled boys.

I look again at my sketch, comparing it to the boy in the photo identified as Teagan and, though decades separate the two pictures, I can now see the similarities. The wide-set green eyes, the thin lips, the large nose.

The "t" on the kill list stopped occurring six years ago which would coincide with his death, or rather his murder by me.

So, of the four boys, Harley and Teagan are both dead, leaving Erwin and the still-unidentified fourth boy unknown. The unidentified boy is "w" and his name stops thirteen years ago when Annabelle and I were taken. Does that mean he's dead, too, or maybe he left the area? Going with dead, who killed him then, and how is it that Erwin is the only surviving boy from this photo?

Except, of course, whoever took it.

Teagan Ray—not a drifter, born and raised in Georgia. Reported missing by his wife but the body will never be discovered because it's decomposing in a lye-lined grave. A seemingly normal man with a wife and a job as a maintenance man.

Seemingly normal, just like Harley, the chef, and Erwin, the teacher.

Using Becka as a lure, Harley abducts me, my sister, and later, the other girl. He holds us captive, me and Annabelle for a year, the other girl much less. Then, along with Teagan and Erwin, they take turns torturing us. All three of them. Unsettling as it is, the idea is not far off.

Fast forward and Teagan finds his way back to those woods where he and I have our chance encounter and his life ends. Only it wasn't a chance encounter. Vincent knew he would be there.

I look at the "w" unidentified boy. "Who are you and

how do you play into this? Are you the other person I keep sensing?"

My phone chirps with a text from Vincent. I'M WITH UZZO. CAN YOU MEET?

WHAT ABOUT ERWIN?

HE'S IN CUSTODY AS OF 15 MINUTES AGO. UZZO DIDN'T TEXT YOU?

NO. I check the time. Vincent's only been gone from our house roughly an hour. WHERE DID THEY FIND HIM?

A FEW MILES FROM THE TRANSPORT VAN HEADING IN YOUR DIRECTION.

I blow out a relieved breath. WHERE ARE YOU?

He texts me the address and I grab my things as Fallon comes down the hall. He stops when he sees me packing up. "Where are you going? I thought we were going to talk. And what about Erwin? It's not safe."

I hold up my phone. "It's Uzzo and Vincent. They want to meet. They're at those suites a few miles outside of town. Erwin's been caught."

"Oh, thank God."

"I know." I slip my jacket on. "I need to go."

Fallon just looks at me and the disappointment in his face is clear. He wants me here, not racing off.

I step up to him. "You know I love you, right?"

"Of course."

"I promise we will talk. Life is crazy right now and I am so close to figuring this case out. Please be patient."

He doesn't respond and I give him a second, hoping for at least a nod. Instead, he turns toward the kitchen.

"I'll be back as soon as I can."

With a sigh, he nods and before either of us can say anything else, I head out.

The patrol car still sits outside of our home and I step up to the driver's side. The cop lowers the window and I say, "They caught him. I guess you can go."

With a frown, she checks her phone and her radio. "Huh, no one told me."

"I'm meeting Detective Uzzo and Dr. DeMurr." I wave. "Thanks and see you."

She starts the car. "Yeah, see ya 'round."

It doesn't take me long to get to the hotel suites. It's one of those privately owned chains with units accessible from the outside. I drive the perimeter, looking for the number Vincent texted me and I find 6A in the back. I park and hurry through the overcast and cold air over to the door. It's wedged open with a small wood block and I push in.

My gaze touches on the empty living room and the empty kitchen. "Hello?" I call out.

"In here," Vincent responds.

I head down the short hall and step into the open doorway of the bedroom. Over in the corner sits a desk with Erwin standing behind a seated Vincent. Clear plastic ties strap his arms and legs to the chair.

"Hello, Caroline," Erwin calmly greets me. "I see you got my text."

My gaze tracks over to the desk where a hunting knife lays next to Vincent's empty gun case. I move my attention from the knife and gun case to Vincent's face and the calm I see there helps me remain calm as well.

From behind his back, Erwin pulls out Vincent's gun and points it right at me. "I've read every single thing Dr. DeMurr here has written about you. It's intriguing to me that your memories don't quite align with what happened to you and your sister."

I swallow. "And what happened?"

"I was particularly fascinated by the fact you gutted that big white dog."

A dog. A girl. Interesting that Erwin is more fascinated by the dog.

Wait a minute, the dog wasn't white. The dog was black.

Erwin nods down to Vincent. "I've got a dog right here. What do you say? Shall we relive the good old days?"

I stare into Vincent's composed face but my brain scrambles with a way out of this.

"You're probably considering your options," Erwin says. "But let me remind you that I have a gun and it has very fast bullets. Do we have an understanding?"

"Yes." I nod. "But I have a question."

"What?"

"Are you sure the dog was white?"

He pauses.

Erwin wasn't there but I bet he wanted to be. They didn't invite him. He was on the outside back then and is now, too. The errand boy.

"You heard all about it, didn't you?" Bitter saliva coats my mouth. "The little girls who were being tortured and you weren't invited to participate."

His eyes narrow. I've hit the mark.

We stare at each other, our breaths the only sound in the room and I wait to see what he'll say or do next.

He smirks. "Interesting we have something in common."

"And what is that?"

Erwin nods to Vincent. "Him."

"Caroline," Vincent says. "He's messing with you. I do not know this man. I met him the same time you did."

Erwin huffs a laugh. "He's lying. We know each other. We go way back."

"Caroline," Vincent speaks again. "He's—"

"I'm curious, do you get serial killer vibes from me?" Erwin asks.

"No." I shake my head. "I get the vibe of someone who wants desperately to belong. You would do anything to be part of the group."

His smile dies off. "I'm the one who provided Harley access to the girls."

I chance a look down to Vincent and Erwin lifts the gun higher. "Don't look at him. Look at me."

With another swallow, I bring my eyes up to his small round ones and I see him as he was in that grainy photo. "I requested to speak with you some time back. Why did you say no?"

Another laugh. "It wasn't part of the plan."

"The plan?"

Vincent interrupts. "I'm the one who denied it. When you requested to speak with Erwin, I told Uzzo privately that I did not think it was a good idea. There was no plan. I didn't want Erwin manipulating you like he's doing now."

"That's right," Erwin agrees. "He's the only one allowed access to you."

I block both of them out as I study the plastic ties that secure Vincent to the chair. They are cinched tight—but not too tight. The plan... "What was your real reason for turning yourself in?"

Erwin pauses as if he isn't sure of how to answer.

"He wanted time with me," Vincent says.

"That's right. I'm a bit of a fan of Dr. DeMurr. But he's not the only one who can manipulate people's minds. I have a degree in psychology, too. I teach—"

"At the schools where the girls attended. I know. How did you break free of the guard and van?"

"Oh, I have my ways." He pauses again, glancing down at Vincent. "I think I'll go off script now."

Off script?

It's slight but the muscles in Vincent's jaw tighten.

Erwin says, "He loves to get inside of your mind, doesn't he? Well, guess what, I'm the one in charge now. Not him. Me."

Reaching down, Erwin pulls tight on one of the plastic zip ties and it cinches into Vincent's wrist. "He's the one tied up and I'm the one with the gun. How do you like that? And to think you were raised by this man. Imagine how far inside of your head he is."

I want to look back down at Vincent but I don't. Off script. The plan. What the hell is Erwin up to?

Vincent clears his throat. Why didn't Erwin gag him?

He sighs. "Fine, back on script. Harley's dead. I wonder what he would think of the reigning Organ Ripper. Do you think he'd be pissed someone took over?"

Off script. On. The plan.

The student surpasses the master, or if not that, co-killers who had a disagreement—the second of which falls more in line with the photo of the four boys. Darkness drew the four boys together but two of them—Harley and one other—took it to a new level. All fingers point to Erwin being the other, yet—

"'Someone who wants desperately to belong'. That's what you think of me? Let's see if you're right." Erwin nods to the knife. "Pick it up."

Slowly my eyes move over to the knife and I try to focus on it but sudden tears fill my eyes. My body sways a little and I tighten my thighs to stay upright.

Erwin kicks the desk, making the knife on the top rattle. "Pick up the knife. I want to see who you are."

What is he talking about? Who does he think I am?

"I said pick it up."

With a shaky hand, I reach for the blade and my fingers wrap around the thick hilt. Something about it seems familiar but I don't know how that is. The last time I touched a knife like this was six years ago in the woods on the day I ended Teagan Ray's life.

Erwin caresses the gun down Vincent's neck. "And here he sits, trusting us with his life."

"Please," I whisper. "Don't do this. You don't need to do this."

"Oh, I'm not doing anything. You're the one who's going to do this and I'm going to watch your face. I think we're all about to find out how warped you still are."

I cast a terrified glance down to Vincent and I see a peacefulness to his expression that gives me pause.

"I need to ask you something," Erwin speaks to Vincent. "In all of your sessions with Caroline, did you ever think your life might end this way?"

"Yes," Vincent is quick to answer as if waiting for that question. "I thought it might be a possibility."

It takes a second for those words to sink in. "*What?*" I gasp.

"Being on a script is fun." With a chuckle, Erwin waves the gun at the knife. "Let's get on with the plan then."

My body sways again and I glance beyond Erwin's shoulder to the glass doors that open onto a small patio. A light rain falls, slowly gaining force, increasing, pounding now on the brick patio until it becomes sheets of water pouring over the glass doors. The sound of it drowns out everything until it's no longer pounding outside, it pounds inside of my body instead.

A distorted image moves through the rain and I step around Erwin and Vincent, moving toward the doors. I'm aware that one of them is talking but I keep stepping until I'm standing at the door. Reaching out I open it but the pouring rain has disappeared to be replaced with a light mist. The pounding through my body goes abruptly silent.

Beyond the patio spans a line of trees surrounded by a foggy haze and through the blur of shadows, a person moves. I step off the patio and across a small patch of grass, heading toward the person.

From a distance, the person watches me approach. As I get closer the person recedes into the darkness. I move closer still, stumbling over downed limbs, and I come up short when the person steps from behind a tree.

Annabelle?

She stands, motionless, staring back, and we watch each other for a still moment. She walks back toward where I came from and I slowly follow her. We emerge from the trees, cross the small patch of grass, step onto the patio, and I cross back through the double doors until I'm in the bedroom with Erwin and Vincent again.

I catch a glance at myself in the mirror, shocked by how gray and sweaty I look.

"What's going on with her?" A voice filters through my foggy brain.

"She's hallucinating."

I look down at the knife in my hand, then up to Vincent still sitting in the chair. My eyes travel over to Erwin and then behind him, through the double doors I see Annabelle looking in. Her image hazes and now I'm not sure if she's real.

"What are you seeing right now?" Erwin asks.

"I see you, Vincent, and Annabelle, right over there through the double doors."

Erwin whips around to look behind him and I ask, "Do you see her?"

"Yes," he says. "I do."

"No, he doesn't," Vincent says without even looking at the double doors. "He's messing with your mind. Don't listen to him."

Terrified tears fill my eyes. I'm going mad. I wave the knife. "She's right there. You don't see her?"

"I do," Erwin says again.

"There is no one there, Caroline," Vincent says, again not even looking. "Annabelle is dead. You know she's dead."

"No, I don't know she's dead." My hand tightens around the knife as I try desperately to make sense of this. "What's happening to me?"

"You're having one of your hallucinations," Vincent tells me.

With a shudder, I shake my head. This can't be. She's right there. In desperation, I look at Erwin and he's smiling. He's enjoying watching me lose my mind. Is this on the script? Is this the plan?

"You're the reigning Organ Ripper," Erwin tells me. "Do you see it now? You got so far inside of Harley's head that you became him."

With the knife still held in my right hand, I push the fingers of my left into my hair and I squeeze my scalp. What's going on?

"Don't listen to him," Vincent says. "He's messing with your mind. This is why I didn't want you to see him again. Caroline, can you hear me?"

Slowly, I nod.

My name is Caroline Christianson and I am in a hotel in Hummingbird, Tennessee.

I close my eyes, telling myself if I open them and she's still there, then she has to be real. I open my eyes back up and I still see her there on the other side of the doors staring in. Why doesn't she come in?

"Can you see me?" I ask her but she doesn't respond. "Can you hear my thoughts?" Again, she doesn't respond. "Do you see the world through the same haze that I do?" Again, no response. "Who have I become?" I ask, fearful she will answer this time.

Kill him. The words sift through the air and I'm not sure who says them.

The sound of a man's voice shouting in agony snaps me back and the knife I was holding, now bloody, slides from my sweaty fingers to land on the carpet beneath my shoes right next to the gun Erwin must have dropped.

Behind me, I'm aware of Uzzo rushing in with a team.

"It's okay," Vincent assures me. "You're okay."

I look at him still tied to the chair, then I look at Erwin's body slumped across the bed and the blood pooling quickly across his stomach. I stabbed him. I stabbed Erwin. And he's not breathing. He's dead. I look at the double doors but I see only the overcast day. There is no Annabelle.

FORTY-TWO

"I came here because I thought Erwin would head toward my home. I felt it would be safer here. Plus, I wanted a private place to think through things," Vincent is saying to Uzzo.

We know each other. In fact, we go way back.

"I put my stuff down in the bathroom, came out, and there Erwin was. He'd broken in through the patio's double doors. I had my gun..." Vincent's voice trails off.

He's messing with you. I do not know this man. I met him at the same time you did.

With a sigh, Detective Uzzo shakes her head. "When the call came in that Caroline left her house to meet us, I knew something was up."

Reaching over, Vincent runs a warm hand across my shoulders. "He used my phone to text Caroline. When she showed up, Erwin had already tied me to the chair. He wanted her to use the hunting knife on me in some sort of sick psychological experiment. There was a struggle between Caroline and Erwin and the knife went into his stomach."

He's the only one allowed access to you.

With a nod, Detective Uzzo makes a few notes in her pad.

Uzzo says, "Leaking Erwin's name to the press was a calculated risk that I take full responsibility for."

Oh, I have my ways.

Vincent gives my shoulder a slight squeeze and I find the gesture to be more of a warning than a comfort.

Uzzo glances up from her notepad to me. "Caroline?"

Why didn't Erwin gag him?

"Yes." I clear my throat, making myself focus. "There's another body. A woman. A smoker. An experiment. Done very violently like Harley. Done in a trailer. Happened last night."

Slowly Vincent slides his hand from my shoulder and though he doesn't say anything, I can tell he's bothered I didn't tell him about this already. He says, "Erwin could have committed this murder after he escaped then."

He loves to get inside of your head, doesn't he?

"How do you know all of this?" Uzzo asks.

"I don't know. I was at Vincent's house. I went home. I began doing some research and then I experienced the murder." The visceral way I felt when Fallon found me has me tensing up. "It was awful."

Reaching down, Erwin pulls tight on one of the plastic zip ties and it cinches into Vincent's wrist.

"I can imagine," Vincent murmurs.

"Your ability to climb inside a killer's head has moved from mirroring to psychic visions." Uzzo looks between us. "Have you two not discussed this?"

He's messing with your mind. Don't listen to him.

"We're working through it," Vincent is quick to say.

Uzzo looks at me and I don't have a response. I can't

explain what's happening to me. I wish I could. She clicks her pen closed and studies her note pad for a second like she's gathering her thoughts. I wait but nothing comes.

Kill him.

"How's it going out at Camp Desonk?" I ask, desperately trying to focus.

"Dots are connecting. We've found traces of blood that have cross-matched to the hair in the rug. That deserted camp is definitely where the kills occurred. One of the cabins had a cage in it, presumably where victims were kept before the kill. On the outskirts of the camp are several beautiful gardens where we've found decomposed body parts, much like the girls we found in the mushroom patch."

The plan. On script. Off.

I clear my throat. "Any traces of honey and charcoal?" I ask and she shakes her head.

Not to say they weren't used but I'm inclined to believe the honey and charcoal is a recent thing done so I would make connections. The reigning Organ Ripper wants me to know my past is connected to all of this.

Pick up the knife. I want to see who you are.

I say, "I didn't want to mention this until I knew more but when we discovered Harley and Erwin went to the same camp for troubled boys, I did some digging. I found a photo of four boys: Harley, Erwin, Teagan Ray, and a boy I have yet to identify but I believe his name starts with a w." I don't look at Vincent but I sense his body tense.

"The more I recall things, the more I think perhaps Harley was part of what happened to me and my sister. One or more of the other boys as well."

Uzzo breathes out. "Shit."

"I also discovered Teagan was reported missing six years ago. If we presume he's dead,"—which of course he is—

"then of those four boys, only one may still be alive. He may be who we're looking for."

"We catch him and justice will be served all around."

"Yes." Still, I don't look at Vincent.

Uzzo thinks about things for a few seconds. "H, E, T, W. Those letters were on the kill list."

I nod. "My thoughts exactly."

"Send me that photo. We need to figure out who the 'w' is."

"And who took the photo," I say. "Any further information on Emerson Logging? As you said, it's not a coincidence that the company owns the acres where Annabelle and I were held as well as Camp Desonk."

"The CEO, one Emerson Marion, lives abroad. The only photo we found is as fake as is his identity."

Emerson Marion.

"Also, this Emerson fellow is on the client list," Uzzo says.

I straighten up. "You decrypted it all?" With a pained nod, she rubs the back of her neck and I eye her movement. Something's wrong. "Why, who else is on that list?"

She shakes her head. "I'm not quite ready to say yet. But know that Emerson Marion's name is there."

A cop comes up behind Detective Uzzo, murmuring something, and Uzzo turns away from us. Through the suite, two paramedics wheel out a body bag with Erwin zipped inside. I don't divert my eyes. I stabbed him and I need to look at what I did.

Vincent turns to me, mumbling, "I don't like how much out of the loop I am."

"And I don't like keeping secrets," I say. "But here we are."

"Uzzo doesn't understand the way we work. Complicated patients require complicated relationships and sometimes it's necessary to color outside the lines. As I did with Erwin."

The plan. Off script. On.

"You arranged his escape, didn't you?"

Vincent lowers his voice. "I did. When I began to understand his true obsession with you and me, I felt we needed to meet outside the hospital where I could utilize my methods."

"And what methods are those? Where he tries to convince me I'm a killer?"

Vincent lowers his voice even more. "No, of course not. I lost control of the situation. He had me strapped to the chair before I realized he had the upper hand."

"Bull shit." I stand up and leave the suite. Outside the light mist has cleared, leaving frigid dampness in the air.

Vincent follows. "Caroline, I truly began to believe he might have been in the woods with you. He knew a lot of details that—"

I shake my head, walking toward my car. "I'm done talking to you."

"Okay, but you're going to be fine," Vincent assures me. "We're going to be fine."

I turn to him. "I don't know how you can say that because it is becoming less and less evident to me, especially with what happened in that room with Erwin. Something is going on with me, specifically with the hallucinations. Why aren't you fully recognizing that? Why are you trying to smooth things over?"

He chances a quick look around but we're alone. No one can hear us. "Trust that we will figure everything out. Just don't stop talking to me. Don't shut me out again. I've known you since you were a little girl. I know who you are.

You know who you are. Never doubt that. Don't let people like Erwin get inside your head."

"But you're allowed in there?"

Vincent sighs. "Caroline—"

"Erwin wanted me to stick that hunting knife into you. How are you so sure I won't? I'm certainly capable. I've done it twice now. You should know." I lean in. "You were there both times."

Vincent quietly studies me and my pulse thuds heavy and dark while I wait for his reply. "I realized early on that you saw things differently than other people, as do I. I see myself in you. You're special and you can use that to help fight the crises that come with living a normal life."

"You didn't answer my question and, for the record, I've never lived a normal life."

"No, I suppose you haven't."

Detective Uzzo steps from the suite, giving us a cursory glance.

"I need space," I tell him, looking over his shoulder at Uzzo. "Can I go?"

She glances between us. "Everything okay?"

"Yes," I answer. "Can I go?"

Uzzo nods and without another glance at Vincent, I leave.

He follows. "One last thing and then I'll leave you alone."

"*What?*"

"I'm taking Becka back out to the spot where you and Annabelle were taken. I think Harley used her to lure you two in. I want to see how she responds to the memory. You're welcome to come if you want. It might help fill in some gaps."

I pause for a second, my hand on the door to the Mini

Cooper. I never told Vincent that I thought Becka was there. He's surmised this from his conversations with her.

"Fine," I say. "Tomorrow."

With a nod to me, he backs away, going to his SUV and driving off. I stand for a few moments, my fingers gripped around the door handle, watching the cops move around the parking lot.

Like Harley, Vincent just used Becka to lure me in. I fully realize this. Yet that's not what has my attention. Instead, the woman does. The one I saw murdered. She's out there somewhere. I know it.

I tasted her.

FORTY-THREE

With hands I find steadier than expected, I drive home through the overcast day. Fifteen minutes later I pull into our gravel driveway to see Fallon standing on the porch waiting for me. I take a second to look at his tall, lean body with his hand propped in his front jean pocket. *Home.* That word settles through me. Fallon is my home.

I open the door, cross the gravel, up steps, and walk straight into him. He wraps his arms around me, pulling me in snug, and I bury my face in his chest. We stand that way for several minutes, me inhaling his familiar and comforting scent and him holding me tight.

"Please tell me I'm not hallucinating this," I say.

Fallon holds me even tighter. "This is not a hallucination. You are here and you feel great."

I take another few luxurious seconds to absorb those words and him.

Still holding me, he presses a kiss to my head. "Vincent called and told me everything."

"Everything?"

"Yes."

"I don't want to remember anything anymore. Every day feels like a horrible dream that I can't seem to wake up from." I breathe in and then back out. "I stabbed Erwin."

"I know."

"I thought I saw Annabelle again."

"I know." Fallon stirs, pressing a kiss to my hair. "I made hot chocolate."

Propping my chin on his chest, I look up at him. "Sounds great."

Fallon places a sweet kiss to the tip of my nose and steps away to grab an insulated mug he'd placed on the porch railing. He rotates the lid, opening it, and sweet steam seeps out. "It's cold out. Do you want to go inside?"

Shaking my head, I zip the last section of my down jacket and take the mug. "Smells heavenly."

With a smile, Fallon leads me over to the swing. He opens his arm, welcoming me, and I slide in right beside him. For several moments we share the warm, dark drink with Fallon gently rocking us on the wood swing. It reminds me of all the times we did this at Vincent and Rachel's home, just sat silently and swung. We've always been each other's support and I don't know what I would do without him.

"I hope you know you're not to blame with Erwin," he tells me.

Shifting, I glance up at Fallon's face. "Surprisingly, I'm not even thinking about the fact I stabbed a man. I'm thinking more about my hallucinations, my sleepwalking, Annabelle... The night she 'called' me, the note she 'wrote' me—I think that may have been me. I wanted to hear her voice. I wanted to see her writing." It's the first time I've admitted the possibility of that out loud. "It's just...I miss her so much."

"I know."

"Do you think my visions of her will go away when I get closure on this case?"

Fallon considers that question. "It's possible but you and I both know what you need to do to get closure on Annabelle."

With a sigh, I nod. "Okay."

He doesn't mask the surprise in his tone. "Okay?"

"Yes, I'll give you the bones to test. But I want this private."

"I have a key to the lab at school. It's not a problem." He presses a kiss to the side of my head. "I'm proud of you."

"Thanks," I say, surprised at the weight already lifting from my shoulders. It's past time I found out about the bones.

He takes a sip of his hot chocolate. "You told me once that killing somebody is the ugliest thing in the world. I thought there was something wrong with me because I didn't feel ugly when I killed my brother for doing those horrible things to my family. I felt good."

It's not often Fallon mentions the events that occurred thirteen years ago, the events that led to him living with Vincent and Rachel. It gives me the courage to share the only secret I have from him. In doing so, I hope that gives him the courage to share whatever secret he's withholding from me.

"How did you feel stabbing Erwin?" Fallon asks.

I don't know. I was hallucinating when it happened. Perhaps that's why I'm not very affected by it. Instead, I think about when I stabbed Teagan Ray. "I felt terrified, then powerful, then confused. Killing him was supposed to allow me to get away from my past."

"We're not talking about Erwin, are we? We're talking

about your captor. You killed him and that's why you weren't originally linking him to the case."

My mouth goes dry and when I glance over at Fallon, I see love and understanding in the brown depths of his eyes.

"Yes," I whisper.

"It doesn't matter. We've both done horrible things. We've done what we've had to stay alive. What's important is our future, not the secrets of our pasts. Okay?"

"I love you, Fallon, do you know that?"

He smiles. "I do."

"You can tell me anything and I will love you for it." I keep my gaze leveled on him, hoping he shares whatever it is that weighs heavy on his heart but instead he kisses me before tucking me back into his side.

That's okay, I'll wait and I'll be patient, just like he always is with me.

We stay that way for several minutes, my thoughts circling, eventually coming back around to Teagan Ray. "You know that sketch I have of my captor? I fed it into facial recognition software. He wasn't a drifter after all. He has a name. Teagan Ray. He knew Harley and he knew Erwin. They all attended the same camp for troubled boys and that is certainly not a coincidence."

Fallon doesn't respond and after a second, I glance up at his face to see him gazing out over the dark yard toward Suzi's house up on the hill. "What is it?" I ask.

"Nothing," he says but I don't believe him. Whatever I just said unsettled him. I think he knows that name, Teagan Ray.

FORTY-FOUR

The next morning, I wake up to find Fallon and the bones are gone.

The truth is, I woke up ready to press him about his response last night. He has me more than curious but he also knows me and that's exactly why he's gone right now. He's not ready to talk to me about whatever it is he knows concerning Teagan Ray.

After getting myself together, I send Uzzo the photo of the four boys with a note: *In order from left to right, Harley Laine, Erwin Myers, Teagan Ray, and the as-yet-to-be-identified boy that I believe is "w"*.

"Good morning," Becka says, walking right in my front door with a messenger bag slung over her shoulder. "Vincent said to tell you he'd be a few minutes."

"You can't just walk in my house." I glance out the front window but I don't see the SUV anywhere. "What do you mean Vincent said he'd be a few minutes?"

She shrugs. "He said he texted you."

I check my phone but I don't see any messages from this morning. One did come in late last night. FIELD TRIP

TOMORROW. Meaning us taking Becka back to the tracks where Annabelle and I went missing.

"Got any OJ?" Becka asks and I wave her into the kitchen.

While she crosses through our dining room, her gaze falls to the folder I have open that displays a multitude of photos including cold cases from other states and the girls found here local. "Looking at my dad's reign of terror, I see."

For a few seconds, I don't say anything as Becka helps herself to juice. The last time I saw her she was crying over being a "monster". Now she seems back to her old snarky self. I envision her as a toddler beckoning me and Annabelle into the woods and the muscles in my neck tighten.

Yes, I want to take her back to the tracks and I would love to do it without Vincent there. I want this girl alone without him as the buffer.

A glance out our front window shows the SUV is still not here. I'm going to make the most of what moments I have with her. I'm going to press.

I tap the picture of Nadia, the girl found in chains, then of Gaby from the motel. "Done after Harley died and by two different people."

"Or by Erwin making it look like two different people." She takes a sip of juice as she sets her messenger bag down. "He did turn himself in after that."

"You and I both know he's not involved beyond supplying Harley access to those girls."

"Okay then, by you. You have been sleepwalking and hallucinating and, given what you experienced as a child, it all may be crawling to the surface now."

Her words, similar to Erwin's, stab into me but I dismiss them. I will not let her get inside of my head. Next, I slide out the photo of Harley, organs removed but left in a pile of thoughtless debris. As I do, I watch Becka in my peripheral vision for a reaction and I note that she turns away slightly so she doesn't have to look at it.

I say, "You helped your dad kill by luring people in. You've also admitted to stabbing at least one of them, the one found in the mushroom patch. Nadia thought she recognized you. Did you stab her, too, to shut her up? Did you rip out her organs in a failed attempt to copy your father and then blame it on Erwin?"

"Why are you saying all of this?"

"I've respected Vincent's request to keep your secrets until we know all the ins and outs but I'm this close to looping Detective Uzzo in."

"Vincent wouldn't like that."

"And I don't care."

Her eyebrows come up. "Are you threatening me?"

"I want to know more about the two girls done after Harley died."

"I have an alibi for both nights."

"An alibi?" I close the folder. "Only guilty people say things like that."

"Do *you* have an alibi?" She comes back. "Where were you during those two murders?"

I don't know but I also don't let her bait me. "You're one of those very smart girls who know all the moves to make and all the things to say."

She moves toward me through the kitchen, her green eyes narrowing, continuing with the baiting. "What exactly happens when you have your periods of lost time? You didn't answer my question. Where were you when the girl found in chains in our garage was being stabbed?"

"Nadia is her name." And I was found wandering the

county road by Fallon with no recollection of where I had been.

"And what about when the girl from the motel was killed?"

"Gaby is her name." And I was found in the field across from our home, again with no recollection of hours that had gone by.

With a satisfied smirk, Becka finishes her juice and puts the glass in the sink. Damn her. She's playing mind games with me and I'm letting her.

I switch tactics, taking on a smirk of my own. "You should know I recently had a memory come to the surface. You lured me and my sister into the woods thirteen years ago, didn't you?"

"I don't know what you're talking about."

"I'm sure you don't," I lie. "Your memory is probably just as foggy as mine, which is why Vincent wants to take you out to the tracks where we were abducted."

"He said that?"

"That's why you're here this morning. But we don't need him. Let's go out there alone."

Her gaze drifts to the front window to see if Vincent has returned but he hasn't.

Yes, I want to see her without him as a buffer. "What do you say, Becka? Want to go with me or are you scared of me?" I lean in, challenging. "Are you scared I'll gut you?"

PART FIVE

Six Years Ago

I enter the open kitchen complete with granite, tile, and stainless steel appliances. Vincent stands at the grill in the center, wiping it with a cloth in preparation for whatever it is he's planning on cooking. I've never shown an interest in cooking or eating for that matter. Cooking in here with Vincent is Fallon's thing, not mine.

"I noticed that you slept with Fallon again last night..." Vincent's voice trails off.

"I don't like having bad dreams and waking up alone."

With a nod, he moves from the grill over to chop herbs that he picked from Rachel's greenhouse. He rotates over to the stove, checking a sizzling skillet, before peeking inside of a bubbling pot.

"All we did is sleep," I say.

Without looking at me, he hands me a knife. "Why don't you tell me about your bad dream instead of Fallon?"

Silently, I take the knife. "I keep seeing myself stabbing my captor over and over again."

He nods to the carrots. "Cut those in strips." He scoops up bell peppers and chopped garlic and slides them into the skillet. "I want you to talk about this stuff with me but no one else. For now at least, no one else."

"Not even Rachel? Not even Fallon?" My gaze slides over to the grinder, still bloody from the meat he put through a few minutes ago. The sight of it makes my mouth salivate and I hate it. I want it to make me nauseous, not hungry.

"No one."

"Because you think I'll scare people," I say.

"No, I think you'll unnecessarily worry those who care for you."

"Hm." I keep my eyes on the bloody grinder. "I'm not eating that."

"I know, Caroline. Just because you don't eat meat doesn't mean the rest of us should abstain."

With a sigh, I turn my back on the grinder, not even wanting it in my peripheral vision. "Do you think there will ever be a day where I don't think about the past? When I don't question it?"

"Are you referring to killing your captor or other things?"

"I think all."

Vincent smiles at me and it reminds me of the pride I used to see in Grandpa's face. "You are a survivor. If you did things you're not quite remembering, it's okay. You went into self-preservation mode. Otherwise, he would have eaten you alive."

I stop cutting the carrots. "That's a poor choice of words."

"Caroline, I wish you hadn't have gone through what you did but we've worked through quite a bit of it and now I want us to focus on the next steps. Let's talk about school. You've been thriving in your online classes. You're fifteen and will be ready for college soon. What are your thoughts on attending a brick and mortar school?"

"I don't know. I like the anonymity of online work."

"What do you think you'd like to study in college? Because I have some suggestions that I think you'll be quite suited for."

My knife slides down through another carrot. "The profiling work you do is interesting to me."

A warm smile plays across Vincent's lips. "You read my mind."

"Given what happened to me though, would I be a good psychological fit for that job?"

"What happened to you was a long time ago and look who you are now. Remember, it's not so much what happened to you in the past but your nature going forward."

"I'm not sure what my nature is anymore, especially after what I did to our captor."

"Yes, you do. You know your nature. You came from a loving family and you are in a loving family now. The time spent with your captor gave you scars to learn and live from. They remind you what is real."

Scooting the cut carrot aside, I pick up another one. If I were Fallon, all these carrots would have been sliced by now. "What would have happened if I'd never gone free?"

"Perhaps you would have ended up like Annabelle."

That comment makes me quiet and still.

He finishes cutting the herbs. "I know it's painful to think of her but you must."

"I just wish...I just wish I could remember everything. So much is still so fuzzy."

"And it may always be that way." Propping his palms on the counter, he studies me for a few seconds. "We could try something. Do you trust me?"

I lift my gaze from the carrots and look into his dark eyes. "Yes."

He nods down to the herbs. "This is a combination of various psychedelics. Woodrose, ayahuasca, cactus, wormwood, dream herb, and a few others. It's a special combination I've developed over the years."

Cautiously, I eye them. "And?"

"Sometimes being in an altered state can allow you better access to the traumatic events of your past." Taking the spatula, he moves the stir-fry around in the skillet. "Look at it more as cleansing your mind."

Reaching forward, I pick up a bit of the chopped psychedelic herbs. "You've taken it before?"

"Yes. Rachel and I both have."

"Has Fallon?"

"No, and I'm not sure this is the right therapy for him. For you, yes."

"'Animals remember trusted voices. They also remember the abuse.' My dad told me that once."

Cocking his head, Vincent studies me. "That's a peculiar thing to remember right now. Are you saying you're an animal?"

"When I was little we adopted an abused dog from the pound. I was just remembering what Dad told me and Annabelle. I'm afraid these herbs are going to make me remember more than the abuse." But didn't I just say that I wanted to?

Vincent wipes his hands on the hem of his apron and I can tell he's trying to read between the lines of my words. "I've told you this before and I'll say it again. You did what you had to do to survive."

"Do I want to remember every detail though?"

"That's up to you. But I would like for you to at least try."

My fingers sift through the herbs. "How do I take them?"

Vincent's face shifts and distorts, slightly at first, then more aggressively. Holding onto the side of the kitchen counter, I lift my hand and waggle my fingers and they blur. He's speaking but his voice comes across thick and plodding, I can't make out his words.

"Does Rachel know you and I are doing this right now?" I ask.

"No."

My lips curl upward. "Ooh, another secret." And more to come, I'm sure.

His hand clasps my arm and I'm not sure where it came from. Carefully, he guides me over to a seat. "This should be more spiritual and positive than anything else. Trust me on that."

"Trust you on that," I repeat, noting my tongue now feels thick.

"Go with whatever you want to say. Whatever you want to do."

I do just that as my lips purse and I whistle those three notes...

"Caroline, it's important that you don't tell anyone about that whistle. Okay? And especially don't ever do it."

"Why?"

"I'll tell you when you're ready. But for now, you need to trust me on that. Okay?"

"Okay." I look around and my head feels like it's separated from my body. "Where's Fallon?"

"He's with Rachel. They'll be back later." Vincent checks my pulse and satisfied, goes back to cooking. "Trauma can leave you powerless. I never want you to feel that way again. I want you to feel only power from here on out."

Nausea rolls through me and I swallow. "I think I'm going to throw up."

"No, you're fine." He lowers the heat on the stove. "I want you to allow the things that you're feeling to wash through you. I want you to welcome it."

I eye the skillet of stir-fry made with ground beef versus strips and yellow peppers versus red. I note, too, the pot of wild rice versus white. "Mom used to make that exact dish."

"I know, you told me and I remembered."

That's right. I did. The food sizzles and crackles as the heat dies down. Vincent serves up a tiny plate of it.

"I want you to start enjoying food again. I want you to stop being afraid of it. It's okay to eat and not feel guilty. Would you like that, Caroline?"

"Yes."

Bringing me the plate, he hands me a fork. "Try a little bit."

The scent of meat, garlic, and something else that I can't quite peg filters into my senses and my mouth salivates.

Vincent watches me. "I'm experimenting a bit with recipes. Try a tiny bite."

Somewhere in the back of my mind, I want to say, *I don't eat meat,* but instead, I grip the fork almost too tightly as I place a bite into my mouth. The combination of flavors and spices melts, soothes, and tantalizes my taste buds. I groan.

Vincent chuckles. "Yes, I thought you might like that. I added a little something special."

A sound coming down the hall catches my attention and Vincent straightens as if he wasn't expecting the footsteps. I smell her before I see her, lemon and ginger, and her scent soothes through my senses. Smiling, I close my eyes and I get a little lost in the colors swirling through my head.

The sound of her heels enters the kitchen and she comes to a stop, apparently taking in the scene. "What did you give her?" Rachel demands, clearly annoyed.

"Just a bit of our herbs."

"I told you she wasn't ready for the herbs."

Still, with my eyes closed, their words float through my head and it makes me chuckle. It's the first time I've ever heard them exchange upset words.

"Fallon," Rachel says, "go upstairs."

Fallon? Fallon's here? I try to open my eyes but the lids are heavy. So heavy.

"I apologize if you think I overstepped boundaries," Vincent speaks.

"I'm the herbalist, not you," she says, still annoyed. "I wanted to be here for her the first time. What were you thinking?"

"Rachel." Vincent's voice is soft. "She was a little agitated and I didn't want to give her prescription anti-anxiety pills."

I was agitated? I don't remember being agitated.

Rachel sighs. "How long ago?"

"About fifteen minutes."

Her heels click across the tile, coming toward me, and she lays a gentle hand on my arm. "Caroline?" She takes the plate I'm still holding and places it on the table.

Still, with my smile, I mumble. "Are you hungry? Vincent made a stir-fry with ground beef, just like Mom used to."

"You fed her meat?" Rachel asks.

"Yes, it was the perfect time to try. She needs to learn it's okay to eat meat."

"Not like this, Vincent. You know the herbs create odd connections. What if she remembers too much?"

"She won't."

She touches me again. "Caroline, can you open your eyes?"

It takes great effort but I slide my eyes open, seeing first the track lighting on the ceiling. I move my gaze down to Rachel and her pretty face blurs as I lose focus. I blink away the blur and my smile slides away as things clear.

"What is it?" She asks. "What do you see?"

My breath comes deep and uneven as I stare at the familiar faces. "Mom?" I look over to the stove. "Dad?" My head wobbles. "Where's Annabelle?"

Dad and Mom exchange a worried glance.

"I'm here," comes a familiar voice over in the corner.

Turning, I see her standing there exactly as I remember her that day in the field of wildflowers. "Annabelle?" I whisper and she smiles.

Several nights later I sit on our back deck, gazing out over the hills rolling down the mountain toward the town at the base. My skin buzzes with the knowledge and the possibilities of taking more herbs tonight. I want to see Mom and Dad again but more importantly, I want to see Annabelle.

A weeping willow towers in the center of the yard, its long arms swaying in the night breeze. Beneath it sits Fallon and Zane, staring out at the same moon I am. Will he be okay if I crawl into his bed again? He hasn't minded so far. He seemed to sleep better, too.

Beside me sits Rachel, humming a song I don't recognize and knitting a gray and white scarf. She told me the gray matched my eyes. Is she going to give it to me when she's done? I hope so.

This is the first time Rachel has been alone with me in some while. I hope that means her hesitancy with me is fading.

Her humming slows to a gradual stop and I sense she's looking at me but I keep my gaze fastened on Fallon and Zane. "How long have you and Vincent known each other?" I ask.

"Oh, forever. We volunteered at a youth program many, many years ago."

Sounds like something they would do.

"We found you sleepwalking again last night. Did Vincent tell you?"

"No." I look over at her.

"You were outside in your pajamas, watching a stray cat eat a mouse. This sleepwalking is a new development. What do you think has brought it on?"

The psychedelic herbs, but I don't say that. It's the only explanation though. I've been sneaking them for days now and every night I've had a sleepwalking episode. The night before last they found me in the kitchen eating raw liver.

Just the thought of it makes my stomach pitch.

But that's okay. I'll put up with some sleepwalking for a chance at seeing Annabelle.

"Every night we've found you wandering the grounds, staring at dead things, or in the kitchen eating questionable items. I worry about you, Caroline. I worry your soul is being drawn to the dark again."

"No, it's not. I'm drawn to you, Vincent and Fallon. I'm not drawn to the dark." I would say I'm more captured by it. But I don't say that because I don't want to worry her. She's not like Vincent. She doesn't accept me as he does.

Reaching out, Rachel soothes a hand over my head and I close my eyes to savor the touch. I lean in a little bit. Mom touched me like this. But I must lean in too close because Rachel shifts away.

Without looking at her, I stand. "Good night, Rachel."

But she doesn't respond and I go to my room to sleep with the bones I both want to and refuse to believe are Annabelle's.

I continue taking the herbs night after night after night. But soon I don't see Annabelle anymore. I don't feel her. Instead, I hallucinate horrible things being done to people. I feel those horrible things and I believe I have done them.

One night I wake from sleepwalking and I'm choking Rachel. "Hold still. Still. It'll all be over in a second. Second."

FORTY-FIVE

Present Day

I stare into the distance, my gaze tracking the switchback of the country roads that lead out to the land my family used to own. Since I was sixteen, I've come here every year on the anniversary of our abduction to say a prayer for Annabelle.

Beside me, Becka stares out the passenger side at the passing trees. I keep an eye on her in my peripheral, hoping to pick up on her mood but she seems a bit bored with this whole thing.

Are you scared I'll gut you? I can't believe those words came out of my mouth. She has a way of digging in though and getting under my skin. And when she challenged my whereabouts, my alibi, I bit back.

And here we are.

Vincent is going to be pissed and I don't care.

From her messenger bag, she pulls out a doll different

from the one she's been working on. This one is smaller with short black hair.

"Who taught you how to make dolls?" I ask.

"My dad."

"What do you do with them when you're done?"

"Some I sell online. Others I keep." She pulls a thread through the fabric hand, loops it to knot, and pulls tight to form a thumb. "I think of them as my friends."

That's a sad thing to say. "How long have you had cancer?" I ask next.

"For as long as I can remember. In remission. Out of remission. In. Out." She sighs. "Sometimes I wish I would be out and stay out."

"Why would you say such a thing?"

She shrugs, still not looking at me. "I'm going to die eventually. Might as well get it over with." Turning away from the trees, she glances over at me. "I'm not depressed. Just practical."

"Hm." I don't know what else to say.

"What's up with you and all the headaches?" She asks. "I see you popping pills all the time."

"Had them for a few years now. They usually come when I'm working. Speaking of—" I nod to my backpack behind my seat— "Do me a favor and fish out a couple of my pills. They should be in the front pocket. And grab me a seed bar. I need something in my stomach."

It doesn't take her but a few seconds to find it all. I take two and wash them down with warm water from my bottle in the console. After that, I check my phone, hoping for something from Fallon about the bones but find nothing. Oddly, Vincent hasn't texted me either.

"Can't be good to take so many," she says.

I take a bite of the bar. "It's fine."

As she puts my backpack away, I see her eyeing me. "You're looking kind of pasty."

I shrug that off.

She continues studying me for a moment before turning back to her doll. "What kind of stuff did you do with your family before your tragic event?"

Tragic event. No one's ever called it that before. "Everything. My family did everything together."

"Must have been great," she mumbles.

"It was." As I turn off onto the dirt service road that parallels the train tracks, I cast her another glance but other than a curious expression, she doesn't seem to recognize the area.

My car creeps down the narrow dirt road with thick trees on one side, tracks on the other, and beyond that the sprawling new subdivision.

Becka's gaze bumps over all the houses in the distance. "Which one was yours?"

I point to a log home some half mile up. "That one with the green roof."

"So, you and Annabelle were taken from here and transported nearly sixty miles to some deserted house in the woods. Ever been back there?"

"Only once." And even then, I didn't step foot inside.

"You were a mere sixty miles from your home the entire time." Becka shakes her head. "That's crazy. Why do you stay in this area?" She shivers. "It would give me the creeps."

"Because my entire family died in this area and I want to be near their memory." I pull my car to a stop, pointing into the woods. "It's about fifty yards in."

"What is?"

"The memorial."

Putting her doll away, she opens her door and I glance at my watch. *My name is Caroline Christianson. It's 11:12 in the morning. I'm at the train tracks where Annabelle and I were taken.*

Grabbing her messenger bag, Becka stands for a few seconds, looking into the woods at the same spot I remember her being all those years ago. With her slightly in front, we make our way into the trees. "I'm curious, do you feel like you know my father better now that he's dead?"

What an unusual question. "I think it's more I feel obligated to understand the entire situation."

Becka steps around a tree, trailing her fingers over the bark. "Dad never said it but I could tell he enjoyed the stalking aspect of the process. Watching, choosing, selecting. I liked being the lure. I liked coming up with new ways to attract the object my dad desired." She glances over at me. "It makes me sad to admit that."

I don't know what to say to that but I go with it. "Are you ready to admit you lured me and Annabelle into the woods that day?"

"Yes." She sighs. "I suspected. But it wasn't until just now and coming back here that I truly remembered that tiny detail."

Tiny detail. I move my gaze away, experiencing an unnerving urge to do something to her right now. Because of Becka, my sister is dead. My parents are dead. And I am forever changed.

I take a breath, telling myself to calm down. To get as much information as possible. "How is it you were here and saw us?"

She shrugs. "Dad was probably hunting in the nearby woods. Saw you two playing. Came back later with me."

"Do you know Teagan Ray?"

Becka shakes her head. "Who is that?"

"A childhood friend of your father's."

She turns to look at me and her eyes widen on a thought. "Do you think he fed me pieces of you and Annabelle?"

I don't respond. She's antagonizing me. *Breathe.*

With another shrug, she turns away. "People think he was a monster but he had remorse. Everything he did bothered him."

I try to focus on her words but muddled thoughts claw at my skull. Harley and Teagan. The hood. The beard. The eyes. The sometimes-raspy voice. *Hold still. Still.* And that horrible whistle. It all strobes through my brain and I wince.

"He talked to someone about it all."

The air around me stills. "What do you mean he talked to someone?"

"Dad had someone he talked to about everything. I never knew the person. But I'm assuming it's Dr. DeMurr. I mean, why else would he have taken me in? I think he felt guilty he couldn't help my dad."

Vincent arranged for Teagan and me to cross paths. According to Erwin, they went "way back". And now I'm finding out he talked with Harley. I'd bet anything Vincent knows the unidentified fourth boy as well.

A high-pitched ring pierces through my skull and I flinch.

I'm not sure what propels me but I shove Becka up against a tree trunk. My hands wrap around her throat and I squeeze. She thrashes against my hold, raking her fingernails down my neck, screaming...screaming...screaming...

The scream replaces the ring in my skull. Everything goes mute and all sound returns in a sudden pop. I blink, realizing I'm gripping the air and not Becka's throat.

"There is something wrong with you." She takes a step back, now holding up a kitchen knife. It's Fallon's favorite and it's sharp. When the hell did she get that? She glances down at it as if reading my thoughts. "I stole it when you weren't looking. You're crazy if you think I'm coming out here without protection."

I take a step back, too, uncomfortable and confused by what I just imagined. "You are the reason we were taken. You are the reason for everything."

Gripping the knife tight, Becka sidesteps, heading back the way we just came. It's clear she's scared of me and I don't care. Let her be scared.

I take a step toward her, stalking now. "You wanted your dad caught, didn't you? That's why you returned the bodies. You were already thinking about being the daughter of the infamous Organ Ripper. Nobody would think poor, sick Becka could be involved. You gutted your father. You killed Nadia to shut her up. You knew your dad's technique. You knew how to carry on the legacy." Another screaming ring races through my brain and I flinch away from the sound. "Vincent knows, doesn't he?"

Becka shakes her head. "You don't know what you're talking about. How is that even possible?" She scoffs. "What, do you think I snuck out of the hospital or something?"

Becka's denial bears down on me and her voice distorts until all sound drops away. I close my eyes, gripping my head, and faces flash through my brain—Harley, Teagan, Becka, Vincent, Rachel, Uzzo, Suzi, Nadia, Irene, Yasmine, Gaby, Fallon...

Annabelle, Annabelle, Annabelle, Annabelle, Annabelle.

"No!" I scream.

FORTY-SIX

A knocking sound filters in, clearing the haziness from my brain. I open my eyes and I startle when I see Vincent staring back at me through the glass on my driver's side window. With his knuckle, he knocks on the glass again.

"You okay?" His muffled voice filters through the glass.

A glance tells me I'm back at home. I blink and look over to the passenger side to find it empty. I look at my watch. *My name is Caroline Christianson. It's 8:14 in the evening. I'm at my home.*

Absently, I unlock and open my door and I quietly step out into the frigid cold. Fallon stands off to the side, concern etched into his face. The air sits perfectly still and I look back at Vincent. "What are you doing here?" I ask.

"Where have you been?" he counters.

"You didn't get my note?"

"What note?" He says.

My gaze drifts over to our front door. I did leave a note taped to the door, didn't I?

"I was worried about you and Becka. We both were.

You've been gone all day." Vincent glances into my car. "Why haven't you answered your phone?"

My phone... Turning away from Vincent I look into my car and there my phone sits in the console. I don't know why I haven't been answering it.

Vincent takes hold of my shoulders and turning me back, he looks deeply into my eyes, studying my pupils. "Where is she?"

I don't answer and instead say, "How long were you seeing Harley?"

If he seems surprised that I know this, he doesn't react, only nods. "Only recently. I didn't know the extent of his issues until this case, though."

His response comes across a little too perfect and thought out. "And how long have you known that Becka lured me and Annabelle into the woods that day?"

"Not long. I was beginning to piece it all together." Vincent squeezes my shoulders. "What's going on? Where's Becka?"

"I don't know."

"She texted me to say she didn't feel safe with you."

My mind spins.

"I don't know what she said to you but, Caroline—" he shakes his head, "I can't protect you anymore."

"Protect me? Protect me from what?" My gaze goes from Vincent to Fallon, back to Vincent, and slowly it dawns on me. "You think I killed those girls?"

Fallon steps forward. "I didn't say that."

I keep my eyes focused on Vincent, trying to read his thoughts. Quietly, he studies me but he doesn't respond and my mind replays the conversation that I had with Becka in the woods. Yes, it replays but what it latches on to is the word alibi. For the murders done after Harley died, I have no alibi. Frankly, I'm not even sure if I have an alibi for the others.

Nausea rolls up my throat. "You think I'm capable of that?"

"Of course not," Fallon says but I can't tell if he means it or not.

"Why don't we focus on finding Becka, okay? I'm going to go look for her and you go inside the house. I'm worried how easy it is for you to be lucid and aware one moment and then the next you're not." Vincent takes my arm and guides me toward the house. "You need to rest."

"No." I pull my arm from his grasp and step away to give myself some distance. "You took Fallon in because his brother was a patient of yours. You took Becka in because her dad was a patient of yours. Did you take me in because Teagan Ray was a patient of yours, too? That's right, I know his real name. He wasn't a drifter, as you said. But you knew that all along, didn't you?"

But it's not Vincent who responds, it's Fallon. "Yes, Teagan was a patient of Vincent's. I've known for years. That's the secret I've been keeping from you. He made me promise not to tell you. Just like I'm guessing he made you promise not to tell me that my brother was a patient, too. Because this is the first I'm hearing of it."

My jaw tightens as I stare up into Vincent's face. Harley, Erwin, Teagan. I haven't shown Vincent the picture of the four boys taken at Camp Desonk. I've only shared it with Uzzo but Vincent knows what I'm referring to when I say, "You know who the unidentified boy is, don't you? You know who "w" is."

"W?" Fallon asks and I don't respond, I just keep a lethal glare pinned on Vincent.

"Who all was in the woods with me? It wasn't just Teagan and you've known that all along, haven't you?"

With a sigh, Vincent tucks his hands into his coat pockets. For a few seconds, he looks at the gravel beneath his loafers and I'm torn with telling him to get the hell off our property and also wanting to hear his words.

"Know that I love you two. I think of you as my children. I would never do anything to harm either of you." Vincent lifts his head to look at me and Fallon. "The things I choose to tell you, to do with you, are in your best interest. Always. I'm not going to defend myself. My actions should speak loud enough. I offered both of you a safe home when you had nothing. Imagine what you would be now if I hadn't stepped in. Yes, I've treated many patients over the years with failed results. Just like I've treated many with success. I consider both of you my great successes."

I am so done with this man. Jabbing my finger in the direction of his SUV, I snap, "Get the hell off our property."

He opens his mouth to say something and Fallon steps forward. "You heard her."

Vincent's expression holds great concern as he rotates away. "Fine, I have to go find Becka anyway."

For several long seconds, I stand, staring at his tail lights as they wind down the country road and disappear around the bend. Neither Fallon nor I speak. There are no words. Vincent is the only father we've known since we were little kids and we just kicked him out of our lives.

The exterior light flicks on from the motion sensor and we turn to see Suzi stepping around the side of our house. She had to have heard everything that was just said.

She walks toward us. The first thing that comes to mind is her greenhouse and the flowers. I want her to know I didn't send Uzzo in that direction. It wasn't me.

I'm about to say just that when she says, "I want you two to know that I gave access to my home and greenhouse to Uzzo and her team. The wildflowers found on the dead bodies have been traced to my home."

"That's bullshit," Fallon says. "You're being set up."

"I agree." I think about the recently decrypted client list and Uzzo's pained expression when I asked about it. "Your name was on that client list, too, wasn't it?"

Suzi nods. "It was. And—" she looks between us, "they went through my deep freezer and found human organs."

Fallon and I exchange a shocked look. When I regain my voice, I ask, "Well did they search all the other clients?"

"Yes," Suzi says. "But my house was the only one with evidence. The names on that private list disposed of things."

Fallon takes a step toward her. "What does this mean?"

"It means I am a 'person of interest.' I can't leave town. I'm also voluntarily going in tomorrow for questioning. Honestly, if it wasn't for Uzzo, I'd be there right now."

I throw both of my hands in the air. "She has to know you're being framed."

Suzi nods. "She does but she also has a job to do."

The three of us stand quietly in our cold and dimly lit yard, our minds racing yet unable to grasp onto thoughts or words. It's Suzi who breaks the silence. "Caroline, I don't like that you had another loss of time, especially with Becka involved."

"I don't either." I turn to Fallon. "And before you ask again, no, I'm not taking those herbs. Not since what happened with Rachel have I taken them and that was years ago."

Suzi looks between us. "What are you talking about? What herbs?"

Quickly I fill her in and when I finish, Fallon reaches

for my hand. "It's the explanation, at least to this part of things. And after everything that just went down, I would not put it past Vincent to be doing it."

"I agree," Suzi says.

Their words lurch through my heart and I don't want to believe it. Vincent knows what those herbs did to me last time. I mean, my God, I choked out Rachel. I wandered off. I ate raw liver. I dug a stick into a dead opossum.

But I also saw Annabelle and that is why I got addicted to them.

Fury crawls across my skin. They're right. Vincent's been giving me those herbs and if I wasn't so emotionally attached to him, I would've seen it sooner.

"He wants me dependent on him." My jaw clenches. "He doesn't like the fact I moved out. That I've been challenging him. This is his way of gaining control, of getting me back. The meals he's fed me, the homemade seed bars, the spices he mixes just for me—they've been in my system all along."

"We are done with him, Caroline. Do you hear me?" Fallon's fingers tighten around mine. "Done."

I nod. "Agreed."

With a disgusted sigh, Suzi shakes her head. "I'm so sorry, Caroline."

On a deep breath, I let go of Fallon's hand. My fingernails dig into my palms. If Vincent were here right now, I would punch him.

Shaking my head, I pace away. What would Rachel say about all of this? She would be furious. She would hate Vincent for this.

I whip back around, looking at Fallon through the night. "Please tell me you have the results on the bones."

Fallon looks at Suzi and I say, "She knows. I showed her."

"I was planning on telling you and then all this happened." Fallon crosses over to me and he cups my face in his hands. "Yes, Caroline. Those bones belong to your sister."

FORTY-SEVEN

I move through the woods, stepping carefully, listening to the melody of the wind rustling through the trees. Sunlight streams down and up ahead I see movement.

Slowly, Becka moves into view, looking right at me. I freeze in place, my muscles tightening, but then she is gone. A rustling behind me has me spinning around. I catch a glimpse of her again, moving away.

I follow but lose sight when she steps through the trees. I listen and the rustling comes from my right. Then my left. Then, once again, silence.

Slowly I advance, sliding deeper into the woods, moving with caution. I approach a thick clump of trees and Becka bolts. I run after her, noting the leaves where she just was and the way they glisten. I touch them, bringing my fingers away, finding blood smeared across my skin.

I track the bloody leaves, pursuing, moving faster, gaining urgency. My breath comes hard, frosting in front of me. I catch sight of another patch of blood, shining dark in the shadows. Up ahead, she steps into view and I stop. Then she turns and runs, and once again, I follow.

I see her, darting, and with a sudden judder, she comes off her feet and crashes backward onto the leaves and dirt.

Panting, I cover the distance, pushing aside limbs and dry leaves. I catch a glimpse of her moving, low to the ground, crawling away. Grabbing the light brown hair on her head, I part the last bit of spindly branches, and slowly, she rolls to her back. Her gaze fixes on me in a silent plea.

I bare my teeth and with a scream, I lunge.

I wake with a jerk, coming straight up in bed. Morning light streaks through my windows and I squint against it. In the distance, I hear Zane barking. Fallon must have let him out.

The sun shifts, beaming in a new way through the blinds and I lift my hand to shield my eyes. Petal stretches across the bed coming for her morning rub. She pushes her tiny head under my hand and I fiddle with her ears for a few seconds. I stare at the wood-framed photo of me and Annabelle sitting across the room on top of my dresser.

She's dead.

Suzi said that knowledge will bring comfort and I wait for that comfort to settle in but it doesn't. Because now that she is for sure gone, I have to face the details surrounding that.

My sister is gone and I have spent years going back and forth on what happened in those woods. I may never remember the details. They are buried deep. The fact is, I'm not entirely sure that I want to. I don't want to face the truth that I may have been forced to eat Annabelle.

The visions I've been having of her have provided comfort. It's the exact reason why I abused the herbs years ago. I would have done anything to see my sister again. But as I learned, the herbs aren't worth it. They bring out another side of me that I never want to surface again.

Vincent.

Fresh and raw anger flares in me that he would do this.

Maybe he was experimenting with the herbs, wanting to increase my connection to the killer and the victims. Or as I thought last night, he was wanting to wear me down to make me more dependent on him. Who the hell knows what truly motivated him?

What I do know is that he stepped way too far over the line with both me and Fallon, and he has been for years. But when you love someone, it's difficult to see through the half-truths, the outright lies, the manipulations...

With me though, Vincent never seemed to keep a secret. He willingly and openly encouraged me to explore his office, the journals, books, the files, the cases...

The files.

No, that's not correct. He never once granted me access to the locked cabinet under his desk. Sure, I've thought of it now and again but I respect privacy and that's where it always stopped with me.

Now though, I want to see what's in that cabinet.

My stomach clenches with an unexpected wave of nausea and I reach for the glass of water sitting on my bedside table.

After a few sips, I check my phone but nothing has come in from Vincent. He said he was going to go look for Becka. If he found her, he would've texted. Despite what's going on between us, he would've texted. At least I think he would've.

Petal swerves beneath my feet as I head into the bathroom. I wash my face and brush my teeth and another roll of nausea moves through me. Maybe I need some toast.

After sliding my toothbrush back into the glass holder, I take a second to look at myself in the mirror—at the shadows under my blue eyes, my pale skin, and tangled dark hair. I look bad. Like been-hit-with-a-train kind of bad.

A few blue and yellow marks dot my neck and I lean in to inspect them. Gently, I place my fingers on them. They're bruises. Left by me? Or—all the air leaks from my lungs—Becka?

"I just came from Suzi's house," Fallon says, moving in behind me. "She's not there. She must have already gone in to be questioned."

Nausea hits me again, throwing me forward, and I retch with violence into the sink. Something brown and twisted comes out of me and I stare at the clump surrounded by bile and a bit of leftover toothpaste.

Fallon stares at what I just threw up in stunned silence. "Wh-what the hell is that?"

FORTY-EIGHT

I explode from the bathroom and through the house, launching myself out the front door and into the snow flurries that have begun to fall. Dropping to my knees, I dry heave but nothing else comes up. I look up and the yard whirls. I know what that was. I've coughed that up before.

Fallon comes out, wrapping a blanket around me and helping me over to the porch. With a shiver, I stare through the flurries falling all around and straight over to Suzi's house. "Vincent went looking for Becka last night. Please tell me he found her."

"I haven't heard from him this morning. Why do you want to know if he found Becka?"

"I had a dream I was chasing Becka through the woods. She was bleeding. She was scared." My shaky fingers grip the blanket and I notice a bit of dirt under my nails. I hold my hand out. "Oh my God, is that blood? Is that dirt? What the hell is that? What if I didn't dream that? What if I was chasing her yesterday? Because what I just threw up—" I swallow the bitterness in my mouth. "I know what that was."

"You're rambling." Fallon sits down beside me on the porch steps, wrapping his arms around me. "Back up. What do you mean you know what that was?"

"The last thing I remember, I was in the woods with Becka and I hallucinated that I was choking her. I didn't." I quickly clarify. "When I came out of the hallucination, she was backing away from me, terrified. Then there's a gap in my memory and I was here in my car. Then there was you and Vincent, and we went inside..." I look at Fallon, both desperate for and horrified of the answers. I show him my neck. "What if I attacked her and she was fighting me off?"

Fallon looks at my neck. "Or she attacked you and you were defending yourself."

"Then where is she?"

"I don't know."

I try to focus on her and what did or did not happen, instead my mind backtracks through the years. "Because of her, we went into those woods. Harley took us. But Teagan was there, too. They bragged about it to Erwin. The hood he always wore. The way he scratched his beard. The raspy voice. That hunting knife. His eyes. Treating our wounds with honey and charcoal. The herbs so we wouldn't feel anything. Playing horrible games with us. The torture. How is it possible my mind merged them into one person?"

"Because Vincent made sure. He manipulated your memories so you wouldn't figure things out."

"Erwin mentioned 'a plan'. Vincent was using Erwin to reel me back in."

"He's used all of us for one reason or another."

"He arranged the 'chance' meeting with Teagan. He wanted to see what I was capable of." I squeeze my eyes shut. "And oh, God, that whistle."

Fallon's body stills. "Whistle? What do mean whistle?"

I open my eyes back up. "One of them used to whistle these three horrible notes." Yet another secret Vincent wanted me to keep. But not anymore. Pursing my lips, I do them now and Fallon shoots to his feet.

"What is it?" I ask.

Squeezing his eyes shut, Fallon shakes his head. "No, it can't be."

"Fallon, look at me. What is it?"

He turns away from me, pressing the heels of his hands into his forehead and breathing out.

Carefully, I get up and I go to him, placing my palms on his back. I'm so relieved when he doesn't flinch away. "Fallon?" I whisper.

"My brother used to do that." Fallon breathes out again. "How is that even possible?"

I stroke my palms across his back to lightly squeeze his shoulders. As I do, I think of timelines. Fallon's tragedy happened the same year as mine, both thirteen years ago. Is it in any way possible his brother was in the woods with us, too?

The picture of the four boys. I've never seen a photo of Fallon's brother but his name was Wesley. On the kill list, the "w" stopped occurring thirteen years ago and that matches the timeline of his death by Fallon, who would have been nine then. I've yet to show Fallon the photo of the four boys but when I do, I have no doubt he'll identify the "w" boy as his brother.

"Do you trust me?" I ask.

Still, Fallon doesn't turn to look at me but he says, "Of course I trust you."

"Will you tell me about it?"

Finally, Fallon turns in my arms and now it's my turn to provide comfort as I grip his hands and look deep into his frightened brown eyes. "It's okay," I tell him. I know the gist of what happened to Fallon and his parents but he's never once shared all the details and I've always respected his privacy.

I nod. "It's okay. I'm right here. It's just you and me."

He takes a deep breath and blows it out slowly. He takes another one and I wait patiently. This isn't easy for him.

He swallows. "We lived in a two-story brick house just over the state line in Virginia. Me, Mom, and Dad. They got pregnant with Wesley when they were in high school. They went on to open up a tiny toy store. Wesley was already grown and out of the house when they had me. I don't remember much about his visits, except I always knew he was coming because he drove the loudest car."

The day we were taken, there was a loud engine. Wesley must have been with Harley. Together they used Becka to lure us in.

"There was always a lot of yelling," Fallon continues. "Dad and Mom didn't like the people he was friends with. I do remember that. I also remember them telling him not to come back."

Fallon takes a second, looking down at our joined hands, his thumb gently caresses the top of my hand. And as he tells me the story, I create it in my mind. I'm no longer standing here in the yard with Fallon, I'm there in his child-hood home...

Turning, I look through the kitchen and into the back hallway to where the screen door sits. I see Wesley there, crouched on the outside, his knife sliding through the screen, his gloved hand coming through and curving up to unlock it. I see him standing in the kitchen, looking at his reflection in the microwave. He's tall and lean like Fallon but where Fallon's hair is blond, Wesley's hair is brown.

I follow Wesley's movements, walking from the kitchen and into the living room, going straight for the stairs. None of them creak as I ascend. I reach the top step and my nostrils flare with the coppery scent of blood that is about to come. I follow its scent right into the master bedroom.

Stains of red scream at me, from the walls to the bed, to the floor. I flinch, not from the sight but the sound.

I see Fallon's parents on the bed lying side-by-side, his father closest to the door. So much blood. Can two people bleed this much? I take a step closer and my brain constructs the gruesome scene as Fallon continues talking.

Wesley grabs their father's hair, yanking his head back and slicing his throat. Their mother wakes up screaming and he stabs her to shut her up.

He heads to Fallon's room but their mother follows, losing blood, trailing her hands along the walls. They fight in the hall, he stabs her a few more times and she dies.

Wesley goes in search of Fallon, opening doors, closing them. He knows Fallon is here. He knows Fallon is hiding.

Wesley enters the hall bathroom. With blue and white tile and a porcelain tub, the room's odd acoustics bounce every sound, like Fallon's expectant breath and the crunch of his hair against the tub where he's hiding. Like the eerie whistle his brother slowly seeps out.

My heart rate elevates. Fallon doesn't realize his brother has found him until he moves the shower curtain aside.

Fallon screams and Wesley smiles as he reaches in, grabbing him by the arm and dragging him out into the hall to look at their dead mother. Dragging him into the master bedroom to look at their dead father. My stomach clenches as Fallon's sobs fill my soul.

A chuckle resonates from Wesley's chest. "How does it feel to be the favorite now?" Then he rears back and hits Fallon. And hits him again. And again. And again.

Fallon cries, begging. Wesley pauses, laughing. Fallon uses the pause, ducking down and scrambling across the room, slipping in his parent's blood. The brother lunges and they are a tangle of arms and legs. Fallon catches him hard in the face with a bony elbow. He digs his nails into his face.

Wesley lets go and Fallon clambers over his mom's dead body, trying to get away. A towel wraps around Fallon's skinny neck and his body catches air as his brother yanks him back, choking him in a sick game. They slip on more blood, going down hard, and Fallon gets away.

But only because Wesley wants him to. He wants the chase.

Through the dark house, Fallon runs, flying down the stairs, rushing for the front door but Wesley catches him, slinging him back, and pummels him with his fists.

My brain fast forwards as Fallon's voice lowers, continuing to describe the horror, and now I see the family seated around the table. Their mom and dad both stabbed and slumped in chairs.

What should be a pleasant and homey scene is, in fact, grim. Wesley moved the bodies. He wanted his version of a family dinner.

Whistling those three horrible notes, he glides around the table, laying out cutlery.

Fallon's voice pulls at me as he continues talking softly and my heartbeat thumps heavy and steady. I see little Fallon, purple and swollen, sitting in his usual spot, staring at his parents and their deathly pallor.

Steam rises off a pizza that was left at the front door where Wesley had put cash for the delivery person to get.

I inhale, smelling the scent of sausage and cheese.

Wesley makes Fallon eat. Wesley eats, too. But Fallon isn't bound. It doesn't matter. He's too scared to move. The brother's jealous of Fallon and how much the parents adore him. He's making Fallon pay. He's making the parents pay.

Wesley savors his deed, flaunting it, but he lets his guard down and Fallon makes a move. He knows where his father keeps their gun.

Fallon retrieves it. He knows how to take off the safety.

How to cock it.

To fire...

Fallon's voice fades as he finishes talking and opening my eyes I focus on his face streaked with tears. Letting go of his hand I wipe under his eyes. "It's going to be okay. We're going to be okay. I found a picture that connects Harley, Erwin, Teagan, and a boy I now know is your brother. They all went to the same camp for troubled boys. They shared a similar dark interest."

"You were taken in the summer. I killed Wesley in the winter. He hurt you," Fallon whispers.

"And then he went on to hurt you. All four of those boys are dead now, deservedly. There is only one person left and that is whoever took the photo. Emerson Logging owns the property where we were tortured. Emerson Logging also owns Camp Desonk where the boys met and Harley later went on to kill his victims. Emerson Marion is the CEO of the logging company. He's also on the client list. I would lay a solid wager that whoever Emerson Marion is, he is also the person who took that photo."

Fallon sniffs, wiping his cheek on his shoulder.

I continue, "Vincent is a common thread with those four boys. Do you know that cabinet under his desk that he keeps locked?"

"Yes."

"I want to break into it. I want to see exactly what Vincent is hiding."

Fallon gives that some thought and his eyes go over my shoulder back to the house. "What are we going to do about your neck and what you threw up?"

But before I can answer, Uzzo pulls into our yard.

FORTY-NINE

I remain seated outside on the porch. After Uzzo pulls in, followed by the CSI van, Fallon wraps another blanket around me to keep me warm and slips moccasins on my feet.

"What are we going to find when we go out to the woods where you last saw Becka?" Uzzo asks me in this pained voice that says she'd rather be anywhere than here questioning me.

The only way she could know to ask that question is if she's either talked to Vincent or if Suzi told her. There's no way Suzi would have said anything. This is on Vincent.

"Well?" Uzzo prompts.

I search for an answer but end up shaking my head. The truth is, I'm not sure. I don't know if Vincent did indeed go out there last night. I don't know what he did or didn't find. He hasn't contacted me or Fallon. He's only contacted Detective Uzzo.

For a few seconds, she stares at me with a sad, yet stoic expression. But the sad is what I latch onto. She's thinking of what Vincent alluded to last night—that I'm involved with one, if not more, of the kills and that I did something to Becka.

The truth is, it's obvious that we had an altercation but I simply can't remember the details.

Uzzo waves a cop over. "Take her but wait for me for processing."

Leaning down, a cop grabs me under my right elbow and pulls me up. He starts to put cuffs on me and Uzzo shakes her head no. "She'll cooperate."

I nod to let the cop know that I will and with stiff legs I follow him over to the patrol car. The CSI team heads past me and into the house to collect evidence, much like I imagine they did at Suzi's home, which makes me wonder what they're going to find here. What was planted in my house and who planted it?

They're going to find what I threw up. That much is clear.

One of the younger cops looks at me with the same sad expression as Uzzo. Everyone thinks I did this. Hell, they may even think I'm the one who planted Suzi's home with the things they found there.

Fallon stands off to the side with Zane and we look at each other, holding a long gaze before the cop tugs my elbow and I'm marched the rest of the way to the patrol car. He opens the back door, his palm going to my head, and he tucks me into the back before closing the door.

Petal wanders out of the house, jumping up onto the porch rail to watch. Zane breaks away from Fallon and runs toward the patrol car, barking and whining, and looking right at me through the glass.

I watch in anguish as Fallon comes up behind him and

gently tugs him back. Again my eyes find Fallon's familiar brown ones and I see only love and support in them.

Uzzo turns away from me to walk the trail over to Suzi's home. But in that second it occurs to me, why would she be going to Suzi's home if Suzi has already left for the station?

FIFTY

A soft rap on the office door has me and Vincent glancing up from the round table and the chess match we've been silently playing for the past half hour. In the doorway stands a cautious and awkward teenage Fallon.

"Would you like to discuss why you've been standing there for fifteen minutes watching us?" Vincent asks.

This surprises me. I was so into the chess match, I didn't sense Fallon was there.

"I like that sort of thing," he quietly speaks. "Watching, observing."

Vincent smiles. "You're very much like Rachel when you do that."

Rachel...I sigh. I miss her.

Vincent makes a move on the board and carefully I eye it.

Fallon steps into the room. "I used to feel like there was this gap between you and me," Fallon says to Vincent. "But now I feel like we're becoming friends. Like you and Caroline are."

"Well, when people have intimate knowledge of each other, the gaps begin to fill in. It makes me sad though, that *you don't have more of a familial feel for myself and Caroline."*

Finally, I speak, addressing Vincent. "It's because you have more of an active interest in me."

This statement seems to take Vincent off guard and he looks again at Fallon. "Do you feel that way?"

"Yes, I think you put her on a pedestal."

"It is my goal to be a source of stability for both of you. It was never my intention to make one of you feel less." Vincent pushes back from the chess match and turns fully to face Fallon. "Communication works best with complete honesty—"

"Yet I don't sense complete honesty in either one of you," Fallon speaks. "I feel like I know only a version of each of you."

I don't have a response because he's right. He's so very right. "I'm complicated."

"And I'm lonely and damaged." Fallon takes one last step across the Oriental rug, coming to stand right beside our table. He doesn't look at Vincent. Fallon looks only at me when he says, "I see enough of you and I like you, Caroline."

A genuine smile creeps into my face and I glance over at Vincent to see him inscrutably studying us. Fallon and I both came here as patients under Vincent's care but Vincent and I have always shared a level of emotional intimacy that he's never had with Fallon. Yet Fallon and I share an under-standing and I don't think Vincent likes that very much.

"Fact is," Fallon says, still addressing me, "you're my best friend."

"And you're mine."

"Am I? Sometimes I wonder."

"Why would you say that?" Reaching out I take his hand, ignoring Vincent's stare. "Fallon, are you worried *about being alone? Are you worried I'm going to leave or something?"*

"Yes," he quietly admits. *"Rachel's gone and I don't want to be alone here."*

"I won't leave you, Fallon. I promise." I squeeze his hand. *"What can I do to make you feel better?"*

Fallon shifts, looking at Vincent. "I want you to give her some space. I feel like you're becoming obsessed with her." Fallon nods to the chessboard. "I feel like I'm in a live version of that game and that you have ulterior motives for us being here."

As I focus on that memory from when we were teenagers, I stand in my tank top and underwear under the bright lights of an evidence collection room. Looking back, I see it all now. Vincent carefully sharing things with me. Other things with Fallon. Constantly juggling, trying not to play favorites but everyone knew I was the favorite, if only because he was fascinated by me.

You put her on a pedestal.

Defensive moves, strategy, offensive moves—Fallon was right—we've been in a human version of chess since the day we arrived in Vincent and Rachel's home.

Vincent doesn't do anything without a motive. I've always known this and yet, somehow, I still trusted him. It's hard to let go of trust rooted in so many years. Or perhaps I've been brainwashed by his warped and twisted psychobabble.

Two female processors move around me, one from the FBI and the other a local officer. They bag my pajamas and the moccasins I tucked my feet into. They take my sister's necklace and place it in an evidence bag.

"Please be careful with that," I whisper. "It belonged to my sister."

With a nod, one of the collectors carefully combs my hair. Another jots notes on an official log. Pictures are taken of the bruising on my neck. I don't know either of their names and the whole thing is painfully awkward.

But I remain silent, shivering a bit, hoping this will be over soon so I can put some clothes on. One of the investigators lifts the edge of my tank top that I wore to bed and studies the hem. The other investigator asks me to step onto a white paper sheet and she scrapes my skin in various locations.

I took a quick shower before bed so they're not likely to find much. But as I think this, she lifts my fingernails and scrapes under them as well. Dull red residue flakes out, falling onto the white paper I'm standing on. It didn't look red under my nails. She doesn't glance up at me but we both know what those red particles most likely are.

Blood, not dirt, blood.

"I can't do this," the local investigator says, stopping for a moment to lean back on her heels. She looks up at me, clearly struggling with the situation. "It's like I'm in some odd *Twilight Zone* episode."

I stare back, unsure where this is headed.

"I was working in the ER all those years ago when you walked out from the woods. I tended to your injuries. I'm sure you don't remember. You were just a little girl."

I remain silent, too numb to speak. I study the features of her pretty round face but she's right, I don't remember.

"We both know what I'm finding under your nails," she says and I nod, because yes, I do know what she's finding under my nails.

"How did it get there?" She asks.

"I'm not certain."

"I didn't want to find anything on you." She glances

down at the red flakes. "But there it is." She looks back up at me. "We all know they use you around here to solve crimes they can't."

The FBI lady clears her throat, signaling we're not supposed to be talking. The door opens then and Detective Uzzo steps in. She takes a second to survey the scene before nodding for the two investigators to continue. Closing the door, she leans up against it, folding her arms. "Vincent told me you've been sleepwalking. When were you planning on telling me that?"

Pressing my lips together, I glance down at the red flakes.

"You knew your state of mind. It's one thing for you to help profile but to completely lose yourself in it? It was irresponsible to push beyond your limits. Do I need to remind you just three short months ago you had a nervous breakdown? You should've told me it was getting too much for you."

I want to be angry but Uzzo's right, I leaned too far over the edge and now I hate this and me. I don't want to face whatever it is they find. It's my job to interpret a scene and what I'm interpreting right now is not good.

My brain wants one thing but my intelligence says another. The clump of light brown hair I threw up. The flakes of blood. The bruising. I was the last person to see Becka. The horrible realization of it all settles in.

I killed Becka and then I must have taken a bite, if not more than that. The thought has fresh bile climbing my throat. Did I kill her in self-defense? I don't know.

Three short months ago. Uzzo's words replay. I had a nervous breakdown. I moved in with Fallon. And unbeknownst to me, that's when the first girl went missing, the one who was eventually found in the mushroom patch and who Becka admitted to stabbing.

My thoughts trail back to when I saw the decomposed body in the morgue. I remember the vision and how Harley stepped in, roughly pushing Becka aside, followed by the entrance of a familiar evil. I knew that evil. It was there in the woods with me all those years ago.

At the time, all of that was muddled with the knowledge I didn't have. But now, piecing it all together. The eerie whistle that I now know was Wesley. The repetitive cadence of *Hold still. Still...* that belonged to Harley. The scratching of the beard that was Teagan. The sometimes-raspy voice that Erwin imitated. Which one had that raspy voice though?

Erwin wasn't there but he knew who was. Vincent knew Erwin knew who was. He needed to shut Erwin up. The plan. Reel me back in, yes, play with my mind but also shut Erwin up. Vincent accomplished both.

Because Vincent is covering for one last person. The person I believe took the photo and perhaps the one, too, with the raspy voice—Emerson Marion.

FIFTY-ONE

Dressed in white jogging pants and a white hoodie, I sit in Detective Uzzo's office with Vincent seated on one side of me and Fallon the other. I haven't seen Vincent since last night. I have no clue what he found when he went looking for Becka. I don't know anything. I was led in here to Uzzo's office and Vincent was already here, waiting with Fallon. If I was anyone else, I'd be in an interrogation room right now.

I don't want Vincent here but I'll tolerate his presence because there's nothing I can do about it. I'm not calling the shots.

Uzzo surprises me by looking first at Fallon as she holds up the photo of the four boys that I gave her. She taps the one I now know is Fallon's brother. "Do you recognize that boy?"

"Yes, he was my brother," Fallon confirms.

Uzzo nods. "Three of these boys are confirmed dead and one, Teagan Ray, was reported missing six years ago. All four of these boys are linked to the kill list we decrypted from Harley's files. H-E-T-W. It's our working theory they had some sort of twisted pact with a fifth person. A person who likely took this photo and wasn't involved with the kills but liked to watch."

My gaze slides over to Vincent. "A person who liked to control. To direct. To manipulate... Unless the 'e' represents Emerson Marion and not Erwin. Because from the start I got the impression Erwin was on the outside, desperately wanting in. The 'e' on the kill list occurs sporadically. So yes, Emerson likes to watch but occasionally participates. He has to keep that skill set tuned as well."

It happens so quickly that I'm not sure I see it in Vincent's eyes—calculated darkness so evil that it reaches across the small space and chokes me.

A hot haze builds in my head and tiny bumps spread over my skin. The urge to move away from this man who raised me riots inside of me. But some unseen force weighs me down and I find myself unable to move.

In my periphery, I see Uzzo making notes and as she does, a pounding starts in my chest and rolls down my arms to buzz my fingertips. It fills my ears in a thrashing white-wash of sound. Emerson Marion took the photo. He knew all four boys. Erwin wasn't the "e". Emerson was.

A person who likes to control, direct, manipulate. Likes to watch but occasionally participates. Emerson Marion, the CEO of Emerson Logging. The owner of the property where Annabelle and I were tortured. The owner of Camp Desonk.

Vincent's head cocks a bit as he stares back at me, his gaze full of calm concern and controlled curiosity. Gone is the evil I sensed and now I'm not sure if I did feel it or if I'm having another one of my episodes.

Fallon's fingers slide over to press into my knee and

Vincent moves only his eyes as he glances down to the comforting gesture.

Chess.

I'm in a human version of the game and this is not my move. I need to keep silent and see what's next. What else does Uzzo want to say and how will Vincent respond to it? What did Uzzo find at my house? What did she find on my body?

She shuffles some papers, pulling out next a photo of the rug taken from Harley's home. "The kill list, coupled with the evidence taken in and around Camp Desonk and this rug, has permitted us to make connections we were struggling with. At this point, there is only one sample we've yet to make a DNA match on. It was found at the camp, not in the rug." She holds up a photo of shiny black hair. "It belongs to an African American female. We know that much."

I stare at that photo and something sour clenches through my stomach. "Harley didn't want the female's name on the kill list. He was scared to put her hair in the rug. She held significance to someone."

Those words and their implication slam into me hard. The unknown African American female held significance.

Rachel.

So, Harley killed Rachel to what? Show he was smarter than Vincent? To show dominance? Were they playing their own twisted game of chess?

She didn't leave because of me. Harley took her and then he killed her.

I glance over to Vincent but I don't see the surprise I expected. He already knew.

Uzzo makes some more notes and while she does,

Vincent speaks, "I think it's important for us to maintain focus. You brought us in here for a reason?"

Uzzo doesn't respond, simply shuffles some more papers before lifting her gaze to look at me. "We analyzed what you threw up and the blood that we scraped from under your nails." Uzzo's gaze stays steady on mine. "It does match Becka Laine."

My eyes close. I knew it.

"We can't know for sure about the bruising on your neck but the angle of the marks indicate the person who left them, presumably Becka, was on top of you," Uzzo says.

"So Becka was attacking Caroline," Fallon clarifies. "Which means Caroline defended herself."

Uzzo nods. "It's our working theory. But we need to know where the body is."

A long beat of silence goes by, filled only by the quiet stress in the room. Like I've been doing for the past several hours, I search the crevice and cracks of my brain but nothing comes to me.

Fallon jabs an accusing finger at Vincent. "This is your fault. *Yours.* You knew she was breaking but you kept right on pushing because she was 'saving lives.' Look me in the eyes and tell me any different. I told you to stop using her."

"Not even I realized the extent of her mental state," Vincent quietly says but the words are staged. He's been waiting to say them.

Fallon explodes. "Bullshit! It's your job to know that!"

Reaching over, I touch his arm, offering silent comfort. He needs to calm down. Uzzo will kick him out of the room and I need him here.

Fallon's fingers dig into the leather armrests, his knuckles popping white, and his jaw tightens with the urge to scream. When we were kids, he would do that when the stress got too great and he needed to let out his frustration and sadness. He would scream. I always envied that scream because he seemed so different after. Renewed. Ready to begin again. I'm afraid if I were to scream right now, I wouldn't be able to stop.

Across the desk, Detective Uzzo pinches the bridge of her nose and shakes her head but she doesn't speak. Instead, she looks at Vincent, who glances away.

With a sigh, Uzzo opens a folder and slides out a photograph. "I sent a team to the tracks and the woods where you took Becka and this is what they found." She turns over the photo.

It's a picture of the tree with the memorial for me and Annabelle. It's where I last stood with Becka. Yellow tabs mark the surrounding area, identifying a few sprays of blood. It's not a huge amount but it's enough. Vincent went out looking for Becka. Maybe he found her body and cleaned up. Maybe these few sprays of blood are simply tiny areas he overlooked. It's not the first time he's cleaned up a dead body. He knows what he's doing.

But as I stare at the photo, my brain desperately searches for a way Becka can be alive.

"I was so confident that I could help you," Vincent mumbles, and his words cling heavily in the air.

I ignore him, looking back at Uzzo. "I can't confess to something I don't remember." Yet as I say those words my thoughts trail off, realizing how spot on I am. If I did kill someone, I wasn't in a frame of mind to remember. Everything was, and still is, fuzzy. It always is when I've been sleepwalking.

Because of the herbs.

My gaze swerves over to Vincent. He's been giving me those herbs since the moment I began helping with this case. It wasn't just to make me more dependent on him. He's been manipulating my mind, my memories. Saying he thought he could help me. The sleepwalking. Mentioning my mental state. He's been setting me up to take the fall and at the same time working on my defense. He wants me going down for this so I'm locked away in a Psych Ward where only he has access to me.

"There's more," Uzzo says and my gaze moves from Vincent back to the detective. "We found your jewelry."

"My jewelry? You mean the bracelets I make?" The bracelets Rachel taught me how to make. "Okay. And?"

"We found human hair woven into the threads. Hair that matches Harley and the two girls done after his death—Nadia and Gaby."

Those words reel through my mind and I shake my head. "Now you're saying I'm a serial killer taking trophies? So let me see, I got so far inside of Harley's head that I began to mirror his actions after I killed him in that garage?" My words die off as Becka's questions filter in. *What's your alibi, Caroline?*

Uzzo props her arms on her desk, drawing my attention back to her. "My biggest fear is learning you knew what you were doing all along."

"*That* is your biggest worry?" I slide up in my chair. "I should think your biggest worry is confirming Emerson Marion's real identity. Because I'm being framed. As is Suzi. Which, by the way, where is she? I thought I would see her when I got here."

"Becka's missing and likely dead, Caroline, and the evidence of that is all over you, as is Harley, Nadia, and

Gaby." Detective Uzzo pushes back from her desk to stand. "And for your information, Suzi never showed up."

"Are you saying she's missing?"

"I don't know what I'm saying but I do know her car is still in her garage and she is nowhere to be found." Uzzo raises both slim gray brows. "Care to respond to that?"

No, I don't. The fact is, I'm screwed.

FIFTY-TWO

FBI Agent Tanaka calls Detective Uzzo out and the minute she's gone, I look right at Fallon. "Could I have killed Becka and not known it?"

Fallon takes a second, studying me like he's trying to figure out how to respond. "I honestly don't know, Caroline. Maybe it's for the best that you've been sleepwalking. It will work in your favor."

"Fallon's right," Vincent says. "We need to start thinking of what to say, hints to drop, carefully timed comments. We need to establish your mental fragility. Luckily, your history already leans toward this."

I want to turn and confront Vincent with everything—Becka, the herbs, the boys in the photo, Rachel, Emerson Marion, Suzi, and about a million more things—but I don't and instead, I keep looking at Fallon. He's my safe spot. Suzi told me to find a light and colorful place to focus on and Fallon is it.

Something in his expression shifts. It's slight and if I didn't know his face so well I wouldn't see it. He doesn't think I did this. He's saying what he thinks Vincent wants to hear.

Smart.

I turn away, looking at Vincent. The air between us stretches with tension and I welcome it. "You fed me those herbs knowing how I respond to them. There is no way I killed Nadia and Gaby. If it had been just Becka, I might believe I got so far into the killer's head that I couldn't find my way back out. But it wasn't just one murder and I know who I am."

"I had to do something to cover for you."

"You are such a good liar that I don't know if you think I did this or if it's one of your elaborate plans."

"Why would I have an elaborate plan?"

"Because you're mad I left. You're jealous of my relationship with Fallon and Suzi. You lost complete control of Becka to the point where, according to Uzzo, she attacked me. And you're obsessed with me."

"It saddens me that you feel this way."

I shake my head. "No, I know who I am. I didn't do this."

"You know who you are at this moment," Vincent says. "But that isn't always the case, is it? You've always been intrigued by murder, almost as if they are inspirations to you becoming someone else."

"An interest you cultivated," Fallon snaps.

"*You* want me to be someone else, don't you? You want me to be that girl who stabbed Teagan. I never was though, was I? Is that why you took Becka in? Was I not quite turning into the psychopath you wanted? Oh, she is though, isn't she? Or rather, wasn't she?"

Vincent shifts in his seat to fully face me. "Are you a

killer, Caroline? Right now. This young woman sitting beside me. Is this who you are?"

I shift to fully face him, too. "You kept our secrets. All these years. You made Fallon keep secrets about me. You made me keep secrets about him. You're quite the puppet master, aren't you? Treating us, brainwashing us into doing your bidding? Erwin, the other boys, us. Wind us all up and watch us go." A scoff scrapes up my throat. "Is that fun for you? Do you get off on that?"

Vincent doesn't respond, just keeps his gaze level on mine. I give the space a second, waiting to see if that evil from before makes another appearance but it doesn't. He's got the same focused demeanor as always.

Uzzo opens the door, her gaze moving over all three of us. "Everything okay?"

No one responds. I want so much to tell Uzzo everything—all my secrets, Fallon's, and most importantly Vincent's, but the more I talk, the more unstable I will seem. The only thing I can tell her and provide evidence on is that I killed Teagan Ray. I mean, at this point, one more murder on my record probably won't make a difference.

Uzzo looks at Vincent. "I need to see you."

With a nod, Vincent gets up and Uzzo quickly follows with, "Fallon, step outside until we come back."

Fallon gives my hand a reassuring squeeze before following them out and closing me alone inside.

Several minutes roll by as I stare at the closed file on Uzzo's desk that contains the evidence quickly mounting against me. I stare at it and my mind whirls. I need to get out of here. I'm seconds away from being charged with murder and I didn't do this. I can't accept Becka is dead. I won't accept I killed her, even in self-defense. I need to see the body.

And I'm sure as hell not accepting I did Harley, Nadia, and Gaby.

The only way I'm leaving is if I get up and walk out. There is only one way out of this office—behind me and into the main hallway. Other than Fallon, I have no clue who else is in the hallway right now. It could be crawling with the FBI.

Or it could be empty.

Sliding out of my chair, I cross Uzzo's office to her coat rack, taking her blue trench and dark beanie. I tiptoe over to the door and inch it open. From his spot leaning against the wall beside the door, Fallon glances over his shoulder at me. I don't say a word and neither does he. He knows what I'm thinking.

Reverse the situation and I would put myself in danger to help him. There is no question of that.

His warm brown gaze leaves mine as he glances up and down the hall, then he slips my car keys from his jacket pocket and slides them to me. He pushes off the wall and taking the door, he opens it wide, blocking the view as I scoot out and along the wall to the exit door at the end.

These are not the actions of an innocent person.

Those are the words that go through my brain as I push through the exit door and run for my car.

FIFTY-THREE

Through the dusk I go, my foot on the pedal of the Mini Cooper, blazing through the mountain town. Its lights dim as I move onto the highway that winds back through the country. Up ahead lies the setting sun.

As I drive, I allow my thoughts to wander as they may. In the shadows of my mind, I see the first girl, Irene, laying on the bed in her dorm, everything washed in dark strokes. In the corner of the room, movement draws my attention. A distinct shape shifts forward, prowling toward the body. I study that shape. It's a person but I can't make out male or female, young or old.

Next, I see Yasmine, the girl lying in the park, again everything painted in shadows. From across the park, the dark shape lurks forward, an inhuman silhouette, slowly taking shape. I try to see it but it shifts and blurs.

Then I see Harley, his body mutilated on the garage floor, his organs lying in a glistening lump. And Gaby, the girl from the motel, done with a similar skilled hand of whoever did Irene, Yasmine, and Harley. Though Harley's death had a different motivation, different aggression to it.

Again though, everything is washed in shades of dark gray. The first two killed before Harley died and Gaby after. Then there's Nadia, the girl in chains, made to look like The Organ Ripper had done it.

The shadows shift and merge, morphing into a black figure that rises in the dark, taking the shape of Vincent but as quickly as it is there, it's also gone. His words float through my thoughts. *You catch these killers by getting into their heads but you also let them into yours.*

No, Vincent is the one who is too far in my head. He's always been too far in my head.

The dream I had of me chasing Becka flashes through my mind. Her body hasn't been found, just the clump of hair I threw up. If I were really in the reigning Organ Ripper's frame of mind, why didn't I eat more? The thought makes my stomach pitch and I dry heave. I don't know how her hair was in my stomach unless I was chasing her and grabbed her hair but then why would I have put it into my mouth?

Did I bite her in self-defense?

I accused her of planting the bodies of Irene and Yasmine so we would follow the trail to Harley. I accused her of killing Harley and taking over his legacy. Logic tells me she was in the hospital when all of this happened but the hospital is a perfect alibi. It's not a prison. She can come and go. The question is, how far inside of her head did Vincent get?

The road to his home sits just up ahead and I downshift to turn. It doesn't take me but a few moments to weave my way up the long driveway to his home. To what used to be my home. I pull through the gate, circle around the fountain, and park.

I know the code to his security and I still have a key to

the front door. I'm through and into his office without an issue.

Crossing over the Oriental rug, I weave behind his large desk and look down at his locked filed cabinet. It's the first time I've ever stepped behind his desk.

The cabinet contains a digital keypad and I think for a few seconds. It would be something significant. His birthday. Rachel's birthday. Their wedding date. Fallon's birthday. Mine.

I try several combinations, none of which work. I sit back for a second and my gaze roams over his many bookshelves, the framed photos, and the items he's collected from his travels. An odd sensation crawls along my skin. With a shaky finger, I reach forward again, this time typing in the date I was found.

The keypad beeps and the cabinet releases.

Son of a bitch.

I slide the cabinet open, expecting to find files but instead I find various things: a small recorder, tapes, a memo pad, a photo album, and a wooden box about the size of a small jewelry box. Nothing is labeled. I grab the album first and flip it open.

The first picture is of a couple with a small boy. Beneath the photo in neat print is written *Dad, Mom,* and *Vincent.* He said his parents died when he was a boy, which is when he entered foster care. Vincent looks to be around eight or so. None of their faces hold happy expressions and the father looks quite angry.

Next, I find a certificate of ownership for one Emerson Marion of Emerson Logging. Emerson Marion, the person I believe took the photo of the four boys. The "e" on the kill list. A person who likes to watch but occasionally participate. Emerson Marion, the owner of the property where we were tortured.

How is it that he has this? Is this proof that Vincent and Emerson Marion are the same?

Those puzzle pieces in my mind twist and turn, wanting to lock together, but at the same time refusing to.

I flip to the next photo. It's of the four boys, their arms around each other, grinning over the mutilated corpse of a dog. As always, Erwin hovers on the cusp, not quite belonging but still there.

Bile rises my throat but I make myself flip to the next.

This one is of a group of boys taken at Camp Desonk in a posed photo. Ten or so dressed in shorts and tees with the camp counselors standing behind them, one on each side. My gaze quickly finds Harley, Teagan, Erwin, and Wesley. I don't recognize any of the other teenage boys. But I do recognize the camp counselors—Vincent and Rachel.

Rachel. Our words from so long ago come back to me...

"How long have you and Vincent known each other?" I ask.

"Oh forever. We volunteered at a youth program many, many years ago."

This is where they must have met. Camp Desonk for troubled boys. Did Rachel know that three of these boys went on to torture me? No, I'm sure not. Vincent kept her in the dark just like everyone else.

If only she could have looked into the future, she would have known to avoid Harley. He killed her in the same spot where she once tried to help him.

But this is proof of how Vincent came to know the boys. They all shared the same sick proclivities and he took an interest.

In the margin are a few notes. I recognize Vincent's writing.

H is most interested in the taste. W is violent and enjoys torture. T likes to wear a hood. E has begun a ritual called "showing gratitude" by re-healing wounds with honey and charcoal and decorating the bodies with flowers. Of the four, E intrigues me the most.

E intrigues him the most? Not what I expected.

I flip to another photo, this one of Harley dressed in a chef's uniform. In the margin, the note: *H on his graduation day from culinary school. Thanks to my guidance he has turned his specific tastes into a successful business. I am proud to be a client and consider him a great success.*

My throat involuntarily closes. *...proud to be a client.*

The next photo is one of me when I first arrived here. The note: *I am mesmerized by C. Even at five she was reading well beyond her years and has developed a curious ability to mirror others.*

Reaching down into the cabinet, I get the tape recorder. There's a tape already in it and I press play. There's a long pause and my heart suspends beating, waiting. I'm about to press the STOP button when my father's voice fills the room.

"Thank you for inviting me to your office," Dad says, his voice low, sad. I catch and hold my breath.

"Yes, well, I've thought a lot about you two since first meeting Caroline in the ER six months ago."

Dad sighs. "I don't have anyone to talk to."

"You do now."

My heart lurches from suspension to full-on thunder and with a shaky finger, I press the FAST FORWARD button.

"She's withdrawn. Quiet. Doesn't sleep. Has episodes

of violence." Dad's voice cracks. "I don't know what to do. And the worst part is, I want to give up. Is that wrong?"

"No, it's normal. And...it's okay to give up. Your wife did and it's okay for you, also. No one will think less."

"Who will take care of Caroline?"

A long pause, then in a soft and deep voice, "Know that I will."

His tone festers and spreads in the space around me. I jab my finger on the FAST FORWARD button. Vincent speaks, "Caroline is now ours."

A stabbing pain pierces my skull and I ignore it as I fast forward. "T's conscience is moving in. He's slipping from my control. It's time that he's gone and I have a plan that will also bring closure to Caroline's demons as well."

Fury explodes deep in my chest and with a scream, I throw the recorder across the room. It hits the wall and shatters and Vincent's voice slurs and warps before finally coming to a stop.

My fingers dig into my scalp and I yank hard, relishing the strands of hair pulling against my skin. I breathe. In. Out. In.

My father committed suicide because of Vincent. Not because of me.

I make myself reach back into the cabinet, snatching up the memo pad and ripping it open.

An entry dated some fifteen years ago: *H had a daughter and named her after his first human kill. The mother died during childbirth. Quite sad. She's a cute little girl. Being around her makes me want one for myself.*

Another dated four years ago: *She wants to come back but I told her no. She walked out and she needs to live with that decision. It's in the best interest of all, especially C.*

Rachel wanted to come back? Even after what I did, she wanted to come back but Vincent wouldn't let her.

Another note, this one three months ago: *C had a nervous breakdown. I fear I pushed her beyond her limits. She has moved in with F and has bonded with the neighbor. I want C back. I've devised a plan.*

White light flashes behind my eyes and my vision blurs to red. I squeeze my eyes shut and a whimper vibrates up my throat and out my lips.

Blindly I reach down into the cabinet and grab the wood box. I place it on Vincent's desk, flip the tiny metal latch, and wedge open the lid.

A photo of the dilapidated house where we were kept is the first thing I see. A handwritten note paper-clipped to it reads: *I struggle with how to handle what they've done. Why did they keep this from me? Did they not think I would understand?*

The screams of Annabelle rebound through my head in a muffled echo, as if soundproofed with cotton. Erwin was part of it, too. How could I have been so wrong about him? All four of them tortured me and my sister and the other girl.

The other girl...my gaze latches onto the next item—a swatch of red hair tied with twine and attached to it is a rolled-up piece of parchment. With unsteady fingers, I unroll the starchy paper to read the single word: *Natalie.*

The name clouds and distorts and several tears plop heavily onto the paper. A debilitating ache knifes through my heart and with a cringe, I press my palm to my chest. Natalie was her name. Natalie.

Closing my eyes, I take a second and when I'm ready, I pick up the next item—a swatch of Annabelle's sundress.

"No," I moan, clutching it to my breast, rocking it as if the torn fabric was a baby.

Her laugher fills the air from that day we raced toward the tracks and her smile as she looked back at me. The way she used to roll her eyes when I would dance. How she would shove handfuls of marshmallows into her mouth and try to talk.

"Oh, Annabelle," I whisper. "I miss you so much."

With a shaky breath, I open my eyes and I recoil at what I see next. They took photos of our torture.

My gaze freezes on a picture of my face twisted in undiluted panic and pain. I'm no longer here in this office, I'm back there.

Me.

Annabelle.

Natalie.

A raspy voice.

The smell of cooking skin.

Screams.

Hold still, still.

Those three eerie notes.

Violently, I shake my head. "No-no-no-no-no."

"I'm here," a voice says, simple and quiet, and the calmness of it touches the deepest corner of my soul.

I look up and I see them both—Annabelle and Natalie—on the other side of the desk, holding hands and staring at me. They are healthy and beautiful little girls.

My heart beats fast, pulsating every nerve in my body and the air around me. My sister nods down to the box where the grisly photos have been turned over and an old school paper sits visible. It belonged to Annabelle, where she practiced her printing. Above the i's are the stars versus the dots.

Vincent must have gotten this from my family home before it sold. He wrote that letter I found in my house. It wasn't me, it was him. He knew how to copy my sister's style. I'm sure it was Vincent who called me that night, too, imitating Annabelle, making me believe my sister might still be alive.

The last item glints in the overhead light and carefully I pick it up. It's my necklace, and like everything else, there's a tiny note attached: *E confessed to everything. Sadly, A didn't make it but C did. I promised E and I'll try my best.*

I read and re-read those lines, trying to make sense of it. He promised Erwin what?

Carefully, I put everything back in the box and I look across the desk at where now only Annabelle stands. Not Natalie. She smiles and the warmth and sweetness of it wash through me.

"I love you," I tell her but when next I blink, she is gone and somehow I know this is the last time I'll ever see her. I search the recesses of my heart for the regret, guilt, and horror that's always there surrounding my thoughts of Annabelle. But instead, there's love and loss and I know without a doubt what I have to do for final peace.

I clip the necklace around my neck and I grab everything for evidence. I race into the kitchen and slide a knife from the rack. And as I run to my car, I dial Fallon. He doesn't pick up. "Fallon, listen to me. Stay away from Vincent. He is more involved in this than either of us realized. I have the proof right here in my car of so much stuff. Suzi's missing and I think Vincent took her to the house in the woods. I'm headed there now. Tell Uzzo."

FIFTY-FOUR

I drive like a demon through the night, whipping in and out of traffic and passing in the right shoulder lane. More than one honk trails my wake and I ignore it all as I swerve through vehicles.

I voice-text Uzzo the same information I told Fallon. As I do, I nearly rear-end someone and yank my wheel just in time. The interstate gives way to my exit, traffic thins, and I open my car to full speed as I race out into the country.

Eventually, I near my turnoff and I downshift, cutting off onto the gravel road that leads to the woods and my destination—the deserted house where we were tortured.

Overgrown weeds scrape the sides of the car and I flick on my dimmer lights to navigate. Gravel gives way to dirt and both spit under my tires, rattling off the underbody.

I downshift again, my tires rolling over the rough-cut path. It's been six years since I've been here and killed Teagan Ray.

With a deep breath, I round the last bend, and a downed tree blocks my path. I stop my car, its engine still purring, and I stare through the windshield at the tree and the path beyond. I'll go the rest of the way on foot.

Killing the engine, I grab a flashlight from the glovebox and the knife I took from Vincent's kitchen and I step out into the darkness. The trees and bushes form dark lumps and I navigate in and around them, heading in the direction of the house. From here, I think it sits about a hundred yards in.

It takes me several minutes to cover the distance and as I draw near, a soft glow permeates the woods. I kill my flashlight, take a few more steps, and I crouch down, surveying the glow.

Overhead through the winter trees, the clouds shift and the moon shines down to illuminate the dilapidated one-story structure. Screams of long ago fill the air and I resist the urge to cover my ears.

Within the house, a shadow shifts, like a flame flickering. I creep closer, coming down behind a tree, staring hard at the soft glow seeping from the window. I wait to see the shadow flicker again but nothing happens.

I scuttle forward, my fingers digging into the handle of the butcher knife, and I come down behind another tree. I lean around it, searching the area. With the darkness and the angles, I can't tell for sure but things seem empty. Yet the soft glow inside means someone is here or was here.

I wait for several minutes, my senses tuned, but still detect nothing. Staying low, I move from the safety of the tree and over to the window. I lift and peer in, shocked to see Becka sitting in an old chair with her wrists tied to the armrests.

Blood trails down the side of her face and the memory slams into me.

Becka knocks me onto my back, lording over me, the

knife poised and ready. She bares her teeth, coming at me. I knock the knife away. We struggle. But she's fast, pinning me to the ground. Her fingers wrap around my neck, digging in. I stare up at her, her cheek a mere inch from my mouth, her light brown hair stuck to it. I open my jaw wide and I bite hard, coming away with a bit of skin but more hair than anything. She headbutts me and the part that I bit slides unwanted down my throat.

The same chunk of hair I threw up.

Vincent must have seen our fight. He must have watched me run off and brought Becka here. But where is Suzi?

In a numb haze, I make my way across the frozen ground toward the front door. The last time I was here, I didn't go inside. Turning, I look at the rusted fire pit and the tree where I stood, where I dug up Annabelle's bones, where I stabbed Teagan Ray.

Beyond the tree, deep in the woods, lies his grave. A grave Vincent helped me dig.

An eerie thought settles through me. What other graves are back there?

Grasping the peridotite necklace around my neck, I turn back to the door. "My name is Caroline Christianson and I am alive." I let go of the necklace and, with the butcher knife gripped in my left hand, I use my right to turn the rusted knob. The door creaks inward.

Everything I am traces back to this horrid place.

Straight ahead and down the steps sits the small basement where they kept us. I see it now...

The basement door opens and my eyelids flutter. I try to open them all the way but I'm too weak. Through my lashes, I see Vincent. He stands for a few seconds staring down. The air around me shifts as he comes into the basement, picks us both up, and carries us up the stairs and lays us side by side on the dirty floor.

He takes a few seconds to look at us, then with a sigh, he says, "What were you thinking?"

"I'm sorry," Another voice, this one quiet, remorseful.

"I thought you were past this," Vincent says.

"It's all Harley's fault. He's the one who took them. For Becka. But then Wesley got involved and then Teagan, and—"

"You're better than them. You should've set an example."

"I know," the voice murmurs.

"Which one were you telling me about?" Vincent asks.

"That one. Caroline is her name." The other person shifts. "What are we going to do?"

Vincent takes in a breath. "Finish this one and I'll figure out what to do with this one."

"I-I can't kill her," the other person mumbles. "There's barely anything left of her. Just let her die."

"Yes, you can kill her, Emerson, and you will. Put her out of her misery. If you want me to help you cover this up, then you will."

"Promise?"

"Yes." Leaning down, Vincent takes a few seconds to put a necklace on me. "There, now you'll have something of hers." The other he slides into his pocket.

I look straight into Annabelle's wide unblinking gaze. But she's alive. I see her soul way in the depths.

"Pick her up," Vincent says. "Follow me."

The other person carefully picks up Annabelle. I see only their feet as they disappear out the back door.

It opens, closes, and footsteps recede.

My arms shake violently as I push up, the whole time

staring at the back door. I need to go get help. If I don't go now, I'll never make it.

Air sucks from my lungs as I emerge from the memory. *E confessed to everything. Sadly, A didn't make it but C did.*

E is Emerson, not Erwin. Emerson Marion, whose name is on the title to this property and Camp DeSonk, as well. Emerson is not an alias for Vincent.

I promised E and I'll try my best.

Promised to cover it up.

E has begun a ritual called "showing gratitude" by re-healing wounds with honey and charcoal and decorating the bodies with flowers. Of the four, E intrigues me the most.

Emerson, not Erwin.

They didn't expect to come back and find me gone. But I was. I found my way to the road. I stumbled out from the trees and that woman who was driving by saw me. Vincent then tracked me to the ER. He cemented himself into the lives of me and my dad. He manipulated my father. He arranged to take me in.

My body sways a bit off-balance. Details come back to me in vivid strength. Wesley was the one who tried to force-feed each of us the other and we refused. I didn't consume Annabelle. Vincent let me believe that I did. My sister is dead but it's not because of me. Emerson finished her life.

Emerson.

Those cogs in my brain click, latching on.

Lifting my foot, I step over the threshold. *Hold still. Still. It'll all be over in a second. Second.* "My name is Caroline Christianson. I am okay."

FIFTY-FIVE

Over to the left sits Becka next to the lantern glowing in the corner. I tell my feet to move and they shuffle sideways, inch by inch. The three-note whistle echoes through my thoughts and my heart picks up pace.

I mouth, "My name is Caroline Christianson. I'm alive. I'm okay."

I don't allow myself to look anywhere but at Becka as I come down in front of her. The doll she was working on earlier sits in her lap and the messenger bag over in the corner.

"Becka?" I'm about to press my fingers to her neck to check for a pulse when she lifts her head and looks right at me. The movement is so unexpected and sudden that I have to grip the chair to stay upright.

A board creaks and gripping my knife, I slowly get to my feet. My gaze trains on the shadows in the back corner and once again I whisper, "My name is Caroline Christianson. I'm okay. I'm okay."

The shadow shifts and I brace myself, ready to lunge

when Rachel steps into view. My first inclination is to run to her, to hug her, but I don't.

A darkness that's never been there before stretches between us and smothers the room. She's showing me her true self.

Everything in me seizes.

Strands of her hair were found at Camp DeSonk. But Harley didn't kill her. Her hair was found because she was there, watching. Sometimes participating.

Her dark eyes go down to the knife gripped in my fist. "Careful with that. We both know what you're capable of."

A few seconds go by and we simply stare at each other, not blinking, not breathing, and my mind races with memories long past...

In the back yard, I stand watching Fallon and Zane play catch. A sensation claws my neck that I'm being watched. I glance over my shoulder and up to the master bedroom where Rachel stands, staring down. I smile a little and wave but she doesn't return the gesture.

Later after dinner, I overhear her and Vincent in his office. "You're hesitant around her," Vincent says. "She's picking up on it."

"You're the one who made me take her," Rachel whispers. "I'm trying my best."

With a gasp, I come from the memory. "You didn't want me. Vincent did."

"You were my therapy. Raising you was penance for what I participated in."

Oh, my God. No. "Emerson?" I whisper.

"Emerson Rachel Marion," she rasps. "My maiden name."

The rasp claws through me and I have to fight to stay

focused. "Suzi's missing. Where is she? She's got nothing to do with this."

Her lips twitch and I hate that she's amused by me. "I don't know. I couldn't care less about your neighbor. Vincent cares though. He cares about everyone but me. Correction, he cares about you. He *used* to care about me."

My legs tremble and I tighten my thigh muscles to keep myself in place. Rachel is obsessed with Vincent and Vincent is obsessed with me. What a disgusting triangle.

I turn to Becka and her gaze slides to the knife gripped in my fist. She wants me to kill Rachel.

I should kill them both.

I back away from Becka, unsettled with the thought I just had. I don't know what Rachel has in mind but whatever it is, it involves me dying and probably Becka, too.

From her back pocket, Rachel pulls out an iPhone, and my stomach drops. That's Fallon's. She touches her finger to the screen and my voice fills the air, "Fallon, listen to me. Stay away from Vincent. He is more involved in this than either of us realized. I have the proof right here in my car of so much stuff. Suzi's missing and I think Vincent took her to the house in the woods. I'm headed there now. Tell Uzzo."

Sliding the phone back into her pocket, Rachel says, "Unfortunately Fallon never got the opportunity to tell Detective Uzzo."

For several horror-filled seconds, I think she means that Fallon is dead. But she disappears into the shadows and with measured and slow steps, she reappears dragging a tied and gagged Fallon across the dirty floor.

I suck in a cry, taking a step forward and Rachel holds up a finger. "He's fine. And he will stay fine. Fallon was, and still is, my favorite. I won't hurt him. But I also can't have him in the way."

Fallon's frightened, yet angry, gaze latches onto mine and it's the anger that I grab hold of. Anger's good.

He nods to let me know he's okay and I nod back. With a grunt, Rachel props him up against the wall. And with a tender smile, she touches the top of his head. "You turned into a handsome man."

Taking a few steps away, she looks at me. "You're right. I never wanted you. Vincent made me take you. And the more months and years that went by, the more I hated you. But if I wanted to please Vincent, I had to keep mothering you." She laughs. "You should know Vincent has been feeding you human meat and organ for years. You only *thought* you were eating vegan meat. He was experimenting, always experimenting with you."

Like Vincent, she's trying to get inside my head so I refuse to let my brain and body respond to her words.

"Especially the most recent woman who smoked. Coupled with the herbs he was slipping you, it did exactly what he thought it would it do. It allowed you to make connections."

Fresh bile bitters my mouth and I focus hard on staying present. I was right, my mirror neurons were on hyperdrive because of Vincent and his sick games.

"Caroline is quite incredible," Rachel mimics Vincent, rolling her eyes. "If I have to hear that one more time, I'm going to stab my eye out."

She was the watcher, the healer. Sometimes the killer.

"He made me believe we were framing you. We were going to lock you away and he'd finally have me back." She scoffs. "I know him and his games and I still fell for it. Lock you away, sure, so he could have full unlimited access to you. Why did I ever tell him about you? Why did I ever bring him here and confess? I should have just let you two die in that basement."

My lungs deflate in a rush of air. "Every person linked to this hell hole and that you met at Camp DeSonk is now dead. Surely, you had to know you were next."

Her jaw hardens. I don't think she did know that.

"Vincent suspected Harley was letting Becka take a more active role," I say. "No longer just a lure but a participant in the kills. But Harley didn't discuss it with Vincent first and it pissed him off. He doesn't like losing control of a situation. Plus, he was developing a curiosity about Becka, just like he did me. And *that* pissed you off."

Rachel narrows her eyes.

I continue, "Three months ago, I had a nervous breakdown and moved in with Fallon. Three months ago is when the first local girl turned up missing. This had nothing to do with Harley mourning the possible loss of Becka. This had nothing to do with him feeding her dead girls in medicinal cannibalism. This was always about me. And you and Harley had no idea."

Becka scoffs.

I point at her. "With her being sick though, Harley latched on. Anything to help his Becka, right? But then the girl returned to the dorm, the girl returned to the park—you treated their wounds. You decorated their bodies. You returned them. Because Vincent knew exactly what would pull me back in. All while he kept his hands clean."

"I hate him," Rachel whispers. "How is it he continues to manipulate me?"

"Because he's good." I nod over to Becka. "He wasn't expecting this one to be so devious though. He wasn't expecting her manipulations or for her to gut Nadia."

More of it pieces together in my mind. "You and Harley

were friends and you killed him. I bet that was hard, wasn't it?"

She doesn't respond.

I keep going. "The honey and charcoal, the wildflowers. Yes, Vincent wanted me to make connections. He wanted me to know you were there all those years ago. He told you to kill Annabelle and then he allowed me to think she might be alive. He called me. He left me a note. He fed me the psychedelic herbs knowing full well how my body responds to them. I thought I was going insane and he let me think it."

"I almost told you everything so many times," Rachel says. "If anything, so you would leave and never come back."

I hate them both. And the hair found woven into my bracelets. That was him, too. A complete framed job. "Where is Suzi?"

"In the basement," Vincent speaks. "Where she's going to hopefully rot."

FIFTY-SIX

I whip around as he steps through the door I left open. His gaze touches on me first, then Becka, Fallon next, and Rachel last.

I bet she hates he looked at her last.

In my periphery, I see Becka grin. She's glad Vincent is here. She probably thinks it means she's going free. Maybe it does.

"Suzi's in the basement," Vincent says. "I put her there yesterday, intending on leaving her there, if possible."

Rachel scoffs. "Nice to see you finally get your hands dirty."

His eyes narrow and with careful movements, he paces into the room. As he does, something shifts in his expression —a wicked excitement that wasn't there a second ago. This scene wasn't part of his plan but he's envisioning the new possibilities.

The hair on my neck shifts to stand.

His attention is focused solely on Rachel and I inch back as I slide the knife I still hold out of his line of sight.

Rachel doesn't back down and instead lifts her chin.

Her defiance makes his lips curl. Vincent loves getting inside the mind. Well, it's time for me to get inside of his.

I speak to Becka, loud and clear. "What's your end game? To capitalize on Harley's success? To branch out on your own? To take over *my* spot in Vincent's life? Or maybe you simply have no self-control and you have no end game in mind."

She shifts and the doll on her lap tumbles to the floor. "All of the above, I suppose."

My gaze drifts to the doll and a gradual realization settles over me. Harley wove that human trophy rug. He taught Becka how to make dolls. He taught her how to use all parts of the kill. Those dolls are her "friends". "You've hidden pieces of the dead girls in your dolls."

She smiles. "They need organs, too."

I don't respond because there is nothing to say. Those dolls are carrying around tiny petrified organs of real girls. No wonder Vincent has an active interest in her.

I look over at him, surprised to see him staring curiously at me and no longer focused on Rachel. Reaching out, she touches his fingers, wanting the attention back. Good, she can have it. Their fingers twine together and she smirks at me. She thinks they're on the same team. Despite everything he has done to her, he's still in control.

Of her he is—but not me.

He's still looking at me. He might be holding fingers with Rachel but I'm the one in his head. I keep my gaze leveled on him. "You were surprised to discover Becka stabbed that girl found in the mushroom patch. Harley was giving her an active role without your consent. And Rachel was there to watch the whole thing. Harley and Rachel lied to you. They told you that *they* killed her because that's what you instructed them to do."

"But they defied you and you only fully realized that after we visited the morgue. It makes you wonder how many other times they lied to you. And Becka, she's doing the same thing. She dug up that mushroom patch without you knowing it." I pull the neck down on my hoodie, showing him the bruises. "She attacked me. Talk about stepping over lines. Talk about *defying* you."

"B-but—" Becka stammers and Rachel's smirk fades.

I keep going, my gaze zeroing in on Vincent's ticking jaw. "Thirteen years ago, all of them defied you. They brought three little girls out here and they tortured us. All of them have paid for that but Rachel. You thought if she raised me, it would be good for her but she resented every day. She hates me as much as you love me. It's why you told her never to come back."

I lift my shirt, reminding him of the scars. "Look what they did to me."

The ticking in Vincent's jaw stops but his glare does not. Rachel must sense his building rage because she shifts away, now not so sure about her united front with him.

"I'm sorry," she pleads.

"I've never defied you," I keep going. "I've always respected you. But look at what Rachel has done here. She's got Fallon and Becka tied up and is fully intending on killing me. *Me.*"

Rachel shakes her head. "I am not—"

I point at Becka. "And she has done nothing but manipulate the entire situation. Think about Nadia. Becka killed and gutted her without your permission. Do you remember when I stabbed Teagan? That was all because of you. I would have never done that without your consent. Just like Erwin in the hotel room. I would have never done that had you not said, 'kill him'.

So, what I want to know is—" I jab my finger first at Rachel and then Becka, "why are you letting them get away with all of this? You've done all this because you miss me. Well, I miss you, too. If you'd only have told me how much you missed me, I would've understood. I love you, Vincent. You are the one true father I know. I will never be a disappointment like the others." I lower my voice, making sure these last words sink in. "Please don't let them kill me."

Vincent is there one second and, before I have time to blink, or even breathe, he's reached over, taken hold of Rachel's head, snapped her neck, and flung her body aside.

I stand frozen, my eyes wide, staring down at Rachel's lifeless body. My brain scrambles. I don't know what I was expecting my words to do to him but that was not it.

Vincent turns a slow circle, stopping to gaze at Becka, rotating to look at Fallon, and finally coming back to me. His chest heaves and I make my expression one of acceptance and not shock. Fallon's words come back to me. *It's like playing chess when you're dealing with Vincent.*

Playing chess, strategy, next move.

Vincent's calculating gaze stays focused on me and I see it all—the darkness, the evil, the sinister mastermind. He's been slowly shaping me into a monster that I will never be but that he needs to see.

I shift my body ever so slightly closer and my fingers tighten around the knife I still hold. I bring it out from behind my back.

This man let me believe I consumed my sister. He manipulated my entire life, all for his sick and twisted curiosity and experimentation.

The knowledge of what I'm about to do should make me sick to my stomach, it should clench through me in fear but it doesn't. I don't want this to end any other way.

I shift forward again, my pulse inching up. My lips quiver into a smile and his eyes soften with the realization I'm about to give him everything his sick fantasies hold.

"You pick. Fallon or Becka," I whisper, knowing he'll like the choice.

His gaze sharpens on me. "Fallon."

I knew he'd pick Fallon over Becka.

Another shift forward and an eerie calm settles through me. Vincent turns, ready to lead the way across to the room to Fallon and my brain doesn't scramble, it doesn't lose focus. I know exactly where the kidney is and with one final step forward, I firm my grip, tighten my bicep, and I slide the tip of the blade in.

I puncture through his shirt, skin, and muscle, feeling the distinct change in pressure of entering the organ.

Several long seconds suspend as Vincent draws in a heavy breath. He arches back in agony and bows forward with a gasp before falling to his knees. My grip stays sure as I slide the knife out, reposition the angle, and slide it right back in.

"No!" Becka screams.

Things after that slow in motion—the blood that soaks his blue dress shirt, his body slumping to the floor, me following, keeping my grip on the hilt, Detective Uzzo running in, shouting, more blood, someone grabbing me and pulling me away...

EPILOGUE

One Month Later

My Dearest Caroline,

IF YOU ARE READING THIS, it means that I have passed on to another life. I have no way of knowing how I died but I hope it was by your hand. I hope, too, that this letter urges you to re-evaluate your goals and yourself. What do you want for your future?

I have made a great many mistakes through the years but the ones I am most apologetic for involve you and Fallon. I always considered you, and still do, my children and I didn't always provide the best of guidance.

I know I have said it before but I will say it again, every decision I made regarding you and Fallon was done with the utmost love. But sometimes love does blind, as the saying goes.

You have been a source of great confusion to me over the years as I tried to figure out what I had done wrong and/or right in providing direction. I questioned myself from so many angles and what I always came back to were thoughts of protection.

I take responsibility for the person you've become. I hope you know that. I hope you know that I didn't create a monster. Know that I will forever see you as I always have— as a work of art.

May your days be filled with continuing recovery and positive progress.

P.S. Annabelle's grave is fifty yards west of the tree. (You know what tree.) Look for a buried brick that marks her grave. If you lift it and see an A chiseled into the brick, you know you're at the right spot.

WITH LOVE,
   Vincent

I READ and re-read the letter that Uzzo found in a bank deposit box belonging to Vincent. I wait to feel something but nothing comes. I am blessedly blank. There is no dark and cold stain on my soul.

Everything tied back to my past is dead except for Becka. Though she's been put away for a very long time, and God willing, our paths will never cross again.

A knock sounds on our front door and Zane lifts his big head to let out a muffled woof. Laying the letter down on the kitchen counter, I cross through the living room and a quick peep out the side window has me smiling and swinging the door wide. "Hi."

Suzi sees my face and a lovely smile curves across her cheeks. "What are you doing? Thought maybe we could catch a movie or something?"

Grabbing my coat, I shoot Fallon a quick text message. "Actually, I'd like to visit Annabelle's grave."

ACKNOWLEDGMENTS

I am very blessed to have a great team of advanced readers who give invaluable input. Kate Brauning, Dr. Jim, Dora Landa, Kelsey Miller, Amy Williams Parker, Jessica Porter, Patrick Price, and Paige Akins Ulevich. Thank you for stepping into yet another one of my dark tales. You are the best!

ABOUT THE AUTHOR

Things you should know about me: I write novels. Under Shannon Greenland (my real name) you'll find spies, adventure, and romantic suspense. Under S. E. Green you'll find dark and gritty fiction about serial killers, cults, secret societies that do bad things, and whatever else my twisted brain deems to dream up. I'm on Instagram and Facebook.

I also have a website and a very non-annoying newsletter where you can keep up to date with new releases, take advantage of free stuff (like books!), and follow along with my travels. I love old and grouchy dogs. My humor runs dark and so don't be offended by something off I might say. I mean no harm. I eat entirely too many chips. I also love math!

Turn the page for a complete list of books!

BOOKS BY S. E. GREEN:

Twisted Truth Box Set

Includes four bestselling, award-winning novels. Its pages full of visceral and provocative, raw and gritty, heart-pumping, edge-of-your-seat reads.

Vanquished

A secret island. A sadistic society. And the woman who defies all odds to bring it down.

Killers Among

She swore never to be like her late mother. But now she, too, is a serial killer.

Ultimate Sacrifice

A small town. A murdered child. A cult lurking in the shadows.

Did you know reviews are important?

They help authors sell books and readers find those books.

Please consider leaving one!

COPYRIGHT

Cover design by German Creative

Made in the USA
Monee, IL
23 September 2021

78702310R10210